An Uninvited Bride on his Doorstep

―――― ♘ ――――

STAND-ALONE NOVEL

A Western Historical Romance Novel

by

Ava Winters

Copyright© 2021 by Ava Winters

All Rights Reserved.

This book may not be reproduced or transmitted in any form without the written permission of the publisher.

In no way is it legal to reproduce, duplicate, or transmit any part of this document in either electronic means or in printed format. Recording of this publication is strictly prohibited and any storage of this document is not allowed unless with written permission from the publisher

Table of Contents

An Uninvited Bride on his Doorstep 1
   Table of Contents 3
   Let's connect! 5
   Letter from Ava Winters 6
Prologue 7
Chapter One 14
Chapter Two 23
Chapter Three 32
Chapter Four 41
Chapter Five 50
Chapter Six 60
Chapter Seven 69
Chapter Eight 78
Chapter Nine 88
Chapter Ten 98
Chapter Eleven 109
Chapter Twelve 118
Chapter Thirteen 127
Chapter Fourteen 137
Chapter Fifteen 145
Chapter Sixteen 156
Chapter Seventeen 166
Chapter Eighteen 175
Chapter Nineteen 185

Chapter Twenty 194
Chapter Twenty-One.. 204
Chapter Twenty-Two.. 213
Chapter Twenty-Three 222
Chapter Twenty-Four.. 231
Chapter Twenty-Five... 240
Chapter Twenty-Six 249
Chapter Twenty-Seven 258
Chapter Twenty-Eight... 266
Chapter Twenty-Nine 276
Chapter Thirty... 285
Chapter Thirty-One 294
Chapter Thirty-Two 303
Chapter Thirty-Three 312
Epilogue 320
    Also by Ava Winters 329

Let's connect!

Impact my upcoming stories!

My passionate readers influenced the core soul of the book you are holding in your hands! The title, the cover, the essence of the book as a whole was affected by them!

Their support on my publishing journey is paramount! I devote this book to them!

If you are not a member yet, join now! As an added BONUS, you will receive my Novella "**The Cowboys' Wounded Lady**":

**FREE EXCLUSIVE GIFT
(available only to my subscribers)**

**Go to the link:
https://avawinters.com/novella-amazon**

Letter from Ava Winters

"Here is a lifelong bookworm, a devoted teacher and a mother of two boys. I also make mean sandwiches."

If someone wanted to describe me in one sentence, that would be it. There has never been a greater joy in my life than spending time with children and seeing them grow up - all my children, including the 23 little 9-year-olds that I currently teach. And I have not known such bliss than that of reading a good book.

As a Western Historical Romance writer, my passion has always been reading and writing romance novels. The historical part came after my studies as a teacher - I was mesmerized by the stories I heard, so much that I wanted to visit every place I learned about. And so, I did, finding the love of my life along the way as I walked the paths of my characters.

Now, I'm a full-time elementary school teacher, a full-time mother of two wonderful boys and a full-time writer. Wondering how I manage all of them? I did too, at first, but then I realized it's because everything I do I love, and I have the chance to share it with all of you.

And I would love to see you again in this small adventure of mine!

Until next time,

Ava Winters

Prologue

Near El Paso, Texas

April 18, 1874

Logan wiped sweat from his eyes and lowered his hat. The sun was setting behind him so there was no need to protect his eyes from shadows, but he lowered it anyway. He'd never been one for letting others see him cry and anyway, his brothers needed his strength right now, not his grief.

Truthfully, he was surprised at how much his grandfather's loss affected him. He loved his grandfather, of course, but Harold Foley was well past his eightieth birthday when his heart finally gave out. Logan thought he'd reconciled himself to Harold's death years ago. Traveling home from the elderly man's funeral, Logan knew he hadn't. Judging by the expressions on the faces of his parents and two brothers, they struggled with grief as well.

"Hey Logan?" a voice whispered to his left—his younger brother, Gregory.

"Yes?" Logan whispered back.

"Can you fall back with me a spell? I need to ask you something."

"Sure, Greg," Logan replied. He pulled back slightly on Canvas's reigns, slowing the horse to a leisurely walk and falling behind his parents in the wagon. He reckoned Greg needed to talk to his big brother to sort out his feelings about his Pappy's death. He didn't feel at all up to giving advice or encouragement at the moment but it was his responsibility as the eldest to be there for his brothers. He would have to find the strength.

When Jay, the youngest brother, saw his two older brothers falling behind, he slowed his own horse.

"Let me talk to Greg first," Logan said, softly enough so his parents couldn't hear.

"Actually, he should see it too," Greg said.

Logan detected a hint of anxiety in his voice and the hairs on the back of his neck prickled. "What's going on, Greg?" he asked.

Greg pointed behind them to the horizon, brushing a lock of his wavy brown hair from his forehead. He alone of the brothers inherited their mother's waves. Jay and Logan had their father's straight, sandy brown hair. "Do you see riders on the horizon?"

Logan squinted against the glare of the setting sun. He could make out several faint shapes that after a moment's inspection, did appear to be riders. Logan counted a dozen in all. "Yeah, I see 'em."

"Me too," Jay piped up. "Should we tell Pa?"

"Reckon we oughta," Logan agreed.

He flicked Canvas's reigns and the horse accelerated to a brisk trot, closing the distance to his parent's wagon in a few seconds. Dale Foley glanced at his son, sorrow still showing in his heavy-lidded eyes. "What are you boys doing back there?" He asked in a voice as tired as his eyes.

"There's riders, Pa," Logan said. "I counted a dozen."

The elder Foley's eyes cleared almost instantly, and his voice enlivened and at the same time became even more serious. "Where?"

"Behind us."

"Are they gaining on us?"

Logan looked behind him. The shapes were noticeably larger than they were a moment ago. "Yes."

Dale quickly scanned the road ahead. By this time, Greg and Jay had ridden up alongside their father and when Dale turned back, he addressed all three of them. "We'll ride behind that dune over there until the riders pass."

"What's going on?" Logan's mother asked.

"There's riders, Martha," Dale said calmly. "It's probably just a troop of rangers out of El Paso but we're going to sit tight behind that sand dune until they pass." He didn't mention the other possibility that the riders were bandits who would see in the family an opportunity for easy money. Such bandits rarely left their victims alive to report their crimes.

Martha nodded and Logan noticed her eyes cleared and became alert as well. The only emotion that could have so easily overpowered their grief in that moment was fear. A pit formed in Logan's stomach as they rode behind the dune.

Once behind the dune, Dale retrieved the rifles, handing one to each of the boys, then one to Martha and the last for himself. "Martha, stay by the wagon," Dale whispered. "Greg, Jay, stay with her. Logan, come with me."

Logan and Dale crept to the edge of the dune and peered around at the road. The riders were much closer now and Logan could see they rode in a wide fan shape about fifty yards abreast. After a few seconds it became apparent they were not Texas Rangers. After a few more it became apparent the riders were heading purposefully for the dune where the Foleys hid.

Dale swore under his breath and ran back to the others. Logan followed close behind.

"There's a fight comin'," Dale said. "Take cover behind the wagon and chamber a round."

The boys nodded and complied. Martha followed suit. Jay's lip quivered slightly, and Martha smiled and put a hand on his shoulder. "It'll be okay, son," she said. "Just listen to your father and me."

Logan's heart pounded as they waited for the riders. After a moment, he could hear the sound of their horses approaching. Soon, he could hear laughter and whooping as the men approached what they thought would be an easy target.

They'll learn different soon enough, Logan thought to himself. Despite the confidence that thought expressed, Logan couldn't shake the feeling of dread that slowly crept up his spine.

A moment later, the gang began riding around the corner, guns firing. As soon as Logan saw a rider, he fired his rifle. The outlaw fell to the ground, clutching his chest. Logan quickly levered another round into the chamber as his father and brother's rifles cracked. Three more outlaws fell and a fourth flew from his horse as the animal stumbled over the corpses of its companions. The outlaw immediately leapt to his feet and ran for about ten feet before Martha's round found his chest.

Logan heard a stream of curses from the other outlaws and the skittering of sand and gravel as they pulled their mounts to a stop and spun them around to avoid the sudden fury of gunfire that felled a third of their number.

"Get on out of here!" Dale yelled. "Unless you want to join your friends in the pit."

"You first!" an outlaw cried. He spun around and fired wildly with his pistol. Dale fired and the man's head snapped backward, a hole the size of a quarter stamped in his forehead just above his right eye.

"Who wants to be next?" Dale called. Logan knew his father would not react so violently if he didn't feel he had good reason.

The reason became clear quickly enough. One of the outlaws shouted, "Who are you to threaten us? We're the Sundown Gang! We ain't afraid of you!"

As soon as he finished speaking, the outlaw spun around the corner and fired three rounds quickly before returning behind the corner.

"Ma!" Jay cried.

Logan and Dale turned. Logan's blood turned to ice. His mother stood upright in the wagon clutching her stomach. Rivulets of blood ran between her fingers. She looked up at Dale with a confused expression than toppled out of the wagon, landing heavily on the ground.

"Martha!" Dale shouted. He rushed to his wife's side, ignoring the enemy ahead.

"Pa, look out!" Logan cried. An outlaw aimed his handgun at Dale and fired. An instant later, both Logan's and Greg's rifles roared. The outlaw jerked twice in rapid succession from the two rounds then fell face first to the ground.

Dale scrambled back behind the wagon, grabbing his chest and grimacing in pain. Logan crawled over to his father. His heart burned from his mother's sudden death, but he couldn't allow himself to feel anything but adrenaline. Emotion would come later. "Fire at anything that shows it's face on this side of the dune!" he shouted toward Greg and Jay.

Tears streamed down the younger boy's face, but Greg's hands were steady. He squeezed Jay's shoulder and Jay took a ragged breath, then calmed and watched the other side. At sixteen, Jay had never fired on anything more dangerous than a mule deer. A year older, Greg had never fired on a man before but was forced to kill a bear once after it came on their camp. Maybe that gave him a calmer outlook when confronted with the danger they faced now.

The outlaws, having lost half their number, seemed reluctant to return. Greg motioned to Logan that he would watch the other side in case the gang tried to flank them.

Logan knelt by his father. The older man's breath was shallow and a sheen of sweat shone on his face. He looked up at Logan, his eyes glazed.

"Take care of your brothers," he rasped. "And take care of the horse ranch."

"Pa, don't talk like that," Logan said. The tears he fought back when his mother died threatened again. "Greg! Jay! Bring me the possibles bag." Logan knew there was nothing there that could help his father, but he couldn't overcome his urge to try something, anything to save his life."

Jay started for the wagon, but Greg placed a hand on his shoulder. Tears ran down his face too. Logan turned back toward his father, his own eyes swimming.

"Promise me," Dale said.

Logan gulped and drew a shaky breath. Then he set his jaw and squeezed his Pa's hand. "I will, Pa."

Dale nodded. "I love you, son."

After saying those words, he drew a final, rattling breath, then stilled.

Black fury filled Logan but instead of bursting into a rage, he found he felt completely calm and unnaturally alert and clearheaded. He crawled back into position and called his brothers over.

"We're going to flank them," Logan whispered. "Follow me. Jay, cover the rear."

He led them around the other side of the dune. Five of the six remaining outlaws were huddled close to the dune, discussing what to do. One watched the opposite side of the dune, but none watched the side Logan and his brothers emerged from.

In a fluid motion, the three boys raised their rifles and fired. Three outlaws dropped. The other three didn't bother trying to fight back but leapt onto their mounts and rode off. Jay and Greg quickly dropped two more of them. Logan leveled his rifle and stared down the sights at the third. He exhaled softly and squeezed the trigger and the final outlaw fell from his horse.

Logan watched as the horse continued riderless, until the animal disappeared on the horizon. As suddenly as it began the fight was over. Only the gradually softening reverberation of the gunfire off the ridge gave any sign eight people died here.

Logan turned to his brothers. Gregory and Jay were sobbing. He opened his mouth to speak, but the pain, loss, and fear finally overwhelmed him and instead he dropped to his knees and wept with his brothers.

Chapter One

Westridge, Texas

May 27th, 1876

"Why, Miss Winona! You look absolutely fetching in that dress!"

Winona smiled at the portly middle-aged woman behind the counter. "Thank you, Mrs. Black."

Mrs. Black put her hands on her hips in mock indignation. "Miss Winona, how many times have I told you to stop with this 'Mrs. Black' nonsense. Call me Cordelia."

Winona laughed. "I guess it would just sound strange to hear you call me Miss Winona and me to call you only Cordelia."

"Well, if you insist, I suppose you could call me Mrs. Cordelia."

"Well then, thank you, Mrs. Cordelia."

Cordelia beamed. "Now, what can I do for you today, Miss Winona?"

"Just a few odds and ends," Winona replied. She handed Cordelia a scrap of paper and a woven basket.

The shopkeeper scanned the paper and grinned up at Winona. "Have you taken up drawing?"

Winona blushed. "It helps pass the time. I'm not any good but it's fun anyway."

"Well, I don't know about that. I think I'll have to reserve my judgment until I see an example of your work."

Winona's blush deepened, but she agreed to return the following week with a drawing for Cordelia. "Don't tell me what it's going to be!" the older woman insisted. "I want to be surprised."

She left the counter and began gathering the items on Winona's list: paper, pencils, oil sticks, various colors of ink and a set of writing quills. Most general stores didn't carry art supplies, but Winona's mother was an artist of local fame when Winona was a child and Cordelia maintained a stock of artist's necessities in her honor.

While she waited, Winona wandered around the store, looking at the various items on display. When she came across the candy counter stocked with miniature barrels full of rock candy, gumdrops, and various other confections, she smiled. She'd loved coming here with her mother as a child. Her mother would always buy her a small bag of gumdrops and she would savor them one at a time as they walked home. She would tell her mother about school, and they would laugh and just enjoy each other's company.

Her smile faded. Her mother died of cholera just a few days after her eighth birthday. Her father remarried three years later, and her stepmother, Audrey, was the opposite of her mother in every way. She seemed more concerned with her wealth and social status than her stepdaughter's happiness. The worst part was the change in her father. Over time, he'd taken on his wife's worst qualities until now he barely resembled the man she once knew.

"You're never too old for a gumdrop, I always say."

The rich, baritone voice startled Winona out of her musing and she turned to see Clarence Huxtable smiling down at her. Clarence was the manager of the bank and the male counterpart to Cordelia in portliness and kindliness. "I'm sorry to startle you, Miss Winona," he said.

"Oh, that's fine," Winona said. "I was just distracted is all."

"Winona! Your order's ready," Cordelia called from the counter. She glared at Clarence, but Winona noticed a flush come to Cordelia's cheeks as she said, "Clarence, quit bothering that poor girl and let her shop in peace."

Clarence smiled and walked over to the counter. "Well, now that I see you, Miss Cordelia, I promise you nothing else will command my attention."

"Oh, go on with you," Cordelia said, her blush deepening. She handed Winona her basket. "Thank you, dear. You run along. I'll keep Clarence out of your hair."

Winona smiled. "Thank you, Ms. Cordelia." She turned to Clarence. "It was lovely to see you, Clarence."

"And just as lovely to see you," Clarence said before turning back to Cordelia.

Winona kept smiling as she walked out of the store and headed home. She was happy for Clarence and Cordelia. Cordelia's husband died in the same outbreak that killed Winona's mother and for years after that, the poor woman suffered deep melancholy. Then Clarence arrived in town and ever since, Cordelia's smile had returned. Winona thought it was beautiful that the two of them had found love.

She wondered if she'd ever feel love for Jude like they felt for each other.

Jude Koch was the son of Sterling Koch, owner of the Heartland Railroad Company and the wealthiest man in town. Jude took a shine to Winona shortly after the Kochs moved to town and Winona's father and stepmother practically leapt at the chance to secure their union. She agreed to marry him after eight months of courting, and their wedding was scheduled for September seventeenth, the one-year anniversary of their courtship.

Jude was a decent enough man. He was kind and generous, and he was clearly fond of her. She liked him well enough, but she didn't love him. He seemed too fond of his wealth. He didn't lord it over others the way Audrey did, and he didn't seem to carry the same disdain for the working class his father did, but he carried himself with a similar sense of superiority and entitlement.

She'd agreed to marry him more to escape her stepmother's thumb and finally have a life of her own than out of any affection for Jude. He'd gotten less superior over the past several months and Winona hoped that with time, he could shed the last of his arrogance and earn her love.

She turned a corner and began walking through the poorer quarter of town. The houses here were little more than shacks, some of them barely qualifying for that name. Her stepmother disapproved of Winona frequenting these neighborhoods, concerned it might affect her reputation to be seen there, but Winona ignored her. These people were fine folk; they just weren't wealthy. Several of them greeted Winona as she walked.

After a few minutes, she heard voices up ahead. One of the voices was familiar. As she approached the house the voices were coming from, she recognized it as Jude's voice. What was Jude doing out here? Maybe he was finally humble enough to spend time with the less well-to-do residents of Westridge.

As she drew close, however, it quickly became clear Jude's intentions were not benevolent. His voice was raised in threat, and the other voices were clearly fearful of him. Her heartbeat quickened as she turned the corner and saw them. An older couple stood outside of their home, a tar paper shack barely larger than Winona's bedroom, and argued with Jude. The woman's hands were clasped in front of her while the man's were raised in front of him, palms outward, as though to protect himself. Jude stood with his shoulders squared, his hands balled into fists at his side. Winona quickly ducked behind a fence and watched the interaction.

"I don't care what your father says, this is our home and we ain't leaving!" The older man's words were brave, but his voice trembled, and Winona could tell he was frightened of Jude. That didn't make sense to her. Jude had never before struck her as a violent man. What was going on?

"Yes, you are!" Jude barked. "And neither I nor my father are interested in your opinion. You get on up out of here by sunrise tomorrow or we'll tear this—" his lips curled downward, "—hovel down on your heads."

"Please, Mr. Koch," the woman begged. She wrung her hands and even from a distance, Winona could hear she was crying. "This is all we have!"

"Had," Jude said. "By the next time the sun rises, this land will be the property of Heartland Railroad Company."

"Now, look here," the man said. Anger seemed to have driven his fear away. He strode forward and stuck his finger up at Jude. "I don't care what that piece of paper in your pocket says. Everyone knows your father has the judge on his payroll. This is our home. We've lived here since before your father came to this town and poisoned it with his gold, and we'll be here long after you move on."

Jude didn't reply immediately. He looked down at the defiant older man, his face expressionless. Then he smiled. Ice crept up Winona's spine at the sight of it. He smiled, but there was no hint of friendliness on his face. It was the grin of a snake preparing to strike, a predator regarding his prey and anticipating the meal he was about to enjoy.

Jude moved so suddenly Winona didn't at first register what had happened. He reached forward and grabbed the old man, throwing him to the ground. The man fell heavily, grunting with the impact and the old lady shrieked and rushed forward. Jude grabbed her and held her back, preventing her from reaching her husband.

"You let her go!" the man called out, fear for his wife overriding his pain. He got back to his feet and rushed Jude. Jude flashed his snake smile again and slammed his fist into the side of the man's head. The man collapsed to the ground and began trembling violently. The woman struggled and shouted for Jude to let her go but he held her tightly, watching the man seize under him with devilish glee.

Winona watched numbly, shock driving her emotions away. This couldn't be real. It had to be a sick nightmare. She would wake and things would be as they were. Jude would no longer be a monster but a decent, if rather haughty, man. These people would be allowed to keep their homes and her father would not be business partner to a ruthless criminal.

Her father. Did he know about this? She shook her head slowly. No, her father couldn't have known. There was no way. Could he really ally himself with someone who would do something like this? She began breathing rapidly and a moment later her vision swam. She steadied herself against the fence and forced herself to breathe slowly and evenly. When her vision cleared, she saw Jude staring straight at her, shock and horror on his face.

She turned and ran back the way she came, instinct driving her away from this monster she was destined to marry. The thought of breaking off the engagement didn't occur to her in that moment. Nothing occurred to her but escaping from this vile creature, this predator that fed on the weak and innocent.

"Winona!" Jude called.

Winona quickened her pace and turned back onto the main road. She quickly slowed to a walk. Something told her it would be better not to attract attention from anyone. She forced herself to proceed slowly across the street, her heart pounding with every step. She managed to control her pace until she reached an alleyway across the street.

Then she heard Jude call her name once more and her self-control fled. She sprinted through the alleyway, then ran up the residential road behind it. Several passersby called her name, but she ignored them and ducked through another alley. She came out behind the livery and worked her way through the back roads behind the saloons and brothels of the town's aptly named Devil's Corner.

A minute later, she reached the fence that cordoned off the section of land destined to become the town's train station.

She heard Jude call again and began to scale the fence. Her dress and walking shoes made it difficult to climb and it seemed an eternity before she finally reached the top and leapt down to the ground.

"Winona, stop!" Jude called. "Wait!"

Winona ran toward the opposite fence. Past that fence were fields of prairie grass that grew head high after a few hundred yards. If she could make it there before Jude caught her, she could lose him. She hitched her dress up and ran as fast as she could. Her feet throbbed in her calfskin walking boots. When she heard Jude crash into the fence behind her, she reached down and tore the boots off, one by one.

Her feet free of the confining leather, she was able to run much faster and reached the opposite fence just when she heard the sound of Jude's boots hitting the ground behind her.

She climbed quickly and landed on the other side before Jude reached the fence. She looked up and saw him running. His face was twisted in a mask of rage. She went white and turned to flee but her dress caught on the fence. Panicking, she tore it free, leaving behind a long strip of fabric.

Her dress was now open over her right leg nearly to the hip, but she didn't have time to be embarrassed. The tear actually allowed her to run faster, her movement no longer restricted by her skirt. Jude called her name but each time he sounded farther away. Her heart leapt and she quickened her pace further, running through the tall grass until she could no longer hear him calling her.

When she felt she'd lost him, she slowed and put her hands on her knees, gasping. After a moment, she remembered something her grandfather taught her and stood straight with her shoulders rolled back. She walked slowly, taking deep, measured breaths until her heart stopped pounding.

She leaned against a pile of wooden planks destined to become part of the station's boarding platform once work resumed tomorrow. and struggled to collect her thoughts. She couldn't believe what she'd seen. Jude had severely injured that poor old man! Maybe even killed him.

She shivered. How could she have been so blind? She'd been close with him, allowed him to touch her, to kiss her hand. The memory of his lips on her palm made her skin crawl and sent a wave of nausea through her.

She walked through the grass, tortured by her thoughts, until a distant rumble of thunder crashed overhead. She looked up, startled, and a raindrop splashed on her face. She blinked and rubbed her eyes then looked up again. The sky was suddenly dark. Clouds roiled on the horizon, flashing every few moments with lightning.

Winona turned back to the town, but the town wasn't there. At least, she couldn't see it. The grass grew tall as a horse's withers out here and everywhere she looked was a tangled maze of vegetation.

A new panic took hold of her and when lightning crashed to the ground a few hundred yards distant, she lost control and ran blindly ahead. She screamed for help or thought she did, but the noise of the thunder deafened her cries. A moment later, the rain came, steady at first, then torrential, with sheets of water falling from the sky to obscure her vision even more than the grass.

Water coursed down her cheeks, and she couldn't be sure if it was the rain or her tears that stung her eyes. She ran and cried and screamed for what seemed an eternity. Then her foot stumbled into a gopher hole. She fell forward, twisting her ankle with a sickening snap. She screamed but an instant later, her scream was cut off as her head slammed against a rock. The world went black, and the only sound was a soft buzzing that seemed to come from somewhere behind her.

Then there was only silence.

Chapter Two

Logan leaned against the corral fence, chewed on a piece of straw and watched as Darrell supervised a half dozen hands branding the newest shipment of horses: one hundred twenty brood mares, checked for ticks, lice, and worms. They would allow the Foley Ranch to keep up with the growing demand for its horses. The new mares brought the herd to an even thousand head.

Logan pushed himself off the fence and walked up to Darrell. The grizzled foreman was twenty years older than Logan and had worked for Logan's father for fourteen years before his death. He was the best horse wrangler Logan had ever seen and he was eternally grateful to him for sticking around after Dale passed on.

"How many left?" Logan asked.

"Couple dozen," Darrell replied. "It'll take another ten minutes, maybe."

Logan nodded. He watched as the hands quickly and expertly branded each animal on its flank then released it into the herd before the animal even felt the sting of the iron. "Have you moved the cattle yet?"

Darrell shook his head. "We're moving 'em on later this afternoon."

"Where you movin' 'em?"

"Southeast pasture."

"Again?"

Darrell nodded affirmation. "The north pasture hasn't finished growing back yet and I want to keep the shoreline in reserve for winter. Southeast'll carry them until the grass is back in the north pasture."

"Why don't we use the east field? The grass there's at least two yards high."

"We need to clear out some of the undergrowth before we use that. I'll take a few of the boys out with me next week and we'll do some controlled burns. I still want to wait until after they graze the north, but we'll use east after that."

Logan shook his head. "These blasted cattle are more work than they're worth."

Darrell shrugged. "It ain't so bad. Just different is all. Ain't no trouble to move them every so often."

Logan nodded and clapped Darrell on the shoulder. "Thank you for all your hard work, Darrell. I'll see you later."

Darrell tipped his hat to Logan then returned to supervising the branding.

Logan walked toward the far end of the corral where Gregory sat polishing tack. Jay leaned on the fence next to him. Both boys—Logan had a difficult time seeing either of them as men, though both were now of legal age—looked up and nodded a greeting.

"Have to move your cattle again today," he growled at Jay.

Jay raised an eyebrow. "And good morning to you too, Logan."

"Why are you so obsessed with cattle in the first place?" Logan asked irritably. "We're a horse ranch, not a cattle ranch."

"We're not a cattle ranch *yet*," Jay corrected.

"In a few months, we're not gonna be an anything ranch if those cows keep eating us out of land."

Jay rolled his eyes. "This old argument again? I told you Logan, if we rotate the cattle every few weeks, the land will recover, and we won't run out of pasture. Trust me, cattle farmers have been doing this since long before you or I were born."

"Well, that's great, Jay, but what will the horses eat?"

"The horses? Come on Logan, you could keep the entire herd on one pasture the whole year and never run out of grass."

"Yes!" Logan argued. "That's the point! If we focused on horses, we could support another three, four thousand head! If we buy any more cattle, we'll need another fifteen thousand acres!"

"So, let's get fifteen thousand more acres!"

Logan stared at his brother, amazed. Did Jay think land was just given away for free? "Jay, blast it, I'm trying to run a business here."

"*We're* trying to run a business here."

"No," Logan retorted. "*I'm* trying to run a business. *You're* trying to run some kind of experiment."

"It's not an experiment!" Jay fired back, heated. "I've shown you the figures, Logan. Cattle are more expensive to maintain but they fetch a far higher price per pound. If we transition our business to cattle, we'll be able to afford all the acreage we need and then some."

"When you guys are done fighting, you might want to take a look to the northeast."

Jay and Logan turned toward the sound of Gregory's voice. The middle brother pointed to the northeast, and they followed his gaze to see thick, black storm clouds gathering on the horizon.

"Oh, that's not good," Logan said.

"We need to get the cattle," Jay said, pleading. "We need to bring them inside."

"There's not enough room inside for the cattle," Logan said, walking back toward Darrell and the other hands. When he saw Jay begin to protest, he lifted his hand. "But, we'll move the horses to the pens and bring the cattle to the corral."

Jay nodded. "I'm coming with you to herd the cattle."

"No. You stay here with a few of the boys and try to keep the horses calm."

"That's not fair!" Jay protested. "I can help!"

"Blast it, Jay, this isn't some joyride. We have maybe an hour before that storm hits. We need these cattle inside when that happens or your herd's going to disappear before we have a chance to sell them."

"That's exactly why I should go with you!"

Logan threw his head back and stared at the rapidly darkening sky as though praying for strength. "For once, Jay," he breathed exasperatedly. "Just do as you're told."

"I'm a grown man, Logan," Jay retorted. "I ain't some little kid you can bully around."

Logan shook his head. "I don't need this right now."

Jay continued to protest, but Logan ignored him. He nodded to Gregory and the two of them walked to the stables to retrieve their horses. Darrell met them in the stable, his face grim.

"We're going to keep the cattle in the corral," Logan said. "I want you and four of the hands to come help us bring the cattle here. Have the others pen the horses."

Darrell cast a worried glance toward the blackening horizon. "We ain't got much time, boss."

"I know," Logan said. He mounted up and started in the direction of the west pasture.

Gregory caught up to him a moment later. The wind was already picking up and he had to shout so Logan could hear him. "Jay's gonna be real sore at you for leaving him behind."

"Jay's gonna have to learn there's more important things than his pride," Logan spat back.

"You shouldn't be so hard on him," Gregory insisted. "He's got as much a say as either of us do."

"You really want to have this argument right now?" Logan said. He spurred his horse faster without waiting for a response.

They reached the herd a few minutes later. The cattle were restless but not yet panicked. That was good. If they could get the herd moving toward the main pens while they were still somewhat calm, it would be far easier and swifter to pen them than if they had to redirect a stampede.

Darrell pulled up alongside Logan, four other hands with him. Logan turned to address the other hands. "Start driving the herd back to the pens. Darrell, you and Greg ride on either side and keep an eye out for any head breaking away. I'll ride point and lead the herd."

The other men nodded and rode off to complete their assignments. Gregory flashed a pointed stare at Logan. "This ain't over," he said before spurring his horse and riding off.

Logan looked at Darrell. The older man pretended to scan the horizon, acting like he had no idea what was going on. Logan shook his head and rode toward the front of the herd. He hollered and whooped at the cattle, urging them toward the south where the pens and safety from the storm waited. Darrell and Gregory did the same from either side of the herd while the other hands drove them along the rear.

After a few minutes, the herd was moving steadily and calmly toward safety. Logan relaxed a little. They might actually get out of this one with little trouble.

Then the storm hit. It came suddenly, as these storms typically did. One moment, the sky was darkening but still clear. The next it was black as night and the wind picked up to gale force, whipping around the herd and drowning out all noise with its deafening whine. There was a flash of lightning, then another, then a second later a loud double report of thunder. Then the rain fell, sharp, hard spikes of water that seemed to drive into the ground rather than fall on top of it.

The cattle leapt forward as though possessed and what had been a simple herding job suddenly became a fight for survival as Logan ran back and forth across the herd, struggling to keep them headed toward the corrals. The other riders ran back and forth along the herd, ensuring any stragglers were quickly returned to the group.

They headed south as quickly as the cattle would allow, which was not nearly fast enough. The four hands at the rear did everything they could to hurry the cattle but could do little to increase the pace. Logan grew frustrated at the lack of progress. Horses spooked just as easily as cattle but when horses spooked, they ran and with practice, it was a simple enough thing to encourage a herd of horses to run in the direction you wanted them to.

The cattle were different. When they spooked, they moved in circles almost blindly, lowing and shaking their heads, unable to focus even on the direction they were running. Every few seconds they would have to guide a straggler back into the herd. A couple times, cows in the middle of the herd got turned around and the herd would become a giant roiling mess.

Lightning flashed on the top of a nearby ridge and an instant later, thunder cracked so hard it shook the ground. The cows began to bleat with terror and the job of keeping the herd together and moving in the right direction became much harder. Lightning flashed again, barely a half mile off this time. Logan felt ice creep up his veins.

He rode to Darrell and waved the older man down. When Darrell approached, Logan shouted. "That lightning's gonna be a problem any minute now."

Darrell nodded agreement. "It's these blasted cattle. They want to run every which way but the way they need to go."

They split up and Logan rode back to the head of the herd. When Logan reached the front, he felt the hairs on the back of his neck stand up. When the hairs on his arm began pulling as well, he cursed and spurred his horse into a dead run. A few seconds later, the sky turned bright as day and the air behind him suddenly felt warm.

The thunder was loud, deafeningly loud and he knew he only narrowly escaped being struck by lightning. As it was, the force and noise of the thunder disoriented him and he fell from his horse, his head spinning.

He came to a moment later to see Jay bolting toward him, panicked. "Logan!" he called.

Logan stood and Jay crashed into him, knocking them both over. Jay quickly scrambled to his feet. "Are you okay?"

"I'm fine," Logan said, picking himself up again. "No thanks to you." He looked around for his horse and saw the animal riding alongside the cattle at the front of the herd. "Give me a ride to my horse."

"Gee," Jay said as Logan mounted up behind him, his tone sarcastic, "I'm glad you're safe too. You're welcome for the ride. Love you too, Logan."

"You want a hug, you can get one from one of the girls at O'Keefe's. Now take me to my blasted horse."

"Yes sir, Mr. Foley, sir. Whatever you need, sir."

"Jay—" Logan began but Jay snapped his reins and started forward before he could continue. When they reached his horse, he leapt onto the saddle. Jay peeled off before Logan could say anything and Logan shook his head and resumed leading the herd.

A moment later, he caught a glimpse of white fabric up ahead. He frowned and peered through the storm and the prairie grass to see what it was. As he approached, he thought the fabric looked a lot like the hem of a dress.

He felt disquiet grow as he watched the fabric, but it wasn't until another bolt of lightning shattered the sky that he saw the girl wearing the dress. She lay unmoving despite the storm and the noise of the herd.

The herd that was now barely a hundred yards away from trampling her. Instantly, Logan spurred his horse into a dead run. The exhausted animal whinnied reproachfully at him, but he ignored it. His heart pounded as he raced ahead of the lead bull and made for the woman in white. He dismounted and ran over to her. He laid two fingers next to her throat and felt a pulse. She was alive!

She was beautiful. Her skin was creamy white, and her features were soft and elegant, but a noble brow and high cheekbones prevented them from being delicate. He nearly forgot about the storm until another blast of lightning snapped him out of his reverie.

He looked behind him and his heartbeat quickened further. The cattle would reach them in seconds. He quickly put one arm under the girl's shoulders and the other under her legs, then lifted. Without pausing for breath, he ran toward his horse, just out of the path of the herd.He too He collapsed to the ground just out of the way of the rampaging animals.

"It's okay," Logan said to the unconscious woman between ragged gulps of air. "You're safe now. I've got you."

Chapter Three

Logan rode toward the house, holding the unconscious girl in front of him in the saddle. The feel of her, soft and warm in his arms, stirred feelings he'd never had before. He'd enjoyed the company of women only sparingly before, usually on very rare trips to O'Keefe's Boarding House in town. He'd never courted a woman or even thought about marriage.

Why was he thinking about this now? Why did he feel a sudden need to protect and care for this strange girl fate had left in his hands? He pushed the thoughts from his head and focused on getting his passenger home where she could be cared for, but no matter how hard he tried, he couldn't ignore the feel of her skin on his body.

He set her on the couch in the parlor and quickly loosened her corset. He placed fresh linens over her, then went to the kitchen for a cup. He went outside and filled the cup with fresh water from the pump, shielding it from the rain with his body. Then he returned to the house and set the cup near her on the side table.

"For when you wake up," he said. The girl didn't respond. That made sense given she was unconscious. He shook his head. "That near miss with the lightning must have addled my head," he explained. Why was he talking to her out loud? He checked her for injuries.

There were several minor bruises on her arms and legs and one of her ankles was badly swollen, but the most concerning injury was a massive welt on one side of her head that was covered in caked blood. He would need to send for Doctor Caraway as soon as possible.

The storm raged outside and every minute or so, there was another flash of lightning. The house remained warm and dry, and Logan silently thanked his father for leaving his sons such a well-built home. He took a few oak logs from the pile of firewood near the fireplace and soon had a healthy fire going.

He left for his bedroom and removed his riding boots. His feet ached and he spent several moments curling and uncurling his toes until the tingling subsided. Once he felt more comfortable, he stood and finished changing. He brought his rain-soaked clothes to the parlor and left them hanging in front of the fireplace to dry, then sat on a chair near the fireplace.

He worried about the herd, about his brothers, Darrell, and the other hands. He'd left them to finish driving the herd so he could get the strange girl to safety as soon as possible. Each flash of lightning brought his own close call vividly to the forefront. He could only pray their luck would hold and they would reach safety before nature decided to turn its wrath toward them.

Sitting still did nothing to ease his worry so he got up after a moment and put the kettle on to boil. He went to the kitchen, grabbed another mug, and shook in a few of the tea leaves he'd received as a gift from a wealthy rancher he'd sold riding horses to a year back. He preferred coffee to tea, but tea had a calming effect he valued when he was anxious about something. Heaven knew he had something to be anxious about now.

When the kettle began to boil, he took it off the fire and poured some of the steaming liquid into his mug. He allowed the tea to steep for several minutes before sipping. The hot liquid did indeed relax him, and he felt his worry begin to subside.

A moment later, he heard knocking at the door. Darrell waited outside. "I am so glad to see you," Logan said. "Come inside."

When the door closed behind Darrell, Logan asked, "Herd make it in okay?"

Darrell nodded. "They're moving them into the corral now. We'll have to wait until the storm passes to get a count and see if we lost any."

"Be nice if we lost all of them," Logan grumbled.

Darrell smiled wryly but didn't respond. He glanced at the girl on the couch. "She wake up at all?"

Logan shook his head. "Her pulse is strong and her breathing's steady, but she hasn't woken up yet."

Darrell nodded. The worry in the older man's face was clear as day and Logan felt his own anxiety return. "We should send for Doctor Caraway."

"I'll go," Darrell volunteered. "Better you stay in case she wakes up." He grinned sheepishly, running a hand over his grizzled cheeks. "You're a sight more gentle on the eyes than I am."

Logan laughed. "Why Darrell, that's sweet of you to say. For what it's worth, I think you're a fine figure for an old man."

Darrell rolled his eyes. "It's a shame you inherited your father's sense of humor." He headed for the door and opened it. He paused for a moment and scanned the clouds. "Storm's moving on. Should clear up in a short while. I'll get Doctor Caraway here quick as I can."

"Much obliged for your help, Darrell."

Darrell tipped his hat to Logan and left.

Logan returned to the sleeping figure on his couch. He sat in the chair across from the couch and regarded her. The light flickered across her oval-shaped face, casting shadows that accentuated her soft cheeks, petite nose, and the curve of her jawline. Her dusty brown hair fell in soft curls down nearly to her waist. In the firelight, it appeared to shine a bright auburn color.

Logan's gaze traveled down her slender shoulders to her shapely hips, lingering on her elegantly proportioned bustline for a long moment until embarrassment finally overwhelmed him and he looked away, somewhat red-faced. He felt a little guilty for looking so frankly at her. He'd just never been close to someone so beautiful!

Who was this girl? He'd never been so affected by a woman before. None of the girls he'd seen even remotely inspired the same level of interest he had in this stranger before him. It didn't make any sense. He didn't even know her name. She didn't even know he existed. He felt warmth travel up his neck, inflaming his face, and he was grateful she wasn't awake to see the awkwardness she inspired in him.

"Who on earth might you be?" he asked softly. He lifted his mug to his mouth and found it empty, so he put the kettle on to boil again and went to the kitchen for some more tea leaves.

He waited by the fire, sipping his tea and trying but failing to avoid thinking about the beauty of the creature across from him. He still sat there when the door knocker sounded again. He opened it and Darrell walked in, followed by a white-haired older man with kindly eyes. He smiled at Logan, "Good afternoon, Logan. Darrell tells me you had some trouble in the storm."

"I didn't but it looks like she did," Logan said, gesturing to the girl.

Dr. Caraway nodded. "Well, let's take a look and see what we can find." He walked to the couch and stopped. "Lord have mercy," he muttered under his breath."

"What is it, doc?" Logan asked.

"Where did you find her?" Caraway asked.

"Out in the west pasture, near to town," Logan replied. "Figure she lost her way in the prairie grass and got caught in the storm."

Caraway nodded and approached the unconscious woman. He set his bag on the small table next to the couch and retrieved a stethoscope. He knelt over her and gently pressed the dial on her chest. When he'd satisfied himself that her heartbeat was strong and her breathing normal, he put his stethoscope away and began examining her injuries. He ran his fingers gently over her head, stopping when he reached a swollen bruise just behind her left ear.

"Hmmm," he said, gently probing the bruise.

Logan resisted the urge to ask what the doctor was doing. He wanted Caraway to be able to focus on his patient without distraction. He wondered that he should feel so much concern for someone he didn't know.

"It's amazing what beauty inspires in a man," Darrell said.

Logan turned to him and shrugged, feigning nonchalance. "I guess she's alright. I hadn't noticed."

Darrell laughed softly. "If you say so."

Logan's face flushed but he didn't argue with Darrell. Dr. Caraway continued to examine the girl, probing for further injuries. He stopped at her right ankle and frowned. "Hmmm," he said again.

Logan noticed then that the girl's ankle was swollen nearly twice the size of the other one. Caraway gently prodded at the bruise, looking for a break. Finally, he nodded and reached into his bag.

Logan couldn't wait any longer. "Will she be all right, doc?"

"More than likely," Caraway said. "But we have to be careful with her."

He retrieved two small wooden planks and a roll of cotton fabric from his bag. Logan watched as he held the girl's leg still and positioned the planks on either side of the swollen ankle. He turned to Logan. "Will you hold these still for me, please?"

Logan gently took the girl's leg in his hands and held the planks still on either side of her ankle. He felt a thrill as his fingertips brushed her skin. The absurdity of his reaction wasn't lost on him, and he flushed once more. The knowing smile on Darrell's face did little to ease his embarrassment.

Dr. Caraway quickly wrapped the fabric around her ankle, tightly securing the planks and rendering the ankle immobile. When he finished, he reached for one of the cushions and positioned it under her foot so her ankle was elevated. Then he carefully lifted her head. "Will you place a pillow under her head, please?" he asked Logan.

Logan took one of the other cushions and set it under her head. Caraway gently lowered her until she rested against the pillow. Then he stood and looked at Logan. "You said you found her near town?"

Logan nodded. "More or less. She was pretty deep in the west field but still within a mile or so of town. If you're not used to the prairie, it's real easy to get lost in the tall grass. I think she probably wandered off and got lost trying to find her way back to town."

Caraway nodded. "Well, I'll be sure to let her father know you helped her. He can be a difficult man and that wife of his is even worse." He shook his head. "Hopefully they'll understand you were only trying to help."

Logan's brow furrowed. Of course he was only trying to help! How could anyone see it differently? What should he have done, left her out there? Then another thought struck him. "You said you know her parents?"

"Of course," Caraway said. "Why wouldn't I?"

"Well, who is she?" Logan asked.

Caraway's eyes widened. "You don't know?"

Logan felt irritation rise, but bit back a sharp retort and only shook his head.

Caraway looked at Darrell then back at Logan. "This young lady is Winona Ross. Daughter of Heath Ross."

Logan's eyes snapped open. Heath Ross of the Ross Ranch? That couldn't be. What was Heath Ross's daughter doing on his ranch? The Foley Ranch was nothing to sneeze at and Logan was fiercely proud of what he and his brothers had accomplished, but the Ross Ranch was on an entirely different level.

Nearly three times the size of Logan's ranch with well over five times the number of horses, the Rosses were the premier breeders of workhorses in central Texas. There was more than enough land on their ranch for Winona to wander without getting lost in his. He could see now why Dr. Caraway was concerned.

"Her injuries are clearly accidental," Caraway said, perhaps noticing the alarm on Logan's face. "I, of course, will mention that without your timely intervention, Miss Winona would very likely not be with us right now. Heath is a hard man but he's fair. Once he's made aware of the circumstances, I'm sure he'll understand." He turned to Winona. "In any case, she'll need to rest here regardless of his attitude on the subject."

He turned back to Logan. "I'm not worried about the ankle. That will heal soon enough with time and rest. The head injury concerns me more. There's no skull fracture but it's badly bruised and I fear she's suffered a serious concussion. She is to remain on strict bed rest—a week at least. I'll be back then to check on her, but I want to know immediately if there's any worsening of her condition."

"When will she wake up?" Logan asked.

Caraway shrugged. "It's hard to say. Depending on the severity of the injury, she may wake up in hours, or days, or ... Well, let's hope for the best. Her pulse and breathing are strong. That's a very good sign."

Caraway's somewhat feeble attempt at reassurance failed to quell Logan's growing worry. *Hours, or days, or ... ?* Caraway hadn't finished that thought, but Logan knew what was meant. He said a silent prayer that Winona Ross would recover soon, and this time he felt no embarrassment for his concern.

Caraway retrieved his bag and began walking toward the door. He opened it to reveal the storm had passed. The sky was still gray with clouds and a light rain that continued to fall, but the thunder and lightning were miles distant. He paused in the doorway and turned back to Logan. "I'll tell Miss Winona's parents she's here," he said, almost reluctantly. "They'll want to see her right away, I'm sure. I'll make sure they understand she is not to be moved. You boys take care now. I'll see you soon." He turned and left, Darrell following.

Logan returned to the chair across from the couch and sat down. His head reeled. Winona Ross! In his house! He wondered what his father would say. He felt anger, beginning as a kernel in the back of his mind and growing until it suffused him. Heath Ross was the reason Foley Ranch took so much longer to get off the ground than Heath's own ranch.

Five years ago, Heath and his father had a partnership—one that Heath shamelessly broke, nearly bankrupting the Foleys while he lined his own pockets with enormous wealth.

Logan's hands balled into fists. The attraction he felt for Winona only minutes earlier faded. This was the daughter of his father's enemy. She was beautiful—stunning in fact, and Logan was sure she was innocent of his father's transgressions. She was still Heath Ross's daughter though and knowing that her presence here meant he must allow Heath into his home galled him.

She stirred and moaned softly, her brow furrowing slightly. Logan's anger melted away, replaced by sympathy for the poor girl who'd lost her way and nearly died for it. Whatever his differences with Heath Ross, he would put them aside for Winona's sake. She would be allowed to rest and recuperate without getting caught in the crossfire of an old family feud that had nothing to do with her. She would be allowed to recover, and Logan would be there to help her.

A moment later, Darrell returned. "Doc said we should move her to the bed so she's more comfortable. You hold her under her shoulders, I'll get her legs."

As they moved her slowly and carefully to Logan's bedroom, Logan stared down at her soft features and once more felt the strange stirring of emotion inside him.

Chapter Four

Winona's first sensation was of floating on something soft but supportive. A mellow rushing sound accompanied the floating sensation, as though she drifted on a gently flowing stream. She felt an overwhelmingly strong urge to give in to the temptation to simply rest and allow the stream to carry her away. Despite her efforts, it was a losing fight and her consciousness nearly faded again, only returning when she heard voices.

The voices sounded distant, as though traveling a great distance to reach her, or perhaps muted by a wall. Yes, that was it. The voices were coming from behind a wall. She was in a room somewhere and the voices belonged to people in a different room.

She slowly forced her eyes open. The light coming through the window was muted by the heavy drapes that covered the glass but was nonetheless enough to send a searing stab of pain through her eyes. She groaned and closed them, at the same time becoming aware of a powerful, throbbing headache that pulsed through her crown and radiated down her back.

Her head. She'd hit her head. She'd run from Jude and hit her head when she fell in the tall grass outside of town.

Jude.

Her eyes flew open as memories of her encounter with Jude and her subsequent flight through town flooded her. She had to get away! She was ... where was she?

She glanced around the room. It was smaller than her room at home but still adequately spacious. She lay on a rough-hewn oak bed. The mattress was firmer than hers and not nearly so soft but was also more supportive than hers.

She guessed it was filled with straw rather than down. The pillows were down and far softer than the mattress. One lay under her head and another under her right calf, supporting her ankle.

Seeing her ankle must have reminded her body of that injury and she felt a dull throb from the limb that threatened to compete with the sharper pain in her head. She gritted her teeth and forced her eyes to remain open. She had to figure out where she was.

Besides the bed, a small chest of drawers of the same rough-hewn wood as the bed sat against the wall near the window. A mirror, small but ornately carved, sat on the chest. On the opposite wall sat a small table and chair of the same rough wood. A tallow candle on a candlestick was the only light available, though it wasn't lit at the moment. The room itself was constructed of a lighter wood than the furniture; pine, she thought, or possibly maple. There was no rug, unusual for a bedroom, although there was a quilt neatly folded on one side of the bed within arm's reach. Overall, the room was comfortable enough but sparsely appointed compared to her own room at home. A man's room, she guessed. She glanced around and saw a Henry rifle on a hook above the table and a pair of boots next to the door, confirming her suspicion.

What was she doing in a man's bedroom?

She heard the voices again: One, much lower pitched, appeared to be attempting to reason with the owner of the higher pitched voice. When the higher-pitched voice spoke again, icy fear crept up her spine. The voice belonged to her stepmother, Audrey.

"Don't tell me to calm down!" Audrey snapped. "How am I supposed to be calm when our daughter has spent the night with these … these … *men!*"

Winona couldn't quite stifle a chuckle at her stepmother's horror at the thought she might have been near men ... *men*, of all things! The laughter did nothing to help her headache and her chuckle quickly turned into a groan. She brought a shaky hand to her forehead and pressed hard, digging her thumb and middle finger into her temples. This relieved the pain somewhat, though it didn't eliminate it, and in a moment, she was able to lower her hand and focus on the voices. The lower-pitched one was speaking now. She recognized it as belonging to her father.

"I'm only saying things aren't as bad as they seem," Heath Ross said. "Think of the alternative. If Logan hadn't brought her here, she could have died out in that storm."

Audrey ignored Heath and continued to panic. "What will people say? What will Jude say? What will *Sterling* say? Our daughter in a strange man's bed after running away from her fiancé? This could ruin us!"

Winona knew that her stepmother was far more upset over the potential scandal from her presence in a strange man's bed than over her stepdaughter's near-death that day. Now, Winona could spare only a wry smile. She'd long known Audrey's priorities lay elsewhere than her stepdaughter's health and happiness.

"It's okay," Audrey was saying. "It's okay, we can fix this."

Winona heard the light tap of shoes on the floor of the parlor and knew her stepmother was pacing back and forth from anxiety. "We can fix this," she repeated. "You said she's only been here a few hours, right?"

Winona couldn't hear a response and wasn't sure if Audrey was asking her father or someone else, but she seemed satisfied with whatever answer she received because when she spoke again her voice was far calmer than before. "Okay, then we can fix this." Winona wondered idly how many times she would hear that same phrase repeated and chuckled again, sending another stab of pain through her head.

"We can save Winona's reputation if she marries Jude right away."

"Right now?" Heath interrupted. "Audrey, she's unconscious in bed."

"Well, we'll have to wake her up then, won't we? She can't stay here in a strange house forever and expect her social standing to remain untarnished. She needs to come home immediately and she must marry Jude at once. Tomorrow. I'll send for the minister."

A thrill of fear ran through Winona. She couldn't marry Jude—*wouldn't* marry him. Not after what she saw yesterday. Her stepmother couldn't be serious!

Her father seemed similarly incredulous, though of course he couldn't know Winona's own reasons for fearing such a union. "Audrey, listen to yourself. We can't take Winona straight from bed rest to the altar. Besides, it'll be a month and more at least before the Westridge station is completed."

"What has that got to do with anything?" Audrey snapped.

"Audrey, I've been cooperative and gone along with your plans with Sterling Koch, and I'll continue to go along with them, but …"

"But what?" Audrey demanded.

Heath didn't respond immediately and when he did reply, he spoke slowly, choosing his words carefully. "My dear, Sterling is a brilliant businessman, and his railroad will bring great prosperity and prestige to Westridge and to our family, but I feel it's unwise to place all of our cards into his hand."

"What are you implying?"

"I'm only saying I think we should retain some leverage. Jude's infatuation with Winona is our best bargaining chip to ensure we receive a favorable outcome in this deal. In fact, it's our only bargaining chip. If we give it away before we officially gain legal ownership of part of the railroad and exclusive transportation rights for our horses, Sterling will have no more reason to honor his agreement."

Winona felt as though she'd received another blow to her head. She expected her stepmother to value business more than she valued Winona. She didn't expect the same from her father. A tear welled in her eye and slowly coursed down her cheek. It wasn't so long ago her father was as loving and caring as any daughter could hope for. Even after her mother died, when Heath was swimming in a bottle more often than not he still retained tenderness and affection for Winona.

Her hurt transformed with anger. It was Audrey's fault. That blasted hussy invaded their lives and stole her father away. She felt a moment's guilt at these thoughts, but it quickly disappeared. Audrey took Winona's father from her. He no longer drowned himself in alcohol every night, but Winona couldn't believe his new dependence on wealth and social standing was an improvement.

Audrey continued arguing with Heath. "You're mistaken, Heath. Sterling Koch is an honorable man. He made an agreement with us in good faith. He'll keep it as long as we keep our own side of the bargain in equally good faith. If Jude marries Winona as she is now, pure and untarnished, he will give us part ownership of the railroad and exclusive transportation rights. If word gets out that Winona has been in the company of her inferiors, he will have no reason to trust us and no reason to follow through on our business arrangement."

"What about Jude? The boy's still infatuated with her. He'll marry her anyway, no matter what people say."

"You really have a poor understanding of society, Heath," Audrey retorted contemptuously. "Affection doesn't matter. Love—" she spat that word as though it was a curse, "—doesn't matter. All that matters is a person's reputation. Without a good reputation, a man, and especially a woman, has nothing in life. Winona *must* marry Jude immediately and that's final!"

"What about the wedding arrangements?" Heath said. "It will take time to prepare everything."

"Forget about the wedding arrangements! We have more important things to consider."

"But what about the flowers? The musicians? The doves? You wanted this to be the biggest wedding Westridge has ever seen!"

"Well, I wanted Winona to not sleep in another man's bed, but I guess we can't always get what we want, can we?"

"Won't the suddenness of the marriage arouse suspicion? Everyone knows how excited you were for this wedding. If she marries suddenly and quietly, people will talk.

At the moment, very few know of Winona's absence and even fewer know of her presence in this house. If we cancel our well-published wedding plans and rush Jude and Winona to the altar, people will ask questions you—we don't want to answer."

"For heaven's sake, Heath!" Audrey said. Winona could almost see her stepmother throwing her hands in the air in exasperation. "Do you never think things through? Like you said, Jude is madly in love with Winona. It'll be no trouble at all to tell people he couldn't wait any longer to take her as his wife. Heaven knows you couldn't wait to have me in your bed."

The thought of being anywhere near Jude's bed made Winona's skin crawl. A wave of nausea passed through her and for a terrible moment she thought she would be sick. The nausea passed, however, leaving her weak and her head throbbing anew, but without the risk of vomiting.

"All right," Heath said, defeated. "We'll take Winona home and make the arrangements."

"Absolutely not!" a third voice interjected. Winona recognized the voice as belonging to Dr. Caraway. He must have examined her and ordered the bed rest Audrey was fighting so vehemently to end. "She has suffered a broken ankle and a concussion, and she is not to be moved for at least a week, longer if her condition hasn't significantly improved when I return."

"Thank you, doctor," Audrey replied coldly. "I believe Heath and I know what's best for our daughter."

"It would seem otherwise, Mrs. Ross."

Winona's eyes widened again, and she couldn't prevent the thrill of joy that ran through her at hearing her stepmother so defied.

"How dare you!" Audrey cried.

"I have an oath to uphold, Mrs. Ross. Winona is my patient, and I will not allow her to be put at risk for further injury so you can prevent an imagined slight to your reputation."

"Imagined?" Audrey replied, her voice shaking with rage. "How dare you, you small man! What would you know about society, you backwoods quack!"

"Audrey!" Heath cried, appalled at his wife's behavior.

Dr. Caraway seemed unmoved by Audrey's outburst. "Enough to know that even in the most pretentious circles a mother who would value her own reputation over her daughter's health will quickly and rightfully earn the scorn of her fellow socialites, along with everyone else who hears of such selfishness. I can't prevent you by force from taking Winona, but I can and do promise you that everyone within fifty miles of Westridge will know that you denied your injured daughter the rest and care she needs so you can protect your family's money and status. I make it a point to keep my patients' private lives confidential, but I will gladly make an exception in this case if it comes to that."

"You—I'll ruin you!" Fury raged in Audrey's voice but underneath it, Winona could hear panic. Audrey's bluff was being called and she knew it.

"Believe it or not, Mrs. Ross, there are those in this world who value people more than social standing," Caraway replied.

"You allow him to speak to me this way?" Audrey demanded of Heath.

"If the doctor chooses to share his account of these events, I can do little to prevent him," Heath responded. Winona was encouraged to hear a hint of smugness in her father's voice. Perhaps he retained some affection for her after all.

"This is outrageous!" Audrey fumed. "I won't stand for this! Where is Winona? I want to see her."

"You can see her when she's well," Caraway insisted.

"Rubbish," Audrey snapped. "I will see my daughter if I please. If you want to tell everyone about that, *doctor*, be my guest."

Winona heard her mother's footfalls again, accompanied by heavier footsteps she assumed belonged to her father and Dr. Caraway. The footsteps quickly grew louder, and Winona realized they approached the bedroom. She quickly shut her eyes and feigned sleep. An instant later, the door burst open, and Audrey, Heath, and Dr. Caraway rushed into the room.

Chapter Five

Logan strode swiftly back to the house. He hadn't wanted to leave Winona alone in the first place, but he needed to check on the pens. His brothers hadn't returned to the house yet and he feared some injury had befallen them, or one of the hands, or maybe they faced some difficulty with the cattle.

He sent Darrell first, with instructions to report to him as soon as he'd checked up on Gregory and Jay. When the foreman didn't report after a few hours, he could wait no longer. He checked on Winona and, satisfied she was safe, and comfortable, and unlikely to wake for several more hours, he dressed in fresh clothing and headed for the corral. He made it halfway when he realized he'd left his boots at the house and was dressed only in slippers.

Not wanting to turn back, he endured the discomfort in his feet and quickly made his way to the pens. Gregory and Jay were all right, as were the hands. The cattle seemed fine too. Jay reported they'd lost ten head. He seemed devastated by the news, but Logan knew that was a minimal loss considering the storm they'd survived. He found Darrell talking with several of the hands.

He approached him and angrily demanded to know why he didn't report back. Darrell protested he was just about to head back, and Logan apologized before giving him and the rest of the hands the night off. He left Gregory and Jay to watch over the cattle and quickly made his way back to the house.

As he approached, he saw a light inside. His heartbeat quickened and he half ran toward the house, slowing when he recognized Caraway's wagon. The doctor must have returned to check on Winona. He didn't remember Caraway's warning that he would return with Winona's parents until he walked into the house and heard Heath Ross's voice. "When will she wake, doctor?"

"Hard to say," Caraway responded. "She suffered a nasty blow."

Logan burst into the room before Heath could respond. The three of them turned toward him. Caraway's face was equal parts frustration and apologetic. Audrey's was angry and contemptuous. Heath's expression was unreadable.

"You!" Audrey said, striding forward and sticking her finger into Logan's face. "How dare you!"

Before Logan could respond, Heath said, "Doctor, will you please take my wife home?"

Audrey whirled on Heath. "Excuse me?"

Doctor Caraway seemed as unhappy with the suggestion as Audrey and opened his mouth to protest when Heath replied. "I need to speak with Logan alone."

"You will not send me away—"

"I'll see to it you're compensated for your trouble," Heath said to Caraway, ignoring Audrey.

"Heath! Are you listening—"

"Now, Audrey!" Heath boomed.

Audrey recoiled as though slapped. She turned to Logan, shaking, her eyes nearly bloodshot with rage. She turned back to Heath and opened her mouth as though to say something, then spun on her heel and stormed out of the room. Dr. Caraway followed slowly, sharing a look with Logan on his way out.

Heath waited until they heard the front door close behind Audrey and the doctor. Then he said, "How dare you take advantage of my daughter, Logan."

Logan's blood began to boil. "Take advantage? Are you serious? I didn't take advantage of her; I saved her life!"

Heath continued as though he hadn't heard Logan. "What kind of man takes advantage of a poor, injured girl? Have you no honor?"

"Have I—have I no honor?" Logan's hands balled into fists, and he had to stifle an urge to strike the older man. "How can you speak of honor?" he said when he could control his tone. "You stabbed my father in the back, Heath. You had an agreement with him, and you went back on it. You betrayed my father, and you want to stand there and talk to me about honor?" He pointed at the mirror in the corner of the room. "Face that mirror and talk about honor, you snake."

Heath's lips curled and Logan wasn't sure if guilt or disgust motivated the gesture. "That was business, Logan" he said softly. "Some people win, some people lose. That's all it was."

"Yeah, and some people get stabbed in the back by lying, two-bit, good-for-nothing coyotes!" Logan shouted.

"I don't have time for this," Heath said. "You will release my daughter to me right now. She is to be married to an honorable young man with class and I won't have her reputation put at risk by association with—" his lip curled again. "With the son of a failure."

Logan stepped forward and raised his hand. He no longer cared about the fallout of his actions. He was going to beat Heath Ross within an inch of his life for that comment.

"No!" Winona shouted suddenly.

Both men jumped. Logan turned to the bed and saw Winona sitting bolt upright, staring at her father. He lowered his fist, grateful she hadn't seen him about to attack Heath.

"Sweetheart," Heath said. "I—"

"Don't you sweetheart me!" Winona spat. "I will not marry that—that animal!"

"Winona!" Heath cried. "Why would you say something like that?"

"I saw him, Pa," Winona said, tears welling in her eyes. "I saw him. He beat a poor old man in front of his wife. He said he was going to tear his home down around their heads."

Heath and Logan stared at her, too shocked to reply. "I never loved him," she continued. "I never loved him, but I liked him. I thought he was at least a decent man. I thought if I married him, I could at least escape the torture of living in that house with that woman you married. I just can't now. Not now that I've seen him for who he truly is. He's a monster, Pa, and I can't believe you would marry me to someone like him. Did you know about this? Did you know Jude and his father are evicting people from their homes to build this station? How can you support such behavior?"

Heath lowered his eyes and didn't respond for a while. Finally, he said, "This is how the world works, Winona. This is how families like ours build wealth and prestige."

"On the backs of those less fortunate than us? Pa, how can you say that?"

Heath's eyes hardened. "This is the world, Winona. The real world, not the black-and-white fairy tale world you read about in your storybooks. There are those who are fortunate and those who are not. There are those who do what it takes to succeed—" he stared Logan in the eye "—and those who don't."

"What happened to you?" Winona said. She seemed on the edge of tears. "You are not the father I know. You are nothing like the man I grew up with. You've changed. You've become a monster."

Tears began to course down her cheek as she said this. Seeing her in such anguish stirred something inside Logan. He glared at Heath and before the older man could respond to his daughter's accusation, Logan said, "What kind of man would sell her daughter to such a ruthless animal? For what? Wealth? Prestige? The satisfaction of knowing your pocketbook is just a little bit larger than your neighbor's? Winona's right, Heath. You *are* a monster."

Heath opened his mouth but didn't say anything. The anger disappeared from his face, replaced by shame. He stared at the floor as Winona continued.

"You know, Audrey was right. My honor has been tarnished. I wasn't taken advantage of, by Logan or anyone else, but my reputation is at risk. The only way to fix this is by marriage."

Logan stared at her, stunned. Heath looked up, hope returning to his eyes. "I'm glad you see it that way, Winona. Let's get you home and we'll make arrangements immediate—"

"Marriage to one of the Foley brothers," Winona finished.

***

Her father and Logan stared speechlessly at her. Both wore identical expressions of shock and confusion. Logan blinked and opened his mouth as though to say something, then closed it and blinked again. Her father's expression morphed from confusion to hurt, from hurt to rage, and finally from rage to resignation. Without another word to Logan or Winona, he turned and left.

Logan continued to stare wordlessly at Winona. She stared back, also silent. Winona heard the front door open and close, her father's muffled footsteps outside, then his horse's hoofbeats as he rode off. Finally, the noise died down and Winona had nothing left to distract her from Logan.

He was tall, taller than Jude and bigger too, with thickly muscled shoulders and arms and a taut stomach that appeared carved from marble even underneath his wool shirt. His jaw seemed chiseled from the same stone and gave his face a strong, noble look. His hair, a sandy-blonde so dark it appeared nut-brown until the light hit it and illuminated wispy golden highlights. He looked like a fairy tale knight come to rescue her from her controlling father and abusive stepmother.

It was his eyes that captured her, though. If the rest of his appearance called to mind a storybook hero, his eyes conveyed a more dangerous message. Silvery-blue in color and set deeply behind ridged brows, they seemed to pierce through her. She felt vulnerable in a delicious way and made no attempt to hide the effect he had on her but stared steadily and frankly back at him, a flush warming her neck and coloring her cheeks.

After a long moment, Logan finally spoke. "What in the world do you think you're doing?"

His voice was soft and wondering, unable to fathom what he'd just heard. She opened her mouth to respond when the reality of what she'd done set in. Her cheeks reddened further as shock set in. Her heart raced.

She'd just broken off her engagement to Jude, turned her father and stepmother away from her presence and promised marriage to one of three men, one of whom she'd never met before and two of whom she'd never even seen. In only a few minutes she'd irreversibly altered the course of her life.

Fear accompanied this realization, but it quickly faded in the face of resolve. She'd altered her future, but that was what she wanted in the first place. She wanted freedom—freedom from her father's rules, her stepmother's audacious expectations, and society's ideas about what was right for her future. More than anything, she wanted the freedom to choose her own life and she was willing to sacrifice anything to get that.

Well, she had sacrificed everything, but she'd gotten her freedom. She had no idea what the future held, and though that thought terrified her, it also exhilarated her. She was her own woman now, in charge of her own destiny.

"Did you hear me?" Logan repeated. "What do you think you're doing?"

She took a deep breath and met his eyes defiantly. "I think I'm marrying you," she said.

"I think not!" he replied, indignation overcoming his shock. "What makes you think I'm gonna marry you?"

"You have to," she replied. "My honor is at stake. I've spent the night in your house, in your bed. If you turn me out now, I'm no better than the soiled doves at O'Keefe's."

"What are you talking about? You were in my bed, but I wasn't with you. You were recovering from a head injury. You slept alone! I wasn't even in the house most of the time."

"That may be true but that's not how people will see it," she said softly.

"Well, I'm sorry to hear that, Winona, but it's not my fault your family's friends are foolish. I brought you here to save your life, not to win your hand. You'll stay here until the doctor says you can leave, then you're going back home."

"I am *not* going back there!" she snapped, eyes flaming.

He shrugged. "All right, then wherever you want to go that isn't here."

She sighed, frustrated. He might have the look of a fairy tale prince, but he sure didn't have the noble spirit. "Look, Logan, I've spent my whole life trapped in that house. I've never had a choice. I've always had to do what other people told me to do. Do this, say this, wear this, behave like this, marry this man: I'm not a porcelain doll! People can't just decide what's best for me without asking me how I feel. That is *my* future. That's what I have to live with for the rest of my life if I go back there. I'll admit, it's not ideal marrying a man I've just met, but a poor choice is better than no choice at all. I'm not going back," she finished with finality.

"What about my choice?" Logan protested. "Don't I get to have a say? Look, you're beautiful, Winona but I don't want to marry a woman I've just met any more than you want to marry a man just because your parents are forcing you."

Her breath caught in her throat when he called her beautiful and despite her frustration, she flushed warmly again as he continued arguing.

"Look, you're angry at your father. I get it. Lord knows I have my own differences with him. If you want help finding a job or paying for a room at the boarding house for a spell while you get yourself situated ..." he trailed off and stared expectantly at her. Once again, her momentary infatuation disappeared. How could he be so alluring and so frustrating at the same time?

"Don't you have brothers?" she asked. "If you don't want to do the right thing, maybe one of them will."

Logan scoffed. "That's never gonna happen."

"Well, hold on now, Logan," a voice interrupted. "I think we can speak for ourselves."

Winona and Logan turned toward the doorway. Two young men stood there. Both were younger than Logan, the older of the two about her own age and the other perhaps a year or two younger. They smiled at Winona, neither able to hide the frank looks of admiration on their faces as they stared at her. She smiled and glanced at Logan triumphantly. His face reddened and she turned archly back to the other two boys.

"Well, hello," she said, making her voice as sweet as possible. "My name's Winona. What are your names?

"Winona, stop this—" Logan started to say, but the middle brother cut him off.

"Well, good morning, Miss Winona," he said, flashing her a debonair smile. "My name's Gregory Foley but you can call me whatever you want."

She giggled, exaggerating the sound to rub salt in Logan's wound. "Pleased to meet you, Gregory."

"The pleasure is all mine." Gregory bowed slightly then turned to the younger boy. "The shorter, less handsome young man next to me is my much younger brother, Jay."

The younger man glared at Gregory, then turned to Winona. "I'm pleased to make your acquaintance, miss. And I'm only a year younger than him. I'm eighteen. Not that that matters, I—" he reddened, and Gregory patted him on the shoulder playfully.

Winona flashed her most stunning smile at him. "It's wonderful to meet you, Jay. Thank you for welcoming me into your home."

She glanced at Logan again. The oldest Foley brother's face was buried in his hands as he endured his brothers' awkward introductions. After a moment, he looked up and she smiled sweetly at him. He reddened with frustration but before he turned away, she caught a hint of a smile on his lips.

Chapter Six

Jay's face turned the color of a ripe tomato and he grinned stupidly at her, like a child become bashful in front of a pretty schoolmarm. Logan brought a hand to his face and massaged his temples. He remembered being Jay's age and collapsing into an awkward mess around pretty girls, so he couldn't quite blame his brother for his reaction. It just couldn't have come at a worse time.

He looked up to see Winona staring at him. She smiled sweetly at him when he met her eyes and though he reddened with irritation, he couldn't help but feel grudging admiration for her. She'd set her mind to marrying one of them and she knew that getting Logan's brothers on her side would force him to at least consider it.

He wasn't ready to give in yet, however. "All right, boys," he said to Gregory and Jay. "Outside. We need to talk."

"I'm talking to the lady," Jay replied indignantly, puffing out his chest. Winona flashed a stunning smile at him and a mischievous one at Logan, and Logan sighed. He reached out and grabbed Jay's shoulder, dragging the protesting youngest brother out of the room. As he passed Gregory, he called over his shoulder, "Don't make me come back for you, Gregory."

Gregory smiled and bowed to Winona, then followed Logan and Jay outside.

He walked several dozen yards from the house. Jay continued to struggle and protest the whole way and when Logan released him, he stood inches from his face and glared at him. Logan met his eyes and after a moment, quietly said, "You want to try it Jay, you go right ahead."

"Now, now, boys," Gregory interrupted. "It's not polite to fight in front of a lady."

Logan looked at him and Gregory nodded toward the house. Logan turned to see Winona watching them through the parlor window. She smiled and waved at him, and he glared back angrily for a moment before turning back to his brothers. "Guys, this is crazy. You can't honestly be thinking of marrying her."

Jay pulled his eyes from Logan and glanced toward Winona. The anger in his face softened into wonder and infatuation. "You can't honestly tell me you're not thinking about it."

Logan opened his mouth to answer, then shut it. In fact, he was thinking about it. Winona's argument sounded insane on the surface but there were actually several good reasons to consider it. As little sense as it made, people would talk about Winona's presence on the ranch, especially if Dr. Caraway was right, and it was several days before she could leave the house.

People were foolish that way, especially in high society. The truth didn't matter nearly as much as appearances mattered and a weeklong stay in a strange man's bed, with or without the company of said strange man, could indeed cast a black stain on Winona's reputation that may never wash away.

Dr. Caraway and Logan could shout until they were blue in the face that she was there out of medical necessity and for no other reason, and people would still believe she was up to no good. Of course, with care and counting on the silence of Logan and his brothers, Audrey and Heath could prevent these rumors from spreading, but if they failed her reputation would be ruined.

On top of that, having a woman to manage the house and assist in running the smaller pieces of the ranch, like the garden and chicken coop, would allow Logan to focus all of his energy on the horse breeding business. With his energy fully devoted to the ranch, they could grow much faster than previously estimated and perhaps even rival Heath Ross in a few years.

And she was beautiful. Slender shoulders hung above a gracefully curved waist and full hips. Logan was ashamed to admit he noticed this, but her bust appeared full as well, though not so full as to be out of proportion to her narrow waist. In the candlelight of the night before, her hair appeared to be a dusty brown but in the morning light it seemed several shades lighter, only a few shades darker than his own.

It hung in soft curls down to the small of her back, highlighting the curves of her shoulders and hips. Logan had no trouble admitting she was the prettiest girl he'd ever seen. The thought of her as his wife, sleeping in his bed, not alone but nestled in his arms ...

The thought of her in his bed as his wife and not as his guest tantalized him but another, even more powerful thought came to his head. This was how he could get back at Heath Ross. He couldn't kill the man.

That would only result in his own arrest and death, and the loss of the ranch and his brothers' futures along with it. He couldn't bankrupt Heath. In fact, despite Logan's earlier arrogance, he knew if Heath was so inclined, he could likely bankrupt Logan.

This was how he could make Heath pay for the pain he'd caused Logan's family. He could marry his daughter. Heath couldn't bankrupt his own daughter and would be expected to be fair and civil to her husband or risk losing *his* precious reputation.

Her stepmother would be stuck in the same boat and would have to put on a show of kindness and respect to him. Both of them would have to live with the knowledge that Winona was sleeping in Logan's bed, only this time she wouldn't be sleeping alone.

"Logan might not be thinking of marrying Winona, but I certainly am," Gregory said, snapping Logan out of his reverie.

"Enough," he said. "Look, I don't like it, but Winona has a point. It wouldn't be right to send her away with a tarnished reputation. As oldest brother and head of the household, it's my duty to do the right thing and marry Winona."

"Now hold on!" Jay said indignantly. "Winona said she'd marry any one of us, so I deserve a shot as much as you do! Besides," he smiled smugly. "You saw the way she looked at me."

"She looked at all of us that way, Jay," Logan said. "She doesn't care who she marries, she just wants to get away from her parents."

"Exactly! That's why we should all have a chance to marry her. We can play jackstraws to decide."

Logan stared at Jay for a moment. "Jackstraws? You want to play jackstraws to decide who gets to marry Winona?"

"Well, if you have a better idea, let's hear it."

"I do have a better idea. I'll marry Winona. You're still green, Jay. You have to learn to be a man before you can be a husband."

"So, I should be sarcastic and bitter and mistrustful like you? That'll make me a better husband?"

Gregory chuckled and Logan glared at him. "You want to help me out, Gregory?"

Gregory shrugged. "Jay does have a point, Logan. Winona said any of us. In fact, as I recall, she said any of us right after you adamantly refused to marry her. I think we both have as much right as you to marry Winona."

"That's crazy talk! Jay isn't ready to—both?"

"That's right," Gregory said. "Count me in. I'm useless at jackstraws, so I doubt I'll win but if I do, well, I wouldn't mind me a pretty little wife like Winona."

Logan couldn't believe what he'd heard. "Ain't you sweet on Louise Parker?" he asked Gregory.

Gregory smiled wryly. "Well, life is short Logan. I don't know if Louise'll ever feel the same as I do and like I said, Winona would make a fine wife. It's worth a shot, anyway. Besides," his smile widened. "I'm probably going to lose anyway."

Logan sighed angrily. Along with the anger was a fair amount of jealousy, which surprised him. He recalled the smile she gave Jay and Gregory, and though he knew she was exaggerating her affection for them to tease Logan, he still felt a surge of envy that they should receive her attention and he should be denied. He looked up to see Gregory smile knowingly and Jay grinning smugly at him and his frustration grew.

"All right," he said. "Fine. That's how you want to do this? We'll play on two conditions. First, if I win, I win. I don't want any more arguments after. If I win this game, I marry Winona and that's final."

"Same if I win!" Jay insisted.

"Fine," Logan snapped. "The second condition ..." he sighed. He couldn't believe they were actually going to do this. "We never, *ever,* under any circumstances, ever tell Winona we decided who would marry her based on a game of jackstraws."

"Deal," Jay said.

"Deal," Gregory agreed.

Logan sighed. He looked toward the house where Winona continued to watch through the window. "Follow me," he said.

He led the brothers to the barn, out of view of the house. He retrieved their old jackstraws box from a shelf just inside the barn where it lay next to a shoeing hammer and a box of nails. He returned outside and instructed Jay and Gregory to hunker down. He knelt in front of them and held the box up.

"Okay, first one to reach five hundred points wins." He dumped the box upside down. The multi-colored wooden sticks fell and bounced, scattering in a circle eighteen inches wide and laying in a tangled heap on the ground.

Logan looked at Jay. "I'll go first, then you, then Gregory."

Jay glowered. "Why do you get to go first?"

Logan threw his hands up in exasperation. "Fine, you go first!" he said.

Jay gingerly picked up a blue stick that lay atop the main pile of sticks. He set it next to himself and smiled. "Three points."

Gregory considered the pile of sticks then carefully pulled a red stick from the middle of the pile, slowly removing it without disturbing the other sticks. He set it next to himself and grinned at Jay and Logan. "Five points."

"I thought you said you were no good at this game," Jay said reproachfully.

Gregory shrugged. "I guess I'm just lucky today."

Logan glared at the pile of sticks. The only ones within easy reach were the less valuable yellow ones, worth only one point. He stared at the pile for a while but seeing no other option, he finally sighed and picked up a yellow stick. He laid it silently next to him and glared back at Gregory and Jay, who grinned at him. "How many points is that?" Jay asked. "I didn't quite see what you got."

"Just pick a blasted stick," Logan said.

Jay's grin widened and he obliged, selecting another blue stick. "That's six for me."

Gregory studied the sticks for a long time. As he awaited his turn, Logan realized his brothers were actually trying to win. So was he. They were actually playing pick-up sticks to decide who got to marry Winona. He sighed and shook his head. Of all the crazy things he thought he'd do in life, gambling over a woman's hand in marriage by playing a child's game was not one he'd considered.

Gregory finally smiled and selected one of the yellow sticks. "I guess we're tied up now, Jay."

Logan reached for a red stick. If he managed to keep it, he would pull even with his brothers. He gently tried to dislodge it from underneath a small pile of yellow sticks but just before he retrieved it, the yellow sticks fell apart.

Jay grinned triumphantly at him. Logan gritted his teeth and left the red stick where it was. He wasn't too worried. It was early in the game, and he'd always beaten Jay and Gregory before. He would catch up. His confidence couldn't prevent a small kernel of doubt from forming in his chest, however. When Jay successfully retrieved the red stick Logan failed to obtain, he frowned. It would be just his luck if Jay won and got to marry Winona.

As the game continued, Logan built on his early lead and soon enjoyed a comfortable margin over Jay and Gregory. Eventually, Logan passed Gregory and finally the middle brother fell so far behind he withdrew. "I suppose I'll have to pin my hopes for happiness on Louise's fickle heart once more," he said, sighing in exaggerated disappointment. "What a cruel thing the affections of a woman are."

"It was a mistake to let you buy that book of poetry when we visited Austin last year," Logan grumbled.

"Don't be sore just because you're losing," Jay teased.

"The game's not over yet," Logan retorted, carefully lifting a red stick and placing it on his pile.

Slowly, the tide turned in Logan's favor and he gained slowly on Jay. He fought to keep his excitement down as he closed the gap between his score and his younger brother's score. He felt more than a little embarrassed still, but the decision had been made so there was no point in dwelling on that.

After several minutes, both brothers neared the magic total of five hundred points. Jay carefully pulled a blue stick from underneath a pile of yellow sticks. When he successfully added it to his pile, he grinned triumphantly at Logan. "That's four hundred ninety-nine points. Your turn."

Logan glared at the sticks. He had four hundred ninety-three points. In a best-case scenario, he could grab the last remaining red stick, but then all Jay needed to do was select the easiest yellow stick. The game would be over. He would lose, and Jay would get to marry Winona.

He nearly gave up when he saw a small sliver of black poking from underneath a pile of yellow and blue. His eyes widened. The black stick was worth ten points. If he could grab it, he would win. Jay saw Logan's intentions and his smile disappeared. He started forward instinctively, but Gregory put a hand on his arm and stopped him.

Logan carefully grasped the black stick between his thumb and ring finger. He slowly pulled the stick outward, stopping to adjust the direction of his pull whenever he felt tension from the other sticks. Jay and Gregory watched with bated breath as he moved the stick free of the others and set it in his pile.

He smiled at Jay, no longer able to contain his joy. "Five hundred three. I win."

Jay stared at him, shocked. Then he stuck his finger in Logan's face. "That's not fair!" he shouted. "You cheated. You..."

His voice trailed off and a moment later, Gregory spoke up. "That was a fair match, Jay. Congratulations, Logan."

Logan didn't respond. The elation of victory quickly faded under the sobering realization of what had just happened. He was going to marry Winona. This time yesterday the biggest worry on his mind was branding the new broodmares. Now he was going to marry his archenemy's daughter.

"Those blasted cattle," he muttered under his breath.

"What's that?" Gregory asked.

"Nothing," Logan said. "You two go see Darrell and get set to drive the cattle to pasture. I need to talk to Winona."

The two younger Foleys left, Gregory smiling and Jay scowling. Logan walked back to the ranch house, shaking his head. "Might as well get this over with," he muttered to himself.

However, despite the reluctance in his voice and the overall exhaustion of the past twenty-four hours, there was a spring in his step as he walked.

Chapter Seven

Winona lay in bed, taking slow measured breaths to combat the ache in her head. She probably should have stayed in bed when the boys left but her desire to tease Logan overpowered her better judgment. She watched them from the living room window while they talked, waving and beaming at Logan when he looked at her.

She remained there, fighting through waves of nausea and pain until the boys disappeared to the barn to continue their conversation with more privacy. Only then did she stagger back to bed.

She wondered what the boys would decide. She couldn't make out their conversation from the living room and had no way of knowing who would end up taking her hand. She was confident one of them would marry her. If anything, she knew she could charm Jay easily enough.

He was barely a man, and she knew at his age a smile and a gentle touch would be enough to overwhelm any defense he might have against her charms. He wasn't her first choice, but he would be a long way better than Jude.

She almost felt presumptuous for daring to hope her first choice would overcome his pride and agree to be the one to marry her. In the very short time she'd known Logan, he'd frustrated her beyond belief. Willful, stubborn, and irritable, she could only imagine how annoying he'd be if she had to endure his grumbling every day.

Underneath his gruffness lay strength, however. He'd managed to rescue her from certain death in the middle of a heavy thunderstorm. She owed him her life.

He had integrity, too. Despite his strong protestations that she would not marry any of the Foley brothers, he'd never even considered the obvious and easy solution of sending her away and cutting short her recuperation. Perhaps it wasn't the most shining example of nobility to allow an injured girl to recuperate from life-threatening injuries, but compared to a man who would severely beat an elderly man in front of his wife, Logan was practically a saint.

And goodness but he was handsome! She colored as she recalled how his muscles seemed to strain underneath his shirt, as though threatening at any moment to tear through the fabric. Warmth spread through her as she thought of his stunning gray-blue eyes and chiseled jaw. She chuckled softly at herself. In her own way, she was just as shallow as Jay.

The door to the bedroom opened, startling her. Logan walked in and Winona's flush deepened at the thoughts she'd just been having. She looked at Logan, desperate to know what had been decided but equally afraid to ask.

Logan didn't say anything to her at first. He pulled the rough-hewn oak chair over to the side of the bed and sat down, staring at her. She stared back, refusing to speak first, though each second brought her more anxiety that her impression of him had been wrong, and he really was about to kick her out of his house.

When he spoke, it was neither to confirm nor to deny her worries. "Winona, why do you really want to marry me?"

Winona felt a thrill that Logan asked why she wanted to marry *him* and not simply any one of the three brothers. She wondered if he knew she preferred him? She felt another thrill as she realized he might actually want her.

Now was not the time to give in to those fantasies, however. She took a breath and answered Logan.

"My stepmother and father are obsessed with wealth and prestige. In my stepmother's case, this obsession is all-consuming and in my father's case, my stepmother is all-consuming." She couldn't help the anger in her voice as she said this and was grateful to see a flicker of sympathy cross Logan's face. "I'm sure my father loves me, but my stepmother values the family's status above all else and she's warped his view until now he sees things the same way. They want me to marry someone to secure our family's social standing. It's not important that I love him."

"I thought you agreed to marry Jude Koch, though. If that's all this marriage was, why agree in the first place?"

"I couldn't stay in that house with that woman," Winona stated flatly. Tears formed in her eyes. "She's got my father under her thumb. She won't get me. Not anymore."

"I don't know. It seemed like your father was in charge when he sent her home with the doctor earlier."

She chuckled bitterly. "Believe me, she'll have him begging for forgiveness within a day for that. Anyway, I can't do it anymore. I knew they only wanted me to marry Jude for the business connection with his father, but it was better than staying with her. And anyway, I didn't love him, but I liked him and at times he could be very charming."

"You don't like him anymore?"

She shook her head firmly. "No. Not after what I saw. He hit that man so hard, Logan!"

The tears that threatened her eyes began to trickle slowly down her cheeks and she shut her eyes tightly against them. A moment later, she felt Logan's hand on her shoulder. The gesture was awkward and uncertain, but he was trying to comfort her, and she smiled gratefully at him. She took a breath and continued. "I can't marry a man as ruthless and heartless as Jude. Not for any reason."

Logan nodded. "Sure. I understand. I just... Winona, look, I understand you don't want to marry Jude Koch but why leap into marriage with someone you've barely met? I'm sure if you talk to your parents, you can work something out."

Winona shook her head vehemently. "No, Logan. You don't understand how important this is to my stepmother. She and my father will never agree to drop the marriage."

"Well, put your foot down. They can't drag you down the altar."

"You don't understand!" Winona's voice rose, which made her head hurt more. Tears threatened her again and her lip quivered slightly as she spoke. She hated sounding so emotional. It made her feel weak and fragile, like some damsel in distress. She supposed she was a damsel in distress but that didn't mean she had to act like one!

Her anger didn't help her tears and despite her efforts, they began to trickle slowly down her cheek once more. She took a deep breath. "Status and wealth are everything to my stepmother. Everything. Not important, not very important, not the most important thing in the world, *everything.*

Ever since she married my father, all she talks about is how to make more money or gain influence or prestige in society. She's obsessed with it. She married my father because he was the wealthiest man who would have her. She told him that to his face. I remember when the Watleys returned home from Europe and Georgina Watley wore that real pearl necklace.

Audrey wore a sterling silver necklace with a diamond brooch, but everyone wanted to see the pearls because no one had seen a real pearl necklace before. She didn't speak for days. Not for days, Logan. She was so furious she was literally shaking on the ride home.

"I remember after she hadn't spoken a word to either of us for a week, my father took her on a spur-of-the-moment trip to Galveston, leaving me with our neighbors, the Hurleys. They returned a week later, and Audrey was smiling and laughing like a newlywed. She was beaming. I ran to the front of Mrs. Hurley's porch, waving and laughing. I was so excited for my Pa to come home! When they got close, I saw Pa had bought Audrey a new pearl necklace with bigger pearls than Georgina Watley's. That's why Audrey was so happy."

She took another deep breath before continuing. "They didn't even slow the wagon. I was waving and shouting for my Pa to pick me up and they rode on without even slowing. Audrey didn't even look my direction. Pa did. He looked at me as he drove past. Didn't say a word. Just looked at me."

Her lip trembled again, and she bit it until it hurt. The pain lent her strength, and her voice was steadier when she continued. "I learned later they drove straight to the Watley's estate five miles away. My stepmother wanted to go straight to Georgina Watley to brag that her pearl necklace was better than Georgina's." She looked Logan in the eye. "That's how important this is to her. That's how much status means. If she'd go to such lengths over a necklace, imagine what she'll do if her stepdaughter refuses to concede to her arranged marriage."

"Can't your father say something?" Logan asked. "He sent her off earlier and she minded. If you convince your pa not to force you to marry, he'll keep your stepmother out of it."

Winona smiled bitterly. "She always gets what she wants in the end. She only listened to my father earlier because she's confident she already won. If he meant to seriously oppose her, no force on earth would move her. She'll have her way eventually. The only way out is to marry someone else. That's the only way I escape. That's why I need you, Logan."

Logan looked away and sighed. "I understand Winona. I'm sorry for your situation, believe me, I am but you're asking for more than you know."

The hope she'd felt since Logan returned from talking to his brothers shattered. For a moment, she was shocked. Then she was devastated. Then, almost immediately, she was angry. How could he be so heartless? "That's fine," she said coldly. "If you don't want to marry me, I'm sure one of your brothers will."

"Now hold on," Logan said. "I didn't say I wasn't going to marry you, I just …" he sighed. "Winona, you should know my family has history with yours."

"Yes," she replied tersely. "I remember you talking to my father about that. Something about extorting your father out of a business deal."

"He cut my father out of a business deal that would have made them both rich. They were supposed to be partners in a deal to sell horses to the U.S. Army in San Antonio."

"I remember that deal," Winona said. "There were soldiers in uniforms in and out of the house at every hour. Father made a lot of money."

"Half of that money should have gone to my father," Logan said. "That was the deal they made. An even split. Instead, Heath convinced my father to give him his half of the horses the night before the deal to make things easier in the morning. Then he made the deal behind my father's back and kept all the money for himself."

Winona listened to Logan's tale, shocked. Could her father really have done something like that? "I'm so sorry, Logan. I never knew."

He shrugged. "Wouldn't have made a difference. What could you have done? Anyway, I'm telling you this because you should know if we do this, there's no going back. I'll be marrying my enemy's daughter. You'll be marrying your father's enemy. That anger your stepmother will feel if you don't marry Jude? That's exactly what your father will feel if you marry me. You won't just be betraying her, you'll be betraying him."

She nodded. She understood now why Logan seemed so reluctant. It was one thing to marry a woman out of the blue. It was quite another thing when that woman was the daughter of the man who betrayed your father. Still, what choice did she have? Her head throbbed, and she remembered the sharp cracking sound of Jude's fist against that elderly man's head.

She looked Logan dead in the eye. "I still want to do this. I can't marry Jude."

Logan didn't respond for a minute. Finally, he said. "Okay, let's do it."

"Really?" she said. Hope flooded back to her. "You mean it?"

He nodded. "Yes, let's do it. Let's get married."

Before she realized what she was doing, she grabbed his face and kissed him hard, then threw her arms around his neck. He smelled outdoorsy, and his body felt lean and strong. She felt warmth creep up her spine and tightened her embrace, but a moment later he gently pushed her away.

"One more thing," he said. "I'll marry you, but I want to be clear I'm doing this so you can avoid marrying Jude Koch. You're beautiful and I'm sure you'll make a fine wife, but this is not a romantic arrangement. I can offer you a marriage of convenience. Nothing more."

"That's fine," she said. "That's all I'm looking for." She meant those words but couldn't deny she felt a sharp pang of disappointment when Logan told her he didn't want romance. Well, that didn't mean anything. She was in a vulnerable emotional state and Logan was rescuing her from her imprisonment. Those feelings would wear off eventually. Despite these thoughts, she couldn't quite silence the small part of her that wished they wouldn't ever wear off.

"We should do this quickly," she said. "We should marry now, today."

"Today?" Logan replied, incredulously. He shook his head. "No, you can't even leave the bed for at least a week. We'll marry when you're well."

"No," Winona insisted. "Audrey's already making plans to prevent this, I'm sure of it. We need to marry now before she can do something crazy like claiming you've kidnapped me, and I'm being held against my will."

He lifted his hands and dropped them, chuckling. "Why not? Might as well build the nursery too, while we're at it."

"I'm serious, Logan!"

"I know, I know. I'll send for the reverend."

"The reverend?" a voice interrupted. They turned to see Gregory standing in the doorway. "Then my brother has delivered the bad news. I sincerely apologize, my lady. Know that I fought valiantly to save you from this end."

"Will you quit acting the fool?" Logan said, exasperated. "Make yourself useful and fetch Reverend Patrick yourself."

Gregory smiled and said, "Your wish is my command, your majesty." He bowed with a flourish and left.

Winona giggled as Gregory walked off. She turned to see Logan staring fishily at her, which only made her laugh harder, which only made her head ache all the more.

Logan shook his head. "I better go tell the boys I'll be busy all day. I'll see you in a little while, Winona." He stood and left for the corrals.

Winona watched him walk away and smiled. She could get used to living here.

Chapter Eight

Two hours later, Logan stood across from Reverend Elijah Patrick in his bedroom. Winona sat next to Logan, an eager expression on her face. Logan smiled somewhat sheepishly at the reverend, who said nothing for a long moment, then sighed and shook his head.

"The Lord forgive me, but I actually hoped your brother was lying when he told me his brother wished to marry Winona Ross immediately."

Logan began to explain but Winona spoke first. "It's no lie, reverend. Logan and I wish to be married at once."

Patrick looked at Logan incredulously. Logan reddened and said, "It's true, reverend."

"I see," Patrick said dubiously. "Forgive me for my surprise but I wasn't aware the two of you were even acquainted, let alone madly in love."

"We're not in love," Winona said quickly. "This is a marriage of convenience, nothing more."

It was true but hearing her say it hurt. It surprised Logan he should feel disappointment at the sentiment, since he was the one who insisted their marriage wasn't romantic. Still, he couldn't deny it stung to hear her state it so adamantly.

Patrick reddened slightly. He looked from Logan to Winona and back then cleared his throat. "I see. Well, I'm sorry to hear of your ... situation. It's true, the right thing to do in the eyes of God is marry—" he glanced at Winona's flat stomach "—but circumstances hardly appear so urgent we must consummate the union this instant."

Logan and Winona stared at Patrick, confused. What was the reverend talking about? How did he know about their situation? Then, at the same time, they understood. Their eyes widened in horror, and both began protesting at once. Patrick held up a hand after a few seconds. "Please! One at a time!"

"I'm *not* with child, Reverend!" Winona insisted. "That is not why we're doing this."

Now it was Patrick's turn to look confused. "If you're not in love and you're not with child, what convenience could this marriage bring? You would be sacrificing a great deal of wealth and comfort living here." He looked at Logan. "No offense intended, young man."

"None taken," Logan said. We're doing this because ... Well, I'll let Winona explain."

Winona told Reverend Patrick about her life at home; her stepmother's obsession with status, her father's inability to deny her stepmother and her arranged marriage with Jude Koch. She left out some of the more personal details but shared enough to get her message across.

"Well ..." the reverend glanced nervously between the two of them. Logan felt a moment of sympathy for the reverend who only hours ago was blithely going about his duties as minister. Now he was suddenly thrust in the middle of this outlandish situation.

"Winona," the reverend continued. "I understand things at home are ... confusing ... but Jude Koch is an upstanding young man with excellent prospects. I'm not saying you should marry a man you don't love, but maybe you should give him a chance before you settle for someone you barely know." He glanced at Logan. "Again, no offense."

Winona sighed in frustration. The same frustration showed in her face and her shoulders that bunched tightly in her neck. "Reverend, I can't marry Jude Koch."

Sensing something was wrong, Patrick approached the bed. He knelt in front of Winona and took her hand. "Child, what's wrong?" he asked softly. "What happened with Jude?"

Winona took a deep breath but managed to avoid further tears. She told Reverend Patrick about her encounter with Jude in town. The minister's eyes widened when she told him about Jude's violence toward the elderly couple in the town's poor quarter. "I can't marry a man like that," she finished.

Patrick shook his head and stood, speechless. After a moment, he looked back at them. "All right, I'll marry the two of you. I feel obligated to insist you reconsider and find some other avenue out of your union with Jude, but I know you won't heed that advice and I suppose a marriage of convenience is better than being forced to marry a monster."

Winona clapped with excitement and tried to stand to hug the reverend. She made it halfway to her feet before she collapsed back onto the bed, moaning. Logan placed a hand on her shoulder to steady her while the reverend shook his head again. "After this, you need to rest like Dr. Caraway ordered."

"After this, I'll finally be calm enough to rest," Winona said. "Now where do you want me to be?"

"Right where you are," Patrick replied. "I don't want you faint on your wedding day." His voice carried only the slightest hint of sarcasm. He turned back to Logan. "We need two witnesses for the marriage to be binding."

"My brothers are in the living room," Logan replied. "I'll get them for you."

Patrick nodded. "I'll prepare the license." He turned and retrieved his bag from the table near the bed. "Lord forgive me for the foolish union I'm about to bless," he muttered under his breath.

Winona smiled up at Logan, happy but also feeling a touch of trepidation at what they were about to do. He still felt a great deal of apprehension over the marriage, but he forced a similar smile before he went to fetch his brothers.

Jay and Gregory waited in the parlor. Gregory smiled at Logan. Jay looked coolly at him but seemed far less angry than he was earlier.

"Reverend needs witnesses," Logan said.

"Then witness we shall," Gregory agreed.

Jay didn't respond but stood and followed Gregory and Logan without protest or hesitation.

Logan stood next to Winona as Reverend Patrick began the ceremony. He couldn't understand why his heart pounded the way it did or why a surge of lightning ran through him when Winona took his hand. He couldn't understand the flush that warmed his cheeks when he recited his vows or the excitement he felt when Winona recited hers.

He was not in love with Winona, but when Reverend Patrick told him he could kiss his bride, he kissed her with far more passion and tenderness than he intended and didn't stop until she pulled away and looked down, her face bright red.

Logan looked at the others. Gregory and Jay both wore amused expressions. Jay's was still somewhat jealous, but his smile seemed genuine as he regarded the two of them.

Patrick stared knowingly at the two of them and Logan felt his flush deepen. "Congratulations on your marriage, convenient though it is," he said with only the barest hint of irony. "Now if I could have the bride, groom, and witnesses sign the marriage license, I'll be on my way."

Winona felt her face suffuse with color at the Reverend's veiled disapproval. She took the quill he offered and signed her name in beautiful flowing script. Logan took the quill next and signed in much rougher handwriting. His brothers signed next. The reverend added his own signature then folded the document and placed it in his bag. "I'll file this with the courthouse when I return to town." He looked between Logan and Winona and shook his head. "Good luck you two."

He left the room with Gregory in tow. Jay mumbled something about leaving to check on the cattle and followed them out, leaving Logan alone with Winona. Neither of them said anything for a long moment.

"Well, Mrs. Foley," Logan finally said. "We've gone and done it now, haven't we?"

"Yes, Mr. Foley," she agreed. "I guess we have."

***

Later that afternoon, as the sun closed on the western horizon, Logan chatted with his brothers in the parlor while Winona rested.

"So, what's the first thing you're going to do now that you're married?" Gregory asked.

Logan lifted his hands and dropped them. "I don't know. What do husbands do?"

"I can think of a few things," Jay said, grinning mischievously. He seemed to have overcome his disappointment and now relished the opportunity to tease Logan.

Logan glared at his younger brother. "Try not to think too much, Jay. That's never caused anything but trouble."

"Hey, don't blame Jay," Gregory retorted. "You could've picked up a yellow stick if you wanted this to be someone else's problem."

"Oh, lay off," Logan said.

"Look, if you're having second thoughts, I'd be happy to fill in for you," Jay said.

Logan began to respond but stopped when he heard hoofbeats outside. A moment later, the door flew open, and Audrey burst into the living room. Logan could see one of the Ross ranch hands sitting behind the reins of Audrey's buckboard, a resigned expression on his face. The man caught Logan's eyes and lifted his eyebrows in a tired greeting before the door swung shut.

"Good evening, ma'am," Gregory said, extending his hand. "Welcome to—"

Audrey passed his extended hand without a word and stormed into the bedroom. Gregory turned to Logan. "What a charming family."

"Can't you take anything seriously?" Logan scolded. "That woman's husband cheated our father and nearly ruined our family!"

"And now you're married to his daughter," Gregory retorted. "How times change."

Logan didn't respond. He heard Audrey in the bedroom arguing with Winona. Their voices were raised enough the brothers could hear them clearly in the parlor.

"Your father tells me you want to marry one of the Foley brothers. Well, that's never going to happen."

"You don't get to tell me what to do anymore."

"Don't I? Winona, the Foleys are a disgrace to this community. You will not tarnish our family's name by marrying someone so far beneath your station."

"The Foley's have been kinder to me than you ever have! You would force me to marry a violent, dangerous man because of his wealth and connections! You don't care about me. You never have."

"Winona, don't be ridiculous. There are bigger things at stake than your reluctance to marry Jude."

"Exactly." Winona sounded as though she were on the verge of tears. "You only care about your blasted money and prestige."

"Watch your language. What happened anyway? You seemed to like Jude well enough until a couple of days ago."

Winona didn't respond immediately. Finally, she said, "I don't want to marry someone just because you tell me to." Logan wondered why she didn't tell Audrey about the violence she witnessed.

"So, you'd rather marry one of *them?*" Gregory turned toward his brothers and pantomimed indignant shock. Jay began chuckling and Logan glared at both of them, motioning for silence.

"Look around you!" Audrey continued. "This place is a pig sty! It's …it's … it's a hovel! It's falling apart around you. This is far beneath a woman of your station. Of any station at all, for that matter."

Logan felt his blood boil at Audrey's insults. He harbored no personal grudge for her the way he did for her husband, but hearing his home and family slandered in this way raised his ire.

Audrey continued to list the reasons why Winona was foolish to marry Logan. "You're not equipped to be a housewife, Winona. You were raised for better things. How are you going to clean and do farm chores? You've never worked a day in your life! And cooking? You aren't ready for this. With Jude, you'll have servants to run your house for you while you focus on establishing your place in society."

"I'm not afraid of work, Audrey. I can learn to cook. I'm not the first woman who has had to learn to make her own way in the world."

"That's enough," Audrey snapped. "I've had enough of your impertinence. I don't care what Caraway says, I'm not leaving you in this hovel a minute longer. Come now. I'll send Josiah to collect your things."

"No!" Winona raised her voice again. "I'm not leaving."

"You are not marrying one of the Foleys!"

"I already have!"

This declaration was met with silence. Logan and his brothers could feel the vibrant tension, even though they weren't in the room with the two of them.

"That's right," Winona repeated. "I've married Logan Foley today. I am a married woman, Audrey and there's nothing you can do about it!"

There was more silence for a moment. Then Audrey said, so softly the brothers had to strain to hear it. "You fool! You have no idea what you've done. You've made a grave mistake, young lady, and you *will* correct that mistake if I have to force you."

The men heard the bedroom door burst open, and Audrey stormed into the parlor. She stopped when she saw the brothers staring at her. Gregory and Jay looked down, but Logan met her eyes. She looked at him with the purest expression of hate he'd ever seen. He felt a rush of satisfaction, knowing her rage was impotent, and he couldn't resist twisting the knife a little.

"Can I escort you to your wagon, Mrs. Ross?" he offered politely.

"This isn't over, Logan Foley," Audrey spat. "You will pay for this. Mark my words."

Logan didn't respond for a moment. Then he smiled. "You have a pleasant evening, ma'am."

She stiffened and turned a shade redder than Mrs. Haversham's tomatoes. Then she stormed out of the parlor without another word, slamming the door behind her.

The brothers remained silent. After a moment, Gregory turned to Logan. "Well, Logan, you've just married the daughter of our family's sworn enemy and earned the personal ire of her stepmother. What are you going to do now?"

Logan thought a moment. "I'm going to bed," he said. "You two clear out of here. I'm sleeping in the parlor."

"You're not going to keep your wife company?" Jay asked. "What kind of husband leaves his wife alone on their wedding night?"

"Jay, drag your tail out of here or I'll boot you out myself," Logan said.

The younger brothers headed outside, laughing, and Logan ran his hands through his hair in exasperation. He went to check on Winona, but she'd already fallen asleep, exhausted from the ordeal of the past two days.

He returned to the parlor, his own exhaustion weighing on him like a wet blanket. "What a day," he muttered. "What a day."

He collapsed onto the parlor sofa and was asleep before he could contemplate the wisdom of the day's events.

Chapter Nine

Winona gazed at the ceiling, lost in thought.

"I'm married," she whispered. "I'm a wife." She wondered that the thought would bring her such exhilaration. She married to escape Jude and there was tremendous relief knowing she was protected from ever having to entertain a union with him again. She married also to escape her parents' house. It was a chance for her to have a life of her own, one not dependent on her stepmother's plans or her father's approval.

Still, she did have a husband. She was gaining freedom from her parents, and she was sure to have more autonomy as Logan's wife than as Jude's, but she wasn't truly a free woman, was she?

Yes, she decided. She was. True, she was yoked to Logan and expected to submit to him as a good wife should, but he was the husband she chose. This was the life she took, not the one given to her by someone else. It was her life, for good or for ill and right now, that was enough.

She looked around her room at the now familiar oak furniture and gingham curtains. Logan had removed the Henry rifle the night of their wedding, so the walls lay bare now. He'd taken the sheepskin rug from the parlor and laid it in front of the bed, offering the room a small degree of additional comfort.

Her injuries had improved considerably over the week since she'd married Logan. Her headaches had ceased and the bruise on her head had faded to a small purple mark that no longer felt tender to the touch. Her ankle remained tightly wrapped but Dr. Caraway had removed the splints and promised to bring a pair of crutches when he visited today so she could begin to move around the house.

Winona couldn't wait for the chance to explore her new home. She was eager to get to know the house better, the brothers better, Logan better, everything better. She still felt like an outsider. Logan visited every evening but never for more than a few minutes and anyway, she shouldn't have to confine her involvement in the household to that of closeted spectator. This was her home now. She needed to be a part of it.

She was also eager to prove she could be a capable wife. Her stepmother's words hurt her more than she cared to admit.

Her brow furrowed in anger. Who was Audrey to suggest she couldn't run a household? When had Audrey ever run the household, besides to bark orders at servants? Audrey had never cleaned or cooked that Winona had ever seen. What would she know about running a ranch?

Logan warned her of the history between their families. He understandably believed Winona would be discouraged by such news and possibly reconsider the marriage. Instead of discouraging her, Winona found it motivated her. She wanted to rub it in her parents' face that not only was she married to her father's enemy, but she was a capable wife to him as well. She felt a little guilty that wanting to embarrass her parents was part of the reason why she wanted her marriage to succeed, but it was.

A knock sounded at the door and her heartbeat quickened. She realized her hair was untied and hung loosely around her shoulders. "One second!" she called.

She glanced around frantically for her hair tie, but it was nowhere to be seen. After several moments, she heard more knocking at the door and sighed in frustration. "Come in!"

The door opened and Logan entered the room. His hair was slightly matted, and his face wore a sheen of sweat from working all day. Her gaze traveled over his strong, hard body and a flush crept into her cheeks.

"Good day, Miss Winona," Dr. Caraway said.

Winona jumped and colored slightly. She hadn't noticed Dr. Caraway follow Logan into the room. "Good afternoon, doctor."

Dr. Caraway smiled warmly and sat in the chair next to the bed. "How are we feeling today?" he asked.

"Much better," Winona replied. "My headache's finally gone, and the bruise doesn't hurt anymore."

"That's wonderful news!" Dr. Caraway said. "Do you mind if I take a look?"

"Not at all."

Dr. Caraway leaned forward and gently probed at the mark on her head. The pressure was uncomfortable but not painful and after a few seconds, Dr. Caraway leaned back and nodded, satisfied. "The injury to the tissue has healed. That's very good. However, I would caution you against any strenuous activity for at least another fortnight. Even though you aren't feeling any discomfort, there's a chance your concussion is still healing."

Winona smiled wryly. "Where can I go on this ankle?" she asked.

"Speaking of the ankle," Dr. Caraway said. "Let's have a look." He reached for the hem of Winona's dress. "May I?"

Winona nodded. The doctor gently lifted the hem halfway up her calf and examined the bandages over her ankle. He began gently unwinding them. When the bandages were removed, Dr. Caraway gently lifted her ankle and probed at the sight of the wound. Winona winced but the ankle hurt far less than it had before.

After a few moments, Dr. Caraway smiled. "Your ankle is healing quickly. I think we can move forward with the crutches. I'll replace these bandages and get them from the parlor for you."

As he wrapped new linens around her ankle, Winona felt excitement rise within her. She was finally going to leave this room!

"All done," Dr. Caraway said when he finished tying the dressing. "I'll be back in a moment." He stood and exited to the parlor.

Winona turned to Logan and smiled. She was pleased to see him color slightly. He cleared his throat and said, "Good day, Winona."

"Good day, Logan. How are things on the ranch?"

Before Logan could reply, Dr. Caraway returned to the room, holding two carved maple crutches. "Jed Tucker finished these this morning," he said. "Would you like to try them out?"

Winona nodded eagerly and Logan stepped forward to help her up. He placed one hand under her arm and grasped her hand with the other. She felt as though a bolt of lightning ran through her when they touched. She couldn't resist a glance at him. For a brief moment, their eyes met, and Winona was transported away. Then Logan handed her to Dr. Caraway and her reason returned. She colored, embarrassed. Now was not the time to get carried away with these absurd romantic fantasies!

Dr. Caraway helped her place her hands over the crutches and grip them so that they supported her weight. With a little practice, she was able to use them to walk around the room. She slipped once but Logan was there to catch her.

As she righted herself, she felt a warm feeling in her chest. It was a simple gesture and could hardly be interpreted as affection, but it touched her nonetheless. She smiled gratefully at him and the way he averted his eyes and flushed before responding suggested there might after all be some affection in the care he showed for her.

"They take some getting used to," Dr. Caraway encouraged. "Still, you've shown remarkable progress. Continue to be patient with your recovery and you should be back to normal in a few months."

Winona's heart sank. A few months? She felt so much better, though! She hadn't expected to be dancing through the house right away, but she'd thought surely a fortnight's more rest would be sufficient.

Her disappointment must have showed, because Dr. Caraway smiled and placed a comforting hand on her shoulder. "These things take time, Winona. Keep your spirits up. It's only for a while longer."

Winona smiled. "Thank you, doctor."

He beamed and squeezed her shoulder, then turned to Logan. "I'll be by in another week to replace her bandages and check on her progress. Encourage her to walk around but keep her indoors for now. We need to make sure we don't cause a reinjury." He turned to Winona. "I'll see you later, Miss Winona. Take care."

"Goodbye, doctor."

Winona was a little irritated that Dr. Caraway instructed Logan to restrict her movements right in front of her as though she were a child, but her irritation disappeared when Logan offered his arm. She tossed one crutch onto the bed and took the offered arm. He led her from the room into the short hallway that led to the parlor.

She leaned against him heavily for support, but he showed no signs of exertion. He was so strong! He led them through the parlor to the kitchen. A wood-burning stove dominated one end of the kitchen while a table and six chairs of the same rough-hewn oak that composed the bedroom furniture dominated the other end. There was a wash basin and an icebox as well. A tall, wooden pantry completed the furnishings.

The kitchen was well-furnished, though modestly so compared to her kitchen back ho—back at her parents' house—but it was covered in dust and grime. Cracks and splinters peppered the wall and the table and chairs, and the floor lay under a thin coating of dirt. It was clear it had been some time since the room was cleaned.

Logan helped her sit at the table then walked over to the stove. He added wood from a small pile next to the stove and lit the fire. Within moments, the warmth from the fire reached Winona. She settled comfortably in her chair and watched Logan cook.

Fortunately, the tin pan he removed from a hook over the stove appeared far cleaner than the rest of the kitchen. "How do you like your eggs?" he asked her.

"Scrambled," she replied. "You know how to cook?"

He shrugged. "I'm not the fanciest cook in Texas but I can throw some grub together in a pinch. Truth be told, my brothers and I are looking forward to having a real woman-cooked meal." He glanced at her. "When you're well, of course."

"Of course," she replied, smiling with a confidence she didn't feel at all. She'd never needed to cook at her old home. Audrey insisted Heath retain servants for all of the cooking and cleaning. Winona didn't know the first thing about cooking! And now her husband expected her to cook for him. Of course he did. What wife couldn't cook for her husband?

Well, she would just have to learn. If the first few meals didn't work out, she could say she was still affected by her injury. Hopefully, she could learn enough quickly enough that she wouldn't embarrass herself or embarrass Logan.

As the eggs cooked, Logan retrieved several sausage links from the icebox and dropped them into another frying pan. They sizzled and Winona's mouth watered as she caught their scent across the room.

A wave of guilt ran through her. What would Logan think of her when he learned she couldn't cook? Would he see her as just a spoiled brat who'd never needed to work for anything in her life? She hoped desperately she could prove she was more than that.

A few minutes later, Logan returned to the table with two plates loaded with eggs, sausage links and toasted bread. "Eat hearty," he said.

"What?"

"Oh," he reddened slightly. "Just something my Pa used to say at every meal. He'd say, 'Eat hearty,' and we'd all dig in."

Winona looked down at the steaming plate. "That sounds just fine to me," she said.

He smiled and his chest puffed out adorably. "Yeah, I'm not the fanciest cook in Texas but I can throw together some grub in a pinch."

She smiled slightly. "You said that already."

"Oh," he reddened even more. "Well, anyway, I'm glad you like your food."

She did like it. It was filling and delicious and simple. Most importantly, it was *hers*. Her food at her table in her home. "Thank you, Logan," she said sincerely.

He reddened even more, and Winona thought he would make a very handsome tomato. The thought brought a smile to her face and Logan shifted uncomfortably before clearing his throat and saying, "So how are you liking it? Here, I mean?"

She smiled wryly at him. "Well, the bedroom is quite lovely. I'm afraid I'll have to reserve opinion on the rest once I've seen it."

"Oh," Logan said, red-faced. He looked down. "Right."

Winona felt guilty for teasing him. She reached forward and laid her hand on his arm. "I like it here," she said. "Thank you."

He perked up and smiled at her. "Good. I'm glad. How're your eggs?"

"They're delicious," she said and meant it. "I'm afraid you might be a better cook than I am."

He laughed, a rich, hearty sound that clashed with his boyish face. She smiled and a moment later, started laughing too. She regarded him as he wiped tears from his face. It was so strange to think she had a husband! Her husband himself was a stranger.

"Oh," Logan said when his laughter had calmed. "I'm sure you'll amaze all of us once you're up to cooking again."

"Oh, I'm sure you'll be amazed," she said. How on earth was she going to learn to cook? Maybe she could pick up some tips from Logan. Her eggs were cooked perfectly, and the sausage toasted to that perfect balance between juiciness and crispness. She'd had fancier food by far but couldn't immediately recall a time she'd had better food.

After breakfast, Logan offered his arm again and showed her around the house. Besides the parlor, there was a small drawing room with a rough-hewn table similar to the one in her bedroom, and an ornately carved upholstered chair. Even covered in the same layer of dust that permeated everything else in the house, the chair was by far the most expensive piece of furniture she'd seen.

"My mother's," Logan explained. "My grandmother left it to her."

After the drawing room, there was her own room then two other bedrooms belonging to Gregory and Jay. The final room was also a bedroom but much larger and more well-appointed than the others, though not quite so large or comfortable as her old room at the Ross ranch.

In addition to the natural handmade table and chair set present in all of the rooms, there was a bureau chest made of maple, with a large vanity mirror on top. An armoire, also of maple, stood on the opposite wall. The room was dominated by a large four-poster bed with a huge down mattress. The furniture was chipped and dusty and the sheets that covered the bed were torn and disheveled. Everything was covered in the ubiquitous layer of dust. Despite this, the room carried an air of reverence.

"This was your parent's room," Winona guessed.

"It was," Logan said. "It's yours now. I'm going to sleep in my old room, the one you've been using."

Winona was amazed. "Oh, Logan, I can't take your parents' room!"

"Your room," he insisted. "This is your house now."

She smiled gratefully. "Thank you, Logan. That's very kind of you."

He nodded. "You're welcome. I'll go bring your stuff over."

He returned a moment later with her chest, boots and art supplies. Winona stared in wonder. She could barely move the chest, let alone lift it. Logan carried it over his shoulder with one arm and appeared untroubled by the weight. His muscles bulged and Winona's heartbeat quickened.

He set the chest against the wall, the boots by the door and the art supplies on top of the table. "I have to help Gregory and Jay with the chores, but I'll be by to check on you later."

"Okay, thank you."

He smiled at her and stood awkwardly for a moment. Then he nodded and left.

Winona thought of her breakfast with Logan and smiled. It seemed a small thing that they shared a meal together, but it meant so much. It meant she was starting to belong, to really belong. This life of hers was no longer a fantasy to consume her idle hours, it was real. It was real and it was hers.

Almost hers. She needed to give back in order to feel like she truly deserved the life she had. She could start by cleaning the house as soon as she was healthy enough to do so. She looked around at the dilapidated bedroom. "Where do I even begin?"

She sat on the bed and a cloud of dust flew into the air around her. *Well,* she thought, *at least I know where to begin now.*

Chapter Ten

Logan steered the last of the herd over the small hill that separated the east field from the southeast pasture. The straggling cattle lowed indignantly as he prodded them but moved readily enough.

He crested the ridge in time to see Jay riding through the herd, stopping every few seconds to peer over the cattle and ensure everything was as it should be. Logan sighed and shook his head. Jay wanted so much to appear grown up and mature but every time he tried, he just seemed more like the child he was.

One of the cattle bumped Logan's horse, causing the animal to sidestep. The horse whinnied in frustration and the cow lowed with equal annoyance before ambling off to join a few of its friends in a patch of thicker grass.

Logan patted his horse's neck. "It's okay, boy. Just a while longer and we'll get these blasted cows off our ranch." The horse snorted its agreement.

Logan looked below to see Gregory sitting atop his own horse, watching the herd disperse through the pasture. Logan trotted up to him. "Hi, Gregory."

"Mornin', Logan," Gregory responded. "Corral's busted."

"Beautiful day, ain't—what?"

"The corral's busted. The herd tore down almost an entire side of fencing on its way out."

Logan stared at his brother, dumbfounded. "Consarn it, Gregory. Who was running the herd?"

Gregory glanced at him. "Consarn it? What are you, a prospector?"

"Blast it, Gregory, I'm not in the mood."

"You never are."

Logan looked sharply at him, but Gregory's expression remained calm. He glanced back at Logan again then looked out toward the herd. "Jay and I ran it."

"Why didn't you wait for Darrell? Or call me for heaven's sake."

Gregory shrugged. "Jay wanted to run them himself."

Logan sighed angrily and glared toward Jay's distant figure. "Well, that worked out just wonderful, didn't it? Gregory, why didn't you call me?"

"He wanted to run them himself."

"So what? You know he's not ready for that kind of responsibility."

"None of us are, Logan. Yet here we are."

Logan's blood began to boil. "Gregory, blast it, this isn't a game. This isn't a lark. This isn't a joke. This is our home. Our father's home and now ours and we can't afford to make mistakes with it. If Jay wanted to run the blasted herd, he could've run it with Darrell or me watching him. Now we have to spend the rest of the day fixing that fence instead of working on selling horses."

"You could just use the other pens for now and fix the fence later."

"Is that what I should do?" Logan snapped. "Wait until later? No time like the future, right? Why get done today what you can get done tomorrow? Am I the only one who takes this ranch seriously?"

"Jay takes it seriously," Gregory retorted. "I'll let him know you'd like him to stop."

"I can't deal with you right now," Logan spat out.

He wheeled his horse around and galloped away, seething. How could Gregory and Jay be so careless? If they'd waited fifteen minutes, he or Darrell could have helped with the herd and gotten them out of the pens without destroying them. Why did they never think things through?

He reached the corral a few minutes later. The damage was as Gregory described. A hundred yards of fence along one side of the corral was knocked down. In some places, the fence posts were torn from the ground. Most of the wood was splintered and torn, leaving very little usable material. Logan sighed.

They would have to rebuild the fence from scratch. That would take the rest of the week at least, since they would have to work around their other chores.

Well, they could clear the debris today, at least. He rode toward the stables and brought three hands back to help him. He also took an ax to help cut the splintered planks away.

The work was agonizingly slow. Logan used the axe to chop the wood into six-foot sections while two of the hands gathered it and tied the sections in bundles they could drag to the barn later. The other hand tied the fence posts that still stood to his horse and pulled them out, adding them to the piles. The wood was too damaged to be of any use for repair or construction, but it would make good firewood.

As Logan worked, his thoughts drifted to Winona. He spent his morning and evening meals with her now. Every night he would sleep anticipating the morning and every day he would eagerly await the night when they could talk again. She was engaging and cheerful when they talked and proved to be very intelligent. Logan, like his brothers, was taught to read by their mother but had little in the way of formal education. Winona had a tutor throughout her childhood and her knowledge in a multitude of subjects fascinated Logan.

He chuckled as he recalled their conversation earlier that morning. She'd shown him a drawing she'd done of a pond with a bird that looked like a large, white goose in the middle. "I've named this one, *Le Cygne*."

"The what?"

"*Le Cygne*," she said. "It's French. It means the Swan."

He'd stared wide-eyed at her. "You speak French?"

She'd smiled and blushed a little at his admiration. He recalled the warm feeling he felt and smiled as he swung the axe down, separating another section of fence. He'd spent the rest of breakfast asking her to name things in French. She'd obliged, chuckling every so often at his enthusiasm. He couldn't wait to see her for dinner.

His smile faded a little. He wasn't supposed to have these feelings. Yes, she was his wife, but their arrangement was explicitly not romantic. He'd offered her a marriage of convenience and she'd accepted it. He was fine with that arrangement at first. He wasn't fine with it now.

That was a problem. Neither of them could afford to entertain thoughts of romance, what with the ranch falling apart around them and Winona's father no doubt scheming harder than ever to ruin them. How could he prevent feeling romantic thoughts for her, though? Every time he saw her, he was more and more enamored with her.

That was the answer. He would have to stop seeing her. She was more mobile now. She'd had her crutches for two weeks and needed them less as time passed. She was not quite able to resume chores, but she was able to take care of herself more easily when Logan wasn't there. So, he'd have to be there less. He hated it but that's the way it was.

Without a dinner with Winona to look forward to, Logan's mood soured considerably. He called for a break and the hands rode toward the barn for lunch. Logan had a bread roll and some smoked meat in his bag, so he stayed by the corral and leaned against a fence post, content to ruminate alone with his thoughts.

"Dollar for your thoughts?" Darrell's voice called.

Logan turned to see the older man walking up. He chuckled. "You're overspending," he replied.

Darrell smiled. "Well, then how about an even trade? You tell me your thoughts and I'll tell you mine."

Logan sighed. "We're hurting bad, Darrell. The ranch, I mean. I guess I just didn't want to see it, but that Audrey woman was right. Everything's falling apart."

"You mean the corral? Near five hundred head of Longhorn stampeded the fence, Logan. I think that's a reasonable excuse."

"Not the corral. Everything. The house, the barn, the pastures—everything's coming to pieces. There are cracks in the walls of the house, the furniture's chipped and worn, we haven't cleaned in heaven knows how long—what?"

Darrell smiled knowingly at Logan. Logan colored and repeated somewhat defensively, "What? Did I sprout a pair of antlers or something?"

Darrell laughed. "This is because of your wife, ain't it? I ain't never seen you so concerned about tidying up before. Now you want to make everything nice and pretty for the missus."

Logan glared, sending Darrell into another laughing fit. Logan reddened, more from embarrassment than anger. There was some truth to what Darrell said. Having Winona around definitely made him more self-conscious about the state of things. That wasn't everything, though.

"It's not just Winona," Logan said. Darrell stopped laughing and listened intently as Logan continued. "This is my father's ranch, Darrell. He built it with his own hands. Our family didn't have anything before Pa started this ranch. This is all that's left of his legacy and it's falling into disrepair."

"Now, you stop it," Darrell chided. His tone was gentle but firm. "This ranch is not just your father's legacy. It belongs to you boys, too. You and your brothers. And speaking as a man who knew your father for twenty-five years and was proud to call him friend, he would be proud of you for what you've done.

A lot of ranches would have folded after everything that's happened, but you've stayed in business, and you've managed to keep everyone on. We might not be a fancy outfit like the Rosses, but every man here is proud to work for the Foley brand."

Logan smiled gratefully at Darrell. "Thank you, Darrell. That means a lot." His smile faded. "It still hurts to see the place so rundown."

Darrell sighed. "Don't be so hard on yourself. You've done the best you can in very difficult circumstances. Things will look up. You'll see." He smiled slyly at Logan. "They're already looking up for you, at least."

Logan colored. "It's not that kind of marriage."

"Sure, it isn't," Darrell said with just the slightest touch of sarcasm. Before Logan could retort, Darrell clapped him on the shoulder. "Well, I'd best get back to work. Got some yearlings to break for the saddle. You take care, Logan."

"Take care, Darrell."

Logan waited a while after Darrell left, reflecting on the older man's words. He knew Darrell was right. The ranch had seen better days, certainly, but it still managed to support itself and support Logan and his brothers.

That wasn't enough, though. Not while Heath Ross was sitting in the lap of luxury on the back of Dale Foley's hard work. His heart ached. If his father were here, he never would have let Heath ride roughshod over them like that.

The little voice in the back of his head reminded him viciously that that was exactly what had happened. Heath Ross had run roughshod over Logan's father and Logan's father hadn't done a blasted thing about it.

Logan stood quickly and began walking. He slapped his horse on the rump and the animal trotted in the direction of the barn. Logan would often choose to walk back from a ride when he wanted to be alone with his thoughts, so his horse arriving riderless at the barn wouldn't cause alarm.

As he walked, he grew angrier. He alone seemed to care that their ranch was falling apart. Jay had gotten it into his head that the best way to prove he was a man was to fight Logan at every turn. Meanwhile, Gregory seemed to think life was a joke and he could just ignore everything except to laugh every now and then. This was their family name! This was their home! Did they expect Logan to do everything?

Well, if that's what they wanted, that's what they would get. Logan had been too lenient for too long, spread thin trying to manage so many moving parts at once that he lacked the energy to rein Jay in or motivate Gregory. That was going to change.

Winona would soon be well enough to handle the chores and Logan could focus on the business. Then things would run the way they were supposed to run, whether his brothers liked it or not. Beginning with selling these blasted cattle.

That thought sparked an idea in Logan's head. That spark quickly grew and strengthened until it became a fully formed plan. Logan's anger fled, replaced by excitement and by the time he reached the house, he was happily humming a tune.

***

"Over my dead body!"

Jay's hands were balled into fists and his face was twisted in anger. He leaned forward, glaring at Logan.

Logan offered a deadly smile in response. "Be careful what you ask for, Jay."

"Logan!" Winona cried in shock. Gregory watched with a bemused expression but said nothing. Logan called a meeting to announce his intention to sell some of the cattle to pay for repairs to the ranch. Jay, as expected, was less than pleased.

Logan glared at her but when she didn't turn away from his gaze, he looked down, then back at Jay. "We need to repair that corral, Jay. Not to mention the stables, the barn and the house itself."

"You're not selling my cattle!"

"*Your* cattle? As I recall, we bought those cattle with the ranch's money. It's *our* cattle. Besides, I'm not talking about selling all of them. Just two hundred head to cover the cost of the repairs. That still leaves three hundred."

"You don't need to sell two hundred cattle to pay for the repairs, Logan."

Logan sighed and admitted reluctantly, "I want to buy some horses to—"

"I knew it!" Jay shouted. He stuck his finger at Logan's face. "You never believed in the cattle business!"

"What cattle business, Jay?" Logan shouted back. "This is horse ranch, not a cattle ranch!"

"Boys! There's no need to shout!" Winona interrupted.

The boys ignored her, and Jay fired back at Logan, "We shouldn't be a horse ranch. This pastureland is perfect for cattle and there's always a market for beef. Sure, we get less per head, but we wouldn't have to struggle to compete with the larger ranches anymore. We'd be the only ranch in the area selling cattle and we have the best land for it. Horse-breeding is just too much risk."

"It's a risk worth taking! I'm tired of eking out a living. I don't want to just make do anymore. This ranch has the potential to be successful if only we could all work together!"

"Why does that always mean doing what you say?" Jay retorted. "Why can't we all have a say and all work together for what we all decide on?"

"Blast it, Jay, we're selling the cattle." He looked to Gregory for support, but Gregory avoided eye contact, pretending to be intently focused on a loose thread in his shirt.

"Logan, we lost," Jay said.

Logan turned back to his younger brother. "Excuse me?"

"We lost, Logan. Heath Ross won. I'm sorry but he did. He won the horse market. We can't compete with him, we'll never succeed. He's got more land and better land for horses. He's got connections with the railroads and the government. It's a fool's errand to go head-to-head with him. But we can win with cattle! No other ranch can support enough grass to sustain a herd of cattle! We still have the rights to the water from five hundred yards of Elm Creek. If we rotate—"

"Get out," Logan said.

"Logan, just listen to me—"

"Get out!"

"Logan—"

Logan started toward Jay, jaw thrust forward. Gregory suddenly moved until he was in between the two of them. "Easy, Logan."

"Oh, now the silent monk wants to speak!" Logan shouted. "Why don't you follow him outside. I don't want to see either of you."

The two brothers left, and Logan turned to Winona. The look on her face filled Logan with shame but his pride wouldn't let him show it. He glared silently at her until she took a breath and said in an even voice. "I'm going to bed."

Logan moved to help her, but she lifted a hand in refusal. "I can make it all right, thank you."

He lowered his head and avoided eye contact as she walked slowly to her room. When he heard the door close behind her, he swore and kicked the small wooden table next to the couch. It flew across the room and hit the opposite wall, splintering into several pieces.

Logan sighed heavily and sat on the couch. He was ashamed of his outburst, but his anger still outweighed his guilt. Why was everyone against him? Couldn't they see he had the ranch's best interests at heart?

Well, fine. If they didn't want to help, he'd just do it himself. He was used to that by now.

Chapter Eleven

Winona sat up and wiped sweat from her brow, then returned to scrubbing. In moments, moisture beaded once more on her forehead. She managed to ignore it until the salty droplets fell into her eyes, stinging them. She sat up and wiped away the fresh sweat, angrily shaking it off.

She looked around the floor of the kitchen and saw to her dismay that she'd made little progress. She'd worked all afternoon and fully two-thirds of the floor still lay under a thick crust of dirt.

"How can this place be so dirty?" she blurted out. Her face went white, and she stilled completely, praying no one had heard her. When she heard no voices after several seconds, she sighed with relief and returned to her work.

Her back ached. Her shoulders ached. Her arms ached. Her legs ached, everything ached. She thought wryly that if she'd known she was healing from pain in her ankle only to hurt everywhere else she might have broken it again.

It was over a month now since she felt well enough to start doing chores and nearly two months since her arrival and marriage to Logan. She'd thought to have the house cleaned and repaired and be ready to start on the other buildings by now, but she was soon disillusioned of that pipe dream.

She couldn't even begin cleaning for the first few days because the brothers didn't have a single cleaning tool on the ranch. Not even a broom. She'd made Logan a shopping list and he'd sent Darrell into town for supplies—a broom, a feather duster, a washboard and bucket, lye soap, scouring pads and brushes.

He'd grumbled about the cost of the items, but she'd put her foot down and insisted.

It took another week to dust. She couldn't believe how thick the dust was over everything. In every room. She'd had to go outside to shake the feather duster clean four times the first day.

Then she'd started on the kitchen. The walls and furnishings took another week to clean. She didn't even bother polishing the wood or plastering the cracks and chips yet. That would have to wait until she could remove the dirt and dust and grime that clung to everything like rind.

She looked down and realized the soap in her wash bucket was now more dirt than soap. The section of floor she scrubbed was a mire of soapy mud that made the floor seem even dirtier than it had before. She huffed and tossed the scouring pad into the bucket. A dollop of grimy soap water splashed onto her face. She gasped and shook her hands in disgust. She wanted to scream, but didn't want anyone to hear her, so she just collapsed to her knees and tried to keep from sobbing.

After several deep breaths, she managed to compose herself enough to stand. She lifted the wash bucket and headed outside to replace the dirty water with fresh water from the well. It was only twenty yards to the well, but her ankle began to ache by the time she reached it. She lowered the bucket, then laboriously began the process of raising it.

Her body hurt all over. The ache in her ankle strengthened to a steady throb. Her back and shoulders were stiff and sore from days and days consisting of hours and hours spent waging war against the years and years of caked-on dirt and dust that covered everything everywhere in the house.

It was already late afternoon, but the sun beat down mercilessly, sapping what little strength Winona had left. A trickle of sweat ran into her eye, stinging it. She cried out and instinctively brought her hands to her face, letting go of the bucket. It tumbled down the well, crashing into the water below.

That was the last straw. Winona's exhaustion and frustration finally overcame her. She collapsed against the well and wept, her sweat mingling with her tears and stinging her eyes further. She brought her apron up to her face to wipe her tears. Her apron was covered with the dirt and grime of the day's chores and did little to dry her eyes. Finally, she sighed and gave up, allowing her tears to flow until they stopped of their own accord.

Her stepmother was right. Winona wasn't cut out for housework. A month's worth of work and then some and she still hadn't finished cleaning the house. She hadn't even begun to repair the holes in the roof or the cracks in the walls. After the house was the barn, the stables, the vegetable garden – if she could even figure out how to get anything to grow after the brothers left it fallow for so long, and heaven only knew what else. She could work nonstop for a year and never catch up.

"Ma'am?"

The voice startled her. She opened her eyes and was immediately assaulted by bright, hot sunlight. She squinted through the light at the silhouette in front of her.

"Ma'am?" the voice repeated. "Are you all right?"

She still couldn't pick out any features, but she finally recognized the voice as belonging to Darrell, Logan's ranch foreman. "Yes, hello, Darrell. I'm all right, thank you. Just resting a spell."

Her vision was clearing, and she could see Darrell's face now. He wore a dubious expression as he replied, "Might be more comfortable if you rest inside." He extended his hand.

She allowed Darrell to help her to her feet but declined the arm offered to escort her back to the house. "Thank you, Darrell. I'm all right."

"All right," Darrell said, his tone making it clear he didn't believe her. "Do you need anything?"

She smiled gratefully at him. "Thank you, but no. I'm just going to rest in my room for a while."

He nodded. "Okay. You ever want help with anything, just let me know."

"I will. Thank you, again."

"Happy to help." He tipped his hat and headed off to the stables.

Winona walked back to the house. She was touched by Darrell's concern. It was the first time in a while anyone had bothered to think about her. Logan still visited with her at least once a day but since the fight over the cattle last month, their interactions were cool.

That spark of romance she'd felt when they'd had breakfast together the day she received her crutches seemed like a distant memory, set aside in a corner of her mind the way her crutches now sat in the corner of her closet, close by but no longer a part of her daily routine.

She no longer felt a part of Logan's routine either. Of any of the brothers' routine for that matter. Logan and Jay were preoccupied with their differences over how to run the ranch. The closest she came to interacting with Jay was overhearing his daily shouting matches with Logan when they thought she was asleep in her room.

She got precious little more from Logan. Gregory seemed nice enough. He alone of the brothers would spare her time for an engaging conversation but even then, his behavior seemed motivated by a duty of politeness rather than genuine interest in her company. She felt less a part of the ranch now than she had when she was bedridden.

When she reached her room, she collapsed into bed, lacking the strength even to undress. She stared up at the tester over the bed, a thin blue cotton panel with a pink, flower-print pattern. The fabric appeared to have been beautiful once but was now drab and faded.

When she first arrived at the ranch, she felt out of place. She'd thought when she was well enough to do chores, she would feel more connected but a month and more of backbreaking labor hadn't made her feel like she belonged. Everyone just lived in their own separate worlds, sharing a house but not a home.

Then she had an idea. She sat upright, infused with a renewed energy.

She hadn't yet cooked a meal for the brothers. She'd intended to make dinner for them after she recovered but between the brothers fighting and the mountain of chores she had to complete, she'd never gotten around to it. Perhaps it was time she did.

Not tonight, though. She was exhausted from her chores and anyway she still had no idea how to cook. She had a plan for that, however. She would send Darrell into town tomorrow with a letter for Cordelia asking for her famous brisket recipe. She would finish cleaning the kitchen and the next day she would make dinner for everyone. If everyone gathered together for a good meal, it would give them a chance to spend meaningful time together and act like a family for once.

A smile spread across her face. She left the bed and sat at the table where her paper and pencils sat. She began to draw an image of a sunrise breaking over distant mountains and illuminating a pristine valley below. If she had any luck, the sun would rise on her family, too.

***

"Okay, boys. I made this brisket special to celebrate two months since I joined our family. Dig in!"

Winona smiled brightly at the brothers, eagerly awaiting their reaction to the food. They each took a bite of the brisket and she leaned forward in anticipation.

Logan said nothing and his face showed no reaction. His silence stung her more than she thought it would. Marriage of convenience or not, he was her husband and she thought she could at least count on a little support from him. Certainly, she deserved better than for him to act as though she wasn't even there! He took another bite of the brisket and she sighed. He was eating the brisket. She supposed she should be grateful for that at least.

She looked at Jay. The youngest Foley stared at his plate wordlessly, his face expressionless. He hadn't even lifted his fork. Her smile began to fade. This was not having the effect she hoped.

She turned to Gregory. The middle brother ate as absentmindedly as Logan. After a few seconds, he noticed Winona staring at her and smiled. "This is delicious, Winona, thank you."

Her smile returned. "Thank you, Gregory, that's very nice of you to say." She spoke loudly, wanting to get the attention of the other two.

They both ignored her and after nodding to her in acknowledgment, Gregory did the same, returning to his food and his absentminded stare. Her heart sank. She'd put so much thought into this meal, desperate to find some way to bring them together, some way to feel like she belonged here. Now she was watching all of her effort come to naught.

She felt anger rising in her chest. She wasn't going to sit still and let the brothers waste another chance at mending fences and she wasn't going to allow herself to be a wallflower anymore. She made this dinner to give everyone a chance to talk, and everyone was going to talk, blast it.

She turned to Logan and smiled brightly. "So, Logan, how are those repairs coming?"

"Fine."

"Have you mended the corral fence yet?"

"Not yet."

"Oh," she took a breath, forcing down her irritation. She would not allow his surliness to ruin the evening. "Well, is there anything I can help with?"

Logan sighed irritably. "No. Thank you."

"Well, there must be something I—"

"We need supplies, Winona," Logan interrupted. "That's what we need. We need more wood, and rawhide, and pitch, and turpentine. Those things cost money—money we won't have until we sell some more of those blasted cattle."

Jay frowned at Logan's veiled jibe but didn't respond.

Winona tried to change the subject. "Jay, I heard one of the cows is nearly ready to give birth."

Jay sighed and said, "Yes, we're expecting to deliver tomorrow morning."

"Well, that's exciting! The first calf born on Foley Ranch. You must feel so proud!"

He shrugged. "Doesn't matter. We're just a horse ranch after all." Logan's jaw tightened as Jay continued. "Who cares about a lousy calf?"

This was getting nowhere. Winona grew more and more frustrated with Jay and Logan with each passing minute. She wanted nothing more than to scold them for their childishness, but now wasn't the time. She needed this to be a happy meal. She needed to have a good memory as part of this family.

She turned to Gregory. Maybe she would get lucky, and he would consider her worth more than a token few seconds of his time. "Gregory, I saw you reading in the study the other day. What are you reading?"

"Poetry."

"Oh! I love poetry. Who were you reading?"

"Tennyson."

"I love Lord Tennyson!" she exclaimed. "I must have read 'Ulysses' a hundred times as a girl. How are you enjoying it?"

He shrugged. "It's all right."

She stared at him—her smile entirely forced by that point. She'd never known anyone so intent on avoiding human connection as these three brothers were. How foolish she was to think she could grow closer to this family over a dinner. They were barely a family to begin with.

She was pulled from her thoughts by the sound of Jay's chair scraping on the floor. He stood and headed for the door. "Where are you going?" she asked. "You haven't touched your brisket."

"I can't eat that," he said. "I'm going to town for a proper meal."

Winona felt as though a knife were driven into her gut. She leaned back in her chair, stunned speechless. Logan and Gregory stared at Jay in shock. "Get back here!" Logan shouted after Jay. "Apologize to Winona!" Nice of Logan to think of her now that thinking of her gave him an excuse to fight with Jay. Jay ignored Logan and a moment later, she heard the front door slam behind him.

Gregory laughed nervously. "Don't take it to heart, Winona," he said. "Jay's still got his milk teeth. He can't quite manage to chew meat yet, so he gets frustrated and um … storms off." Gregory's voice trailed off as he realized his joke wasn't remotely funny or remotely helpful. He stared at his plate and swallowed anxiously.

"Don't worry, Winona," Logan said. "When he gets back, I'll tan his hide for this. He's got no call to talk to you that way. I'll—"

"Leave it, Logan," Winona snapped. "Dinner's ruined anyway." She stood so quickly her chair fell to the floor behind her. She left it where it fell and stormed off to her room. When she arrived, she fell face-first onto the bed and sobbed bitterly.

Chapter Twelve

Logan swung with a grunt. The mallet struck the fence post with a low, heavy *whump*, driving the fence post two inches further into the dirt.

He couldn't believe Jay! Logan knew he was still more child than man, but he never expected this degree of foolishness! How could he speak to Winona like that? What would Ma think?

He swung the hammer again, driving the fence post down another two inches.

He knew Jay was angry. He even understood it. He and Jay clearly didn't see eye to eye on the ranch. Jay wanted to raise cattle and Logan wanted to remain a horse ranch. Jay was wrong but he clearly didn't see it that way. He was passionate about cattle and Logan wasn't, and in the end Logan had the final say. It made sense for Jay to be angry with him. From his perspective, Logan was shutting him down and denying him a say in the family business.

Logan swung again. The mallet slipped and only glanced against the fence post. Logan adjusted his grip and swung hard. This time it landed true, and the fence post gained another two inches of depth.

Well, maybe he was shutting Jay down, but he had good reason. The Foley Ranch was the finest horse ranch in West Texas and had been for twenty-five years. Sure, there were bigger outfits, but none finer. Logan couldn't allow Jay's harebrained schemes to threaten their reputation. Their business was at stake. Jay was just too young to understand.

That's not really why you're fighting with Jake, the small voice in his head retorted. *The truth is, it doesn't matter to you if Jay is right or not. You just can't handle the thought of Heath Ross winning.*

Logan swung the hammer again. The dirt was more hard packed below the surface and the fence only sunk another inch. He sighed heavily and rested a moment, leaning against the handle of his mallet.

That was the truth. If the Foley Ranch left the horse business to become a cattle ranch, then Heath Ross won, and Logan couldn't stand the thought of Heath Ross winning.

Well, so what? What was he supposed to do? Their father broke his back building this ranch. He worked tirelessly to establish their reputation and then kept working tirelessly to maintain it. He poured his heart and soul into this ranch and then Heath Ross stabbed him in the back.

Most men would have given up, but Dale Foley didn't. He kept working tirelessly and though they'd nearly gone under several times since Heath Ross stole the contract from them, Dale managed to keep them afloat through blood, sweat, and tears. He'd kept them afloat in spite of Heath Ross's betrayal and Logan wasn't about to betray his father's legacy by admitting defeat now. If Jay couldn't understand that then that was Jay's problem.

His conscience spoke again. Strangely, it spoke in Winona's voice this time. *If this ranch goes under because you're too stubborn to know when it's time to make a change, then that's your problem.*

He swung the hammer with all his might. The impact reverberated through Logan's arm and jarred his teeth. It also split the post down the center all the way through.

Logan cursed loudly and kicked the two halves of the broken post. They flew through the air, landing a few yards away. Logan landed heavily and nearly rolled his ankle. He stumbled and lost his balance, falling onto his backside and rolling onto his back. He remained where he fell, staring up at the sky. The mallet lay a few feet from him.

"I'm so tired," he said, "I'm just so tired."

Jay shouldn't have talked to Winona like that. He was justified being angry with Logan, whether or not he was right about the ranch. That didn't give him the right to insult Winona. Logan recalled the look on Winona's face when Jay insulted her meal and guilt and anger flooded him in equal measure. He should talk to Jay. He should make Jay apologize to Winona.

He wasn't going to, though. What would be the point? Jay would just yell at him a little more until they both stormed off. Logan couldn't do it anymore. He couldn't keep fighting. He just wanted to keep the ranch afloat. He was so sick of barely scraping by. He wanted to be comfortable. He didn't care if they were never rich. He didn't need to be wealthier than Heath Ross. He just needed the ranch to do well enough to give him, his brothers and his wife a nice, comfortable life free of hardship and worry.

"I'm so tired," he repeated.

He recalled his plan to sell some of the cattle to pay for the supplies needed to repair the ranch. He'd hesitated, unsure about acting without his brother's consent. He'd never get that. Gregory would just shrug or make some smug comment and Jay would fight him every step of the way.

He would have to do it without them. He sighed and ran his hands through his hair. He would sell the cattle. Just a hundred head. It wouldn't leave them a surplus and it wouldn't let them buy more horses, but it would cover the repairs and shore up their food pantry a little. There was a buyer in town representing an Arizona outfit that was looking to branch out from dairy to beef.

He knew from Darrell that the buyer was rooming at the Westridge Inn. He didn't relish going into town, but he could move quietly and avoid notice. He would head in, meet the buyer and leave right away. On the off chance anyone noticed him, they would probably just avoid him anyway.

If he hurried, he could wash up and meet the buyer that afternoon. Hurrying was the last thing Logan wanted to do right now but he allowed his desire to stop scraping by to motivate him.

He reached the ranch just as Winona was heading outside to refill her cleaning bucket. Despite the awkwardness of the past few days, Logan couldn't help but admire her work ethic.

She'd barely healed when she began cleaning and already she'd nearly cleaned the entire house! He couldn't believe her discipline. He expected her to be a soft, spoiled rich kid unused to the rigors of working on a ranch. Instead, she'd proven a tough, resilient hard worker—harder working than some of his hands. He felt a pang of guilt over his earlier complaint of exhaustion.

"Mornin', Winona," he said.

"Morning, Logan," she replied, her voice ice-cold.

Logan's heart sank a little. "I think I might go into town a little."

Winona tensed. "Do you want me to come with you?" she asked, her tone carefully measured.

Logan's heart sank further. "No, no, it's just for business."

"I see," she said. "Well, take care." She began to lower her bucket into the well, avoiding Logan's eyes.

He stared at her a moment, unsure how to reply. He started to walk away but that didn't feel right, so he turned and said, "Right nice what you done with the place. I haven't seen it this clean since Ma was alive. Thank you."

Winona didn't look at Logan but the tension in her shoulders eased slightly and her tone was softer when she replied, "Thank you."

Logan's spirits lifted a little. "You want me to help you with that bucket?"

Winona hesitated, but only briefly. "Thank you, that's very kind."

"Don't mention it," he said. "It's the least I can do, especially after ... well, it's the least I can do."

She didn't reply as he took the crank and began hauling the bucket out of the well. She glanced at him once, but her expression was unreadable. Still, this was the most contact they'd had in days. Logan was surprised how good it felt to spend time with her, even doing something as mundane as this.

When he finished, Winona accepted the bucket and thanked him, glancing briefly up at him before lowering her eyes. They stood awkwardly for a moment before Logan cleared his throat. "Well, I should go wash up. It's good to see you, Winona."

He may have imagined it, but he thought he saw the faintest trace of a smile as Winona replied, "Thank you." A moment later, "Will you be home in time for dinner?"

Hearing those words was like a fresh infusion of strength for Logan. His shoulders straightened and he stood taller. His head even seemed to clear. "I reckon I will," he said.

She nodded and met his eyes. "I'll make something hot then. Goodbye, Logan."

"Goodbye, Winona."

She headed back for the house. Logan watched her until she disappeared behind the front door.

"Blast it," he said when the door closed. "I should have carried the bucket back for her."

He washed at the spring near the vegetable garden behind the house, lingering longer than he should have. The water was cool and soothing on his dusty, parched skin and he closed his eyes, wishing he could simply lay there and rest and allow the water to flow over him. He heard a branch snap and looked around quickly. No one was there and he chuckled to himself. Now he was getting jumpy. He needed to get more rest.

He dressed and nearly left when it occurred to him that his clothes were covered in dust from a long day of work. He headed back to the house, a little anxious. The sun would set soon, and it was impolite to bother a man after sunset.

He reached the house and nearly bowled Winona over. She jumped back in shock, a pretty pink blush coming to her face as she did so. He felt his own face grow hot and said, "Sorry. I forgot a change of clothes."

"I laid them out on your bed," she said. "I figured you'd want to change before you left for town."

Logan stared wonderingly at her. "Thank you," he said. "That's awfully nice of you."

She smiled. It was faint and brief, but it was unmistakable. She smiled at him and for a brief moment, the world was right again. He couldn't believe her happiness should mean so much to him but there it was. For one crystalline instant, everything was okay, and he was content. "You're welcome, Logan."

They stood silently again but this time the interaction was much less awkward. Finally, Winona said, "You'd better hurry. The sun's going down soon."

"Yes," he said. "You're right. Thank you again."

"Happy to help," she replied.

He headed to his room to find an outfit laid on the bed. His trousers and shirt were brushed and starched, and his belt buckle polished to a gleaming shine. "That woman sure is something," he said to himself.

***

"I confess, Mr. Foley, I was hoping to negotiate for substantially more than a hundred head."

"Well, we're not really a cattle outfit," Logan replied. "We happened on a small herd but we're primarily in the horse business."

The buyer, Joseph Baker, represented the Double Bar S Ranch, a growing outfit in Arizona Territory, raised his eyebrow. "That's an odd thing to say to a potential business partner."

"Well, like I said, we're a horse ranch. Truth is, we're just trying to unload some of the herd to make room for more horses."

"These are quality cattle?" Baker asked.

"They are."

"How much are you asking per head?"

"Ten dollars."

Baker nodded, "That's a fair price. You understand we'll need to inspect the cattle before accepting delivery?"

"Of course," Logan said. Inwardly, he felt anxious. He had no idea how he would manage to keep Jay from noticing people poking around his cattle.

Baker nodded again. "Well, then it's settled. I'll be in contact when I'm ready to inspect the purchase. We'll remit payment upon delivery. I assume you bank with the Wells Fargo?"

Logan reddened slightly. "No," he admitted.

"Oh. Well, that's no trouble. I'm sure First Bank of Westridge will be able to accommodate your deposit."

"Actually, we don't ... We'd prefer a cash payment."

Baker didn't respond at first but gazed at Logan with an unreadable expression. Logan knew the man was sizing him up, trying to determine if Logan was simply a con man and if this deal was worth completing. Evidently, he decided in Logan's favor because after a while, he smiled. "That will take a little longer to secure but it can be done." He stood and extended his hand. "Thank you, Mr. Foley. I look forward to doing business with you."

"Likewise," Logan said.

On the way back to the ranch, Logan wrestled with his emotions. On one hand, he was relieved to know they would soon have the money to repair the ranch. On the other, he felt far more guilt than he cared to admit about going behind Jay's and Gregory's backs. Gregory could be made to see things from Logan's side – if he cared enough to take a side – but Jay may never forgive him for this.

Well, Logan would just have to hope for the best. He was leaving Jay four hundred head of cattle—a hundred more than he'd initially planned to leave. He wasn't being greedy. He was only taking what they needed. Jay would be angry but maybe he could be helped to see this was best for the ranch. He knew he was right to sell those cattle. He was.

Repeating that to himself didn't help to alleviate the guilt.

Chapter Thirteen

Winona finished her dinner and was tidying up the kitchen when she heard the door open. It was Gregory.

Good afternoon, Gregory," she said, smiling.

"Good afternoon, Winona," he replied in his typical pleasantly neutral tone.

"Would you like some lunch?" she asked. She stepped in front of him so he wouldn't be able to pass her without a conversation. She'd had enough of the brothers avoiding her and avoiding each other. She and Logan were finally talking again, and she was incredibly grateful to share her morning and evening meals with him once more, but the other two barely spoke to her.

It was time for that to change. So, she smiled at Gregory pleasantly, but with enough of an edge to make it clear to him he would not be able to avoid this interaction.

His slight smile suggested he knew what she was up to, but he acquiesced without difficulty. "Lunch sounds lovely, Winona. Thank you."

"Wonderful!" she said. "Sit down. I'll bring you some water."

Gregory sat and Winona poured him a glass of water from what remained of the water she'd drawn for herself. He sipped gratefully and smiled at her. "That sure hits the spot after a morning full of hard work."

"You must be hungry, too," Winona replied. "I'll make you a sandwich."

"That sounds wonderful. Thank you."

She smiled and gathered bread and meat for the sandwich. "So how have you been?"

"Oh, fair. There's always hard work to be done and that can be tiring at times, but that's living on a ranch for you."

Before Winona could respond, the front door opened again, and Jay entered.

"Good afternoon, Jay," Winona called brightly. "Would you like to join us for lunch?"

Jay glared at her and passed the kitchen without responding. A moment later, she heard the door to his room slam shut.

She turned back to Gregory. The older brother's smile had faded, replaced with a look of despondence. A halfhearted version of it returned when he noticed Winona's gaze. "Don't be angry, Winona. Jay's having a hard time right now. He's not thinking straight."

"I'm not angry," she replied. To her surprise, she realized this was the truth. She wasn't angry, only sad that her family could be so divided. "It's his fighting with Logan, isn't it? Why do they have such trouble getting along?"

Gregory shrugged. "They're both pigheaded. They have different ideas how the ranch should run, and the best way they can think to compromise is to yell at each other in between long periods of moody silence." He chuckled. "It's kinda funny when you think about it. They don't even realize how alike they are."

"I'm sorry to see them fight so much," Winona said. "I wish there was a way to mend fences between them."

"Good luck with that. They've been fighting almost nonstop since our parents died. It's getting so I can't remember a time when we all got along."

"That's horrible! I'm so sorry."

He shrugged. "What can you do?" He stood. "I think I'll take my sandwich to go. There's still a lot of work to do."

"Oh." Winona was disappointed to see him withdraw into his shell when they were finally having a real conversation, but she didn't know how to stop that. "Well, it was nice talking with you. We should do it again some time."

He smiled but his face was sad and tired, making him look far older than his years. "We should. Thank you, Winona. It was good to have a talk that didn't end in shouting."

He left without waiting for a response. Winona started on her chores, but she was too distracted to focus on them, so she gave up after a while and went to her room to draw. As she drew, she wondered what she could do to help repair the brothers' relationship.

They lived in the same house, but their lives were separate. It was almost like they weren't a family at all. They lived in the town but hadn't been seen in years. They weren't a family, and they weren't part of the town either.

She had to do something to fix that. A plan began to form in her head. As it took shape, she began to feel excitement for it, anticipation that finally some positive turn could come to their lives. She would make the brothers a family again and make their family a part of the community again. It was five years since the scandal that soured them in the eyes of the townsfolk and two years since the brothers' parents had died. It was high time everyone moved on.

When Logan came home, she enacted her plan without hesitation. As soon as he walked in the door, she said, "Logan, I need supplies to mend the furniture and the cracks in the walls. I also need more cleaning supplies and a few more odds and ends. Will you take me into town tomorrow?"

Logan stared at her and blinked twice, unprepared for the question. Finally, he said, "Why don't you put a list together and I'll have Darrell get what you need."

"I'd rather go with you," she said. Before he could protest, she insisted, "I need to get out of this house, Logan. For that matter, you do too. Besides, we're husband and wife. We're going to have to get used to being seen together."

Logan's expression showed he knew Winona was right but wasn't happy about it. "I suppose you're right," he said reluctantly. "Okay, we'll ride in tomorrow morning."

"Oh, thank you!" she cried. She threw her arms around him and hugged him tightly. The embrace lasted only a moment, but it was enough to lift her spirits to the highest they'd been in weeks. She pulled away and smiled at him.

He returned the smile a little dubiously and she laughed. "Don't be afraid. What's the worst that can happen? People will frown at you?"

"I ain't worried about what people think. I'm just worried about how you'll feel."

She thought a moment before answering. "I'll feel like you're my husband and I'm your wife. This is my home, and this is my family and there's not a single thing anyone can do about it."

He nodded and when he smiled again there was a hint of admiration in his face. "That's exactly how I see it."

Winona beamed at him and embraced him again. This one lasted longer and she had time to savor the feel of him in her arms. He had a strong musky odor after a long day tending to the herd in the pastures, but rather than be repelled by the scent, she found herself strangely intoxicated by it. Logan was her husband and whatever their marriage might or might not be, it felt good to know this strong, hardworking man belonged to her and no one else.

The next morning in town, the townspeople reacted exactly as Logan feared they would. Some cast disapproving glances at them while others refused to acknowledge their presence. Most didn't offer judgment but simply gazed at them like they were a spectacle. Which they were, Winona supposed. The daughter of the most respected family in town with the scion of the most despised. It was a noteworthy scandal for a town as small and close-knit as Westridge. She and Logan pretended not to notice the attention as they shopped, though she could tell Logan felt tense. She placed her arm in his and was pleased to feel him relax slightly.

They stopped at the hardware store first for lumber, plaster and a few other tools Winona would use to fix up the house. Then they visited the mercantile where Winona bought several dozen yards of cotton fabric to replace the dilapidated curtains and drapes and a bearskin rug for the parlor. Finally, they found themselves in the general store to purchase the final few odds and ends Winona needed.

Cordelia was out on a picnic with Mr. Huxtable, so they were assisted by Frankie, the boy Cordelia hired to help her with the store. Winona smiled at him when they entered and he blushed bright red, eliciting a suppressed chuckle from Logan. She gave Frankie a list of what she needed, and the boy stared at her like she were some sort of goddess a moment before disappearing to the back to fulfil her order.

The front door opened, and Winona and Logan turned to see who had entered. Winona's face went white as a sheet when her father and stepmother entered. The four of them stared silently at each other for a long moment. Finally, Logan spoke up. "Mr. Ross, Mrs. Ross. Good to see you."

"Good to see you, Logan," Heath replied stiffly. He turned to Winona. "Winona. I see you've recovered well."

"Yes, thank you," she said.

Audrey remained silent but stared daggers at Winona and Logan. Winona met her gaze and smiled sweetly, though the smile stopped before it reached her eyes. "How are you, Audrey? It's good to see you."

Audrey's face turned a sickly grayish-white color, and she didn't respond.

"It's a lovely day out," Logan said. "I'm glad I took Winona up on her offer to come to town. It's been too long since my wife and I have seen folks."

He emphasized *my wife* slightly. Winona's parents reacted noticeably. Heath reddened and Audrey somehow managed to pale even more. "It certainly is lovely weather we're having," Heath replied, seeming to choke on every word.

"Say," Logan said. "How would you folks like to come over for Sunday luncheon a couple weeks from now? Our apples are coming in nicely and should be ready to harvest soon. I'll have Winona bake you some fresh pies and we can catch up."

Winona stared at Logan, shocked. Did he just invite her parents over for dinner? She was too surprised to respond and could only turn anxiously to her father and stepmother.

Audrey looked ready to offer a scathing refusal but Heath surprised Winona even more than Logan by replying in a surprisingly cordial tone. "That's very kind of you, Logan. Audrey and I will be delighted to join you."

Audrey's head snapped toward Heath, her features radiating shock and outrage. Heath continued to smile at Logan and Winona, ignoring his wife. Winona couldn't believe what she was seeing. Had her father finally managed to overcome his dependence on Audrey's approval?

"Great!" Logan said. "We'll see both of you Sunday after next."

Frankie returned then with their supplies, and it was with some relief that Winona excused herself and Logan and left her parents to return home. During the ride back, Winona stared in wonder at the breezy smile on Logan's face. She couldn't recall ever seeing him so happy. She was so glad her efforts to make her family a part of the community again were paying off.

Her good feeling lasted exactly as long as it took them to arrive home. Jay met them at the gate, glaring angrily at Logan.

"You bastard!" He shouted.

"Jay!" Winona cried, shocked at his language toward his own brother.

Jay ignored her and continued to scream at Logan. "What in blazes makes you think you have the right to sell my cattle?"

"Our cattle," Logan retorted, his tone as angry as Jay's. He dismounted from the wagon and walked right up to his younger brother until they stood mere inches from each other. "And I sold them so we could afford to fix up the ranch."

"You had no right!" Jay insisted.

"Jay, you are not in charge of this ranch. If I want to sell some of the cattle, I can do it without asking you first."

"You bastard," Jay repeated.

Winona had enough. "That's enough, you two!" she shouted, stepping in between them. "You two are brothers but you fight like you were sworn enemies! If you want this ranch to succeed, you have to stop fighting! What would your parents say?"

Jay wheeled on her. "Who are you to talk about our parents?" he demanded. "Just because you married my brother you think you can butt in where you don't belong and act like you have a say? Well, you can't."

Logan took a menacing step forward and growled. "Jay, don't talk to Winona like that."

Jay shoved Logan hard. He stumbled backward but managed to keep from falling. "I'm gonna make you pay for this, Logan!" he shouted. He turned and stormed off.

Logan made to go after him, but Winona stopped him. "Let him go, Logan. Fighting will only make it worse."

They unloaded the wagon in silence. The good feeling they'd had all day was gone and forgotten. So much for making things better. Logan avoided eye contact with Winona, and she could tell he felt guilty for going behind Jay's back. Winona didn't blame him. He should feel guilty. Whether or not he had the authority to sell the cattle, it was disrespectful of him to not even tell Jay.

She didn't bother to point that out, however. Heaven knew the day had ended badly enough without her causing more friction. So, she simply sorted the supplies, bid good night to Logan, then headed to bed.

***

Winona breathed heavily as she vigorously swept the porch. She'd spent the last week plastering the walls, mending the furniture and replacing the drapes. She'd even repaired the roof. The house finally looked like a home now.

Winona knew she should feel proud, but she felt anxious instead. She hated to admit it, but it was important to her to show Audrey she could, in fact, handle the rigors of being a housewife. Everything had to be perfect! She couldn't give Audrey even an inch of room to complain about anything.

She didn't even know what to make. Her first brisket had turned out to be a disaster and that was too much food for a Sunday luncheon anyway. She sighed and wiped sweat from her brow. Her whole body ached but she kept sweeping, desperate to leave the house spotless.

It didn't help that she'd been left on her own. Jay and Logan were busy fighting again and Gregory, as usual, was doing his best to avoid everyone, leaving Winona to mend the house and prepare for her parents' visit.

She felt lightheaded and paused, leaning against the broom. Her vision swam and then, without warning, her legs gave out and she collapsed on the porch. The last thing she saw before everything went black was Jay running across the courtyard, shouting for her.

She woke in bed, her mouth dry and her head aching. The brothers stood around her, all wearing looks of concern. Logan knelt by her side, taking her hand tenderly. "Are you all right, Winona?"

She smiled, touched to see him so worried for her. "I'm okay. A little thirsty."

Gregory offered her some water and she sipped gratefully. "I'm glad you're okay," he said.

"Me too," Logan said. He turned to Jay and smiled. "I'm glad Jay was around. You might have been on that porch for hours if he wasn't there to help you."

Jay smiled, pleased to hear Logan's praise. His smile faltered a moment later. "Logan, do you mind if I talk to Winona privately a moment? I have something I need to tell her."

Logan shared a knowing look with Gregory. Winona knew they both understood what Jay needed to say. Logan squeezed her hand then stood and left, Gregory close behind.

Jay stood awkwardly a moment. Winona waited, knowing he needed to do this himself, without any prompting. He cleared his throat and began.

"Winona, I'm sorry for the way I've treated you since you've been here. You've worked so hard to fix up the house and, well, I guess I just let my pride get to me. I didn't want to admit we needed help, but we did. You've made such a difference already. I'm sorry I haven't thanked you before and I'm even more sorry I've been so rude and standoffish. The truth is, I'm glad you're here."

She smiled and took Jay's hand. He stiffened a moment, then relaxed. There were tears in his eyes when he looked at her. "Thank you, Jay," she said softly. "I'm glad to be part of your family."

He smiled then, a real smile and Winona felt her hope for their future as a family return. "We're happy to have you, Winona."

Winona knew there would be more challenges ahead but after Logan's display of affection and Jay's apology, she felt confident they would overcome whatever they had to.

Chapter Fourteen

Logan dismounted and waved to Darrell. The foreman returned the greeting and met Logan at the gate of the newly repaired corral. The money from the sale of the cattle allowed Logan to purchase the wood, rawhide, and tar necessary to finish the repairs to the corral. There was even enough left over to repair the roof of the barn, a project Darrell promised Logan would be completed within the next two days—just in time for the Ross's visit.

"Mornin', Darrell," Logan said when the wrangler reached the gate. He patted the gleaming new post and smiled. "Looks good."

"Yes, it came out real nice, didn't it?" Darrell agreed. "Better than the old one."

"You and your boys did a fine job," Logan replied. "Thank you."

"Just doing my job," Darrell demurred with a smile. "To tell truth, I'm more excited to fix the barn up than I was for the corral. It'll be nice to have a place to store feed without worrying about it spoiling every time a storm comes through."

"That's for sure." Looking around at the solid new corral, Logan felt a swell of pride. The feeling was strange but welcome. It was a long time since Logan could say he felt pride in the ranch's appearance. They had a long way to go yet but it was a far cry from what it was three months ago, before Winona's arrival.

Winona. She was the difference. Once she arrived, Logan and his brothers suddenly had a reason to believe in the ranch and its future. Logan always wanted the ranch to succeed but before marrying his wife he'd almost resigned himself to believing they would never get ahead. Now they had a new corral. In a few days, they would have a solid barn.

The house, too, was night and day compared to the state it was when Winona arrived. For that, Logan definitely had Winona to thank. She had singlehandedly cleaned and repaired the entire house. All by herself. Alone.

He felt a rush of guilt and his smile faded. For the first time, he considered how hard it must have been for Winona to have shouldered all those chores by herself. Darrell must have seen the guilt in his expression because he said, "You know, the boys and I will be all right handling the barn ourselves. If you want to take the day and help Winona around the house, that's fine with us."

Logan nodded. "Reckon I'll do that, Darrell. Thank you."

Darrell smiled and clapped him on the shoulder, then turned and walked back to the other hands. Several of the hands waved goodbye to Logan as he mounted up and rode back to the house.

He entered to find Winona on her hands and knees, polishing the parlor furniture. "Mornin', Winona," he called.

She looked up briefly then returned to her polishing. "Morning, Logan" she said. "Sorry, I can't join you for lunch today. I still have a lot to do before my parents visit. There's bread in the pantry and cheese in the icebox if you want to make yourself a sandwich."

"I'm not hungry but thank you," he replied. "Actually, I was wondering if you could use some help. The boys have the repairs to the barn handled and ..." he blushed and fumbled over his words. Why did he get so tongue-tied around her? He swallowed and continued. "Well, you've been workin' real hard and I'm much obliged and I thought you could use some help."

She smiled at him, slightly amused but mostly surprised and grateful for his offer. "That's very kind of you, Logan. I would love some help."

Logan brightened and knelt down next to Winona. She handed him a stiff brush. He caught a whiff of her perfume—a light, flowery scent—and felt heat rise up his neck. She turned to him and smiled coyly. "I'll keep polishing the wood. Why don't you brush the dust out of the cushions?"

Her face was only a few inches from his as she spoke. Logan's heart began to beat faster as he regarded her bright blue eyes and soft features. Her lips parted slightly as she returned his gaze. Logan nearly leaned in for a kiss but caught himself at the last moment. He pulled back and cleared his throat. He took the brush and said, "All right. I'll get started then."

His voice was a little gruffer than he intended, and he worried a moment Winona might take offense. She only smiled knowingly and held her gaze while he blushed and cleared his throat once more. He stood and shuffled to the high-backed chair a few feet from the couch and began vigorously brushing the cushion on the back of the chair.

A moment later, he heard a soft sliding sound as Winona returned to polishing the wooden legs of the couch. He risked a glance back at her. She was absorbed in her work and didn't notice him staring. His eyes traced a line from her neck down her back to the curve of her hips then traveled upward, taking in the supple roundness of her shoulders and the soft angle of her jawline. Her hair seemed to shimmer like burnished copper in the sunlight coming in through the window.

He stared at her in awe, too distracted to focus on brushing until Winona turned and met his eyes suddenly.

She blushed crimson and said, "Are you going to help or are you just going to stare at me all day?"

He blushed an even deeper shade of red and turned back to the chair, brushing vigorously. She laughed, and his embarrassment grew as he moved to the cushion on the seat of the chair. He worked for a few minutes without succumbing to distraction but when he finished the chair and prepared to move to the couch, he couldn't resist another look at her.

She was staring at his arms and chest, her eyes wide, a curiously intense expression on her face. He smiled and said, "Are you going to help or are you just going to stare at me all day?"

She jumped, startled and her blush deepened until it was redder than a ripe apple. He suppressed a chuckle and squatted next to her. "I'm finished brushing the chair. I was planning to start on the couch but if you need more time to polish—"

"No," she interrupted quickly. "All finished. I'm going to start brushing the drapes now."

"The drapes? We just bought those. They need brushing already?"

"Oh, right," she said. She was flustered and knowing she was flustered because of him gave Logan a warm feeling. "Well," Winona continued, "I'll sweep out the fireplace then."

She walked quickly to the fireplace and began sweeping out the ash in short quick strokes. Logan watched her for a moment, then continued with the cushion.

They continued working until the parlor was spotless. Once Logan finished brushing the couch, he dusted and polished the mantle and the side table. Winona swept the fireplace until not a speck of ash remained, then gave the same treatment to the floor while Logan took the rug outside and beat it until it no longer shed dust.

When everything was swept and brushed, Winona looked around and smiled. "Well, the parlor's nearly there, at least. Now we just need to mop, and everything will be pristine." She turned to Logan. "I'm going to the well for water. Would you like to keep me company?"

Logan couldn't stop the grin that spread from ear to ear. "I would love to, Winona."

She returned his grin and led him out the door. The sun, dimmed by the drapes in the house, assaulted them with blinding sunlight when they stepped outside. They both put a hand up to shield their eyes. They heard laughter and turned to see Jay crossing the courtyard, leading a yearling colt he was breaking for saddle. The horse wore blinders and a training saddle and looked decidedly uncomfortable but allowed Jay to lead him without protest.

Jay grinned at them. "I can let you two borrow Raven's blinders if you want," he teased. "The Texas sun can be a little intense for more sensitive eyes."

"You been reading Gregory's poetry book or something?" Logan quipped. "Get that horse on out of here and leave us to our work."

"Oh, my apologies," Jay replied. He put a hand to his chest in mock consternation. "I would hate to think I've interfered in such important goings-on. Please, continue to stumble around in the blinding daylight. Don't mind me."

"Mind your brother!" Winona called, laughing. "Or I'll give Raven a nice pat on the rump, and you can spend the rest of the afternoon running her down!"

Jay lifted his hands in surrender. "I give up!" he called. "You win!" He turned to Logan, "Control your woman, would you?"

Winona took a menacing step forward and Jay quickly moved on, leading Raven behind him. The horse turned its head furtively and whinnied at them before trotting along after Jay. When Jay reached the end of the courtyard, he turned and bowed theatrically. He forgot to tell Raven to stop first and the horsed bumped into him, knocking him sprawling.

Logan and Winona burst into laughter as Jay scrambled to his feet, red-faced. He smiled at them and bowed again, more successfully this time, then continued on his way.

When they reached the well, Logan lowered the bucket and drew water for Winona. She thanked him and leaned against the well, watching him with a soft smile on her face. He tried to ignore it, but he couldn't stop his face from flaming red. He spent so much time blushing around her he wondered if she'd even recognize him without a flush in his cheeks. Finally, he said, "Why are you staring now, Winona?"

"I'm just glad to see you and Jay get along," she said. "This is the first time since I've met you that you two aren't fighting."

Logan took the full bucket off the hook and lowered it to the ground. Winona was right. To tell the truth, even he couldn't remember the last time he and Jay weren't fighting. Before his parents died, at least. He looked at Winona. "I owe that to you, Winona," he said. "You've helped me see how important it is that we get along as a family. I never would have been able to do that without your help. Thank you."

Winona reached forward and squeezed his hand. The contact was brief, and she released his hand an instant later, but it felt like a lifetime to Logan. He stood taller, his shoulders straightened, and he felt renewed strength flow through him. He picked up the bucket and gestured for them to return to the house.

"Is there anything you want me to do while you mop, Winona?" he asked as they walked back.

She chuckled. "Why do you keep saying my name like that? I'm the only one here. I know you're talking to me."

"Oh," he said. "Well ... I like your name. I like saying it. It's pretty."

"Oh," Winona replied. She looked away and couldn't quite stifle the grin that spread across her cheeks. "Well, I suppose that's all right."

"You're sure that's all right?" Logan teased. "You don't mind if I use my wife's name every now and then?"

She giggled, a pretty, girlish sound unlike any laughter he'd heard before. It warmed him and all at once he regretted his initial reasons for marrying her. He hated Heath Ross and he loved watching the impotent wrath in his and Audrey's faces when he paraded Winona around in town and forced them to acknowledge him as her husband. He still enjoyed this moral victory, and he would be lying if he said he wasn't looking forward to rubbing their faces in it some more on Sunday.

That wasn't the only reason for marrying her anymore, though. He liked her. He enjoyed her company. She was beautiful, and funny, and very kind—even when he didn't deserve it. She was everything he would have asked for in a wife if given a choice and he wished desperately he could make her his wife in more than just name.

"Dollar for your thoughts?" she asked, smiling up at him.

He realized he was still staring at her and looked away, blushing once more, of course. He supposed he'd just have to get used to having that reaction around her. "You and Darrell sure put a high price on my thoughts."

Her brow furrowed. "Darrell?"

"Darrell offered me a dollar for my thoughts once, too."

"Well, that's the saying, isn't it?"

"It's a penny for your thoughts. Not a dollar."

"Oh, well, maybe your thoughts are worth a little more to me."

He looked back down at her. She looked away, grinning and blushing. After a moment, she said. "You should watch where you're going."

He looked up, just in time to see the stairs and avoid tripping. She giggled again as he hopped up the stairs, narrowly avoiding the water that sloshed over the bucket with his abrupt movement. "Wait here," she said. "I'll go get the lye."

They mopped the parlor until the floor gleamed, then they moved to the kitchen. Winona polished the table and chairs in the dining room while Logan cleaned the stove out, sweeping the ash into a pile and dumping it into a bucket to be taken outside and disposed of later. They swept and mopped the kitchen after until both rooms shone like new.

Winona smiled, regarding the work they'd done. "Thank you, Logan. Now if only I could figure out what to make."

"I can help," Logan offered. "I might not be a great cook like you but if you help me, I can be useful in the kitchen."

"Thank you," she said again. "That's kind of you. I'm sure we'll figure something out. Not today, though. I'm exhausted. Let's just have dinner and we can worry about it in the morning. How does that sound?"

Logan gazed into her eyes, smiled and said, softly, "That sounds wonderful."

Chapter Fifteen

Winona glanced anxiously between her father, stepmother and Logan. Logan and Heath talked easily enough and neither seemed particularly hostile toward the other, but Winona could see the unspoken tension in her father's shoulders and the set of Logan's jaw. She shared a look with Gregory and Jay and could see they felt a similar apprehension.

Her stepmother made no attempt to hide her feelings. Audrey sat back in her chair, frowning and glaring at Logan and Winona. She didn't so much as look at her roasted quail or green salad and spoke less than she ate. Winona decided she preferred her stepmother's silence to her sarcasm and made no attempt to engage with her.

On the bright side, the others seemed to enjoy the food. Her father even went out of his way to compliment Winona on the quail. After his compliment, Audrey saw the tension between the men ease considerably. Logan and Heath even had a lengthy conversation about proper pastureland management. If Winona hadn't known any better, she would never have guessed there was bad blood between the two of them.

Her father's politeness encouraged Winona and she forgot all about her stepmother's attitude until her father asked Logan to walk with him outside. Logan looked to Winona for approval and Winona desperately wanted to ask him to stay with her, but she knew it was better to give Logan and Heath a chance to hash things out. So, she nodded and smiled so he'd know it was okay to leave. At least she'd have Gregory and Jay to talk to.

Of course, no sooner had she thought that then Gregory and Jay excused themselves, saying they needed to ensure the herd hadn't migrated out of the southeast field again. That left Winona alone with her stepmother.

Winona forced a smile and said, "You really should try the quail. It's—"

"I will never acknowledge that man as your husband!" Audrey spat.

Winona was shocked for a moment. Then anger replaced her shock. "Well then it's fortunate that our marriage doesn't depend on your acknowledgment."

"Just look at you!" Audrey continued, ignoring Winona. "You've aged ten years since you've lived here. I told you before, you're not cut out to be a rancher's wife. Hard work doesn't suit you."

Winona didn't for a second believe her stepmother, but her words hurt nonetheless. She fought back tears as she replied, "Not all of us consider work beneath us, Audrey."

"Look around you, Winona! Look at this house! Look at this ranch. You're living like a … like a … like a peasant!"

"Well at least it's my life!" Winona shouted. The tears that threatened her now trickled down her cheeks as she shouted at her stepmother. "It's a life on my terms and no one else's! A life free from *you!*"

Audrey shook her head dismissively. "This isn't a life. This is barely an existence." She looked at Winona. "I wanted so much more for you. I expected so much more from you. Now look at you. You're a failure."

Winona was too stunned to reply. A moment later, it didn't matter because the door opened, and Logan and Heath returned. Both seemed far more relaxed. Whatever they'd discussed outside, the heat between them seemed to have cooled.

At least one of us managed to rebuild bridges, Winona thought.

"Winona, Logan, I want to thank you both for a wonderful meal," Heath said. "I hope we can all meet again soon."

"Sure thing, Heath," Logan replied. Did he really just use her father's first name?

Winona and Audrey remained silent. Heath glanced between his daughter and wife and frowned but chose not to say anything. He simply thanked Logan and Winona again and left with Audrey.

"Everything okay?" Logan asked.

"No," Winona replied. "But I don't want to talk about it right now. Let's just clean up and worry about everything else later, okay?"

Logan didn't respond immediately, and Winona feared he would press the issue but finally he simply said, "Okay."

***

Logan surveyed the repairs to the barn roof, nodding approvingly. The building was now weatherproof and could finally hold the vast amount of feed it took to support both herds without fear of spoilage from rain, or predation from birds.

"Fine job, Darrell," Logan said. "The place looks brand new."

Darrell smiled. "Thank you, boss. I can't take all the credit. The boys did all the work. I just stood around and barked orders at them every now and then."

Logan chuckled. "I wish I had it as easy as you, Darrell."

"Naw, you'd go stir-crazy if you couldn't work with your hands."

"I guess you're right at that."

They fell silent a moment. Then Darrell asked. "So how was dinner last night? Gregory tells me you and Heath talked privately a while. How was that?"

"It was fine," Logan said. "I have to admit, I was surprised. He wasn't confrontational at all. We just talked about the ranch a while. He actually gave me some good advice."

"That so?" Darrell said, raising an eyebrow. "What advice?"

"He told me to plant mint and thyme in a pasture at least a month before we move the herd. Horses like those plants a lot. That'll help keep the herd from migrating so much to the wrong pasture. During the winter, we can use bales of mint and thyme instead of the fresh plants."

Darrell nodded, impressed. "That's not a bad idea. Cheap, too. Mint spreads like wildfire once you plant it and thyme's easy to get a hold of. I can get some from the grocer on Wednesday when I to town."

"Great," Logan said.

"So, what else did he say?" Darrell asked.

"He said to take care of his daughter."

"That's it?"

"That's it. Just, 'Take care of my daughter.' Then he shook my hand, and we went back inside."

"Wow," Darell replied. "He doesn't seem all that upset about you marrying Winona after all."

Logan smiled. "No. No he doesn't."

He wanted to be mad at Heath—to hold on to the hate he'd had for the man since his father was killed, but he couldn't. The truth was, Heath seemed almost happy to see Logan and Winona together. He'd treated Logan as an equal the night before. Maybe he'd finally come around to accepting Logan.

Logan didn't know if he could accept Heath, but he could at least see a way for them to stop being enemies. Maybe that was good enough.

***

Winona's pencil skipped again, leaving behind a rough, jagged line that intruded into the shading on the face of the portrait. She sighed heavily and tossed the pencil onto the table. She'd spent nearly an hour perfecting that shading, and now it would have to be redone. Why did it feel like every time she tried to accomplish something things would go well at first, only to collapse around her?

She was pulled from her thoughts by a knock at the door. Probably Logan coming to wish her good night. "Come in," she called.

The door opened and Gregory walked in. "Gregory!" Winona exclaimed. "What a pleasant surprise!"

Gregory smiled and sat on the edge of the bed. "Hey, Winona. I just wanted to say I'm sorry about last night. I heard you and your stepmother talking outside. Jay and I thought if we left you two alone you might be able to work things out with her like you did with us. We should've known better."

Winona smiled. "That's okay, Gregory. My stepmother's arrogance isn't your problem."

"I know," he replied. "It's not yours, either. What I mean is, you're not a failure. Audrey's wrong about that. Actually, I think you're one of the bravest people I know. Leaving like you did, making a life for yourself here ... you really inspire me."

"Thank you, Gregory. It means a lot to hear you say that."

He nodded and then stared pensively at the wall. Winona waited, allowing Gregory to gather his thoughts. He finally said, "When my parents died, I promised myself I would never put myself at risk the way they did. Not in business and not in life. I never wanted to feel that kind of hurt again. I pulled away from my brothers and pulled away from the ranch, from everything.

I thought if I could just avoid conflict my whole life, I would be safe. After meeting you and seeing you fight through everything in your way to have the life you want, I think I've changed my mind. I might not rush off to elope with someone like you did—" Winona chuckled at that— "but I'm not going to hide anymore."

"What do you want, Gregory?" she asked. "In life, I mean. What do you want?"

He didn't respond right away. When he did, his words broke Winona's heart. "I want us to be a family again. Like we were before Ma and Pa died. We're not fighting right now, but we're not a family. Not like we used to be. I miss when it was the three of us against the world. I want that back."

In reply, Winona took Gregory's hand. "The four of us," she said. "It's the four of us against the world now. I promise you, we'll be a family again."

He squeezed her hand and smiled. "Thank you, Winona."

He released her hand and stood. "Well, I should be hitting the hay. I promised Darrell I'd help him move the horses tomorrow. Good night, Winona."

"Good night."

Later, as she drifted off to sleep, Winona smiled as she recalled her promise to Gregory. Come what may, she had her home. She had her family.

The next morning as she tidied up the kitchen, she noticed a book laying open on the table. It appeared to be a bank book. She picked it up, curious, and discovered several entries related to purchases at the ranch. This must be the ledger! She'd wanted to ask Logan about the ranch's finances but never seemed to find the time in the middle of everything else going on. She decided she would ask him about it tonight at dinner.

"Oh, sorry," a voice said. Winona looked up and saw Jay in the doorway. "I left that there this morning. I'll put it away now."

"Is this yours?" Winona asked.

"Yes. I'm in charge of the books."

"Really? I used to help my father with the books back home!"

"That so?" His face brightened. "Can I show you something?"

"Of course!" Winona said, excited that Jay was finally reaching out to her.

He sat next to her at the table and opened the ledger, flipping it to a page in the back with dozens of figures and calculations scribbled on it. She gazed admiringly at the work and asked, "What's this?"

"It's my plan to grow the herd. The cattle herd, I mean. Here, these numbers are projected costs for each hundred head added. These are projected sales assuming we sell each head at ten percent below the market rate."

Comparing the two numbers revealed that investing in cattle would greatly increase the ranch's profits. "This is amazing!" Winona cried. "Have you shown this to Logan?"

Jay's face fell. "Naw. Logan's just like Pa: stubborn and set in his ways. He's convinced that horse breeding is the only way to grow the ranch. I've tried to show him the numbers, but he just dismisses them."

"Why don't we show him again? You and I?"

He shook his head. "Honestly, I'm tired of fighting with him. If we show him this, it just means more fighting and I don't want you fighting with him over this. We're getting along now. That's more than we've done in a while. The cattle can wait."

Winona didn't respond. She wanted to encourage Jay to fight, to tell him that if it meant she stood up to Logan with him then that's what she would do. She didn't, however. The truth was she, like Jay, didn't want to risk the fragile peace that had sprouted between the brothers. She was so close to making them a real family. But how could they be a real family if the whole family didn't have an equal say?

Jay stood. "Well, I appreciate the talk, Winona. It's nice to have someone who'll listen to me every now and then. I'll see you later."

He left with the ledger, leaving Winona to wonder if she was really doing the right thing by keeping quiet. She resolved to speak to Logan about the cattle at dinner that night.

When the meal came however, she found it impossible to focus. Gregory had picked that night to come out of his shell and engaged the three of them in lively conversation the entire evening. When he wasn't in his shell, he proved to have a great sense of humor and quick wit. Winona found herself crying tears of laughter as she listened to the banter between the brothers.

After one particularly sharp jab from Logan, Gregory grinned evilly and said, "Did Winona give you permission to say that?"

Winona burst into another laughing fit and Jay clapped his hands as Logan reddened. "Hey, at least I have a wife."

"A real man wouldn't allow himself to be tied down," Gregory replied. "No offense to Winona, but I choose to remain a free man."

"So, I should tell Louise Parker you're not interested?" Logan retorted.

This time it was Gregory's turn to redden.

"Wait a minute," Winona interrupted. She looked at Gregory. "You never told me you liked Louise Parker! I know her parents! They're good people and Louise is just the sweetest thing! You should talk to her parents! They'll be honored to have you court her."

"Not gonna happen," Gregory replied amidst peals of laughter from Logan and Jay.

"Oh, come on," Winona pressed. "Didn't you tell me earlier you didn't want to hide from life anymore?"

Before Gregory could reply, they heard a crack of thunder. The brothers immediately silenced. Their smiles faded when they heard a second crack of thunder and disappeared entirely when they heard the pattering of raindrops. Immediately the brothers rushed outside, Winona following closely behind. The rain fell in icy sheets and Winona was reminded uncomfortably of the night she arrived on the ranch. Thunder cracked again and Winona knew the animals were in imminent danger.

"Get back inside!" Logan called to her.

"No!" she shouted back. "I can help put the animals away!"

Surprisingly, he didn't argue with her. She felt a swell of pride at his trust. That pride quickly turned to fear when the brothers left her at the corrals and galloped off to help the hands corral the horses and cattle. A few minutes later, Gregory returned with two hands and a hundred head of horses. The hands remained behind and helped Winona lead the horses to stables while Gregory left to find more.

Darrell came next, leading more horses. Then Gregory again. After an hour, she saw Jay and Darrell driving what looked to be the entire remaining herd of cattle into a nearby corral. Then Gregory arrived with another fifty head of horses.

"Where's Logan!" she shouted.

Gregory only shook his head before riding off.

Winona felt her blood turn to ice. She forced herself to focus on stabling the frightened horses, but her thoughts kept turning to Logan as time and again Gregory and Darrell and eventually Jay returned with more horses, but Logan was nowhere to be seen. When they'd finished stabling the horses and there was still no sign of Logan, she feared the worst.

Then she heard Jay shout, "Logan!"

She turned to see Logan struggling through the rain. Over his shoulders, he carried a newborn colt. Winona watched in amazement as he brought the animal into the barn. She slammed the door shut and barred it just before she heard the crack of hailstones on the roof of the stable.

Logan lowered the colt with a groan and turned to her. She threw her arms around him and hugged him hard, closing her eyes and drinking in the feeling of his body against hers. "I'm so glad you're safe," she whispered.

The storm raged around them, but for Winona it no longer held any fear.

Chapter Sixteen

Winona cleaned out the closet of the master bedroom and reminisced on the storm. The last few days were spent assessing the damage from the storm and repasturing the animals. They'd lost ten head of cattle and twenty-three horses—not ideal but far less than they could have, considering how unprepared they were. Fortunately, the storm was fairly short, so most of the fields escaped relatively unscathed.

The west field near the creek was flooded but there was more than enough grazing in the north pasture to accommodate the cattle. The horses could return to the southeast pasture.

The newly repaired corral was sturdy and escaped the surging cattle with no damage. The barn and house held as well but the stable roof was pockmarked with new holes from the hail. The entire roof would likely need to be replaced. That would be a major setback financially, but Winona couldn't bring herself to worry about that right now.

Logan was safe. She was safe. The brothers were safe. Logan was safe.

She didn't realize before the storm how important Logan had become to her. He was no longer simply her husband of convenience. She hadn't told him how she felt yet, but that time would come. She knew now she would not be content being his wife only in name. The thought that she might have lost him in that storm nearly overwhelmed her.

She was pulled from her thoughts when she came across a small box in a corner of the closet. She pulled it out and opened it to reveal a few odds and ends she decided must have belonged to Logan's parents. There was an old Bible with a worn leather cover, a pair of gold earrings, a medal and a small, bound leather diary.

The door to the room opened and Logan walked in. "Logan!" Winona called. "Look what I found in the closet."

He strode toward her, frowning. With no warning, he snatched the box from her and shouted, "What are you doing with those?"

She recoiled in shock. "I was just cleaning. I found them in the closet."

"Why are you going through my parents' things?"

"I'm not going through their things!" she protested. "I just found them in the closet!"

"Stay out of their things!" Logan shouted.

He glared down at her with what he probably thought was an intimidating stare but reminded Winona more of a petulant little boy. She decided it wasn't worth the argument and simply said, "Okay."

***

The next morning as she ate breakfast, Logan entered the kitchen, his hat in his hand. He sat in front of Winona and said, "May I talk to you?"

She looked at him coldly but her look softened when she saw the contrition in his face. "Sure," she agreed.

"Thank you." He took a deep breath. "Winona, I apologize for yelling at you last night. It was wrong of me to get upset. Those things are important heirlooms of my parents. To tell you the truth, I'd forgotten about them, but seeing them again last night just brought the pain of their loss rushing back. I lost control and I snapped at you. I'm sorry."

"Okay," Winona said. "I forgive you. Next time, though, just tell me how you feel. Let's not fight when there's no fight to be had."

Logan nodded and said, "I'd like to make it up to you. Will you come riding with me?"

Winona's eyes widened "Riding?"

"Yes. Will you take a ride with me?"

She leapt up from her chair, overwhelmed with excitement. Logan nearly fell out of his own chair with surprise, and she chuckled. "Sorry, it's just I haven't ridden since before my mother died. Audrey always said it was unladylike and of course, my father agreed with anything Audrey said. Can I really ride a horse?"

"Of course," Logan replied. He smiled. "They're your horses too."

An hour later, they galloped across the west field toward the stream that marked the western border of the Foley Ranch. The feel of the powerful animal beneath her and the wind rushing through her hair made Winona feel free for the first time since she could remember. She looked over at Logan and smiled.

The light from the sun seemed to bathe him in a golden glow and she felt a stirring in her chest. When her feelings threatened to overwhelm her, she spurred her horse faster and raced him to the stream.

They arrived a few minutes later and dismounted to allow the horses to drink and rest.

"Boy howdy, you sure can ride," Logan said.

She laughed. "Thank you. It's been a long time. I'm glad I haven't forgotten how."

"You surely haven't," Logan agreed.

They sat and watched the creek for a while, content in each other's company. After several minutes, Logan turned to Winona. "I should be thanking you," he said.

"For what?"

"I spent so much time focused on the past before you got here. I hated your father. I'm sorry to say it but it's true. I hated him for what he did to my father."

"What happened? I mean, I know he stole the deal with the Army from your father but it's more than just business rivalry, isn't it?"

Logan nodded. "He didn't just steal the contract away. He manipulated my father into allowing Heath to speak for the Foley Ranch, legally. Heath wrote my father completely out of the deal. My father spent the ranch's savings expanding the ranch to support the Army's requirements. When Heath stole my father's share in the deal, he nearly ruined us. We've never fully recovered."

"I'm sorry," Winona said. "My father's changed so much since he met my stepmother and not for the better."

"You really don't get along with your stepmother, do you?"

"I don't" Winona agreed emphatically. "She's completely absorbed with wealth and status. It's a sickness with her. If there was ever any good in her, her lust for money and prestige has killed it. The worst part is she's corrupted my father. The man I knew as a young girl would never betray anyone the way he betrayed your father. It just goes to show how much she's corrupted him."

Logan nodded. His next words surprised Winona. "Well, for what it's worth, I think your father's starting to see Audrey for what she truly is. I got the impression when they visited that he wasn't entirely happy with the way she treats you.

"In any case, I say we leave the past behind. Since you've gotten here, you've managed to repair the house and repair my relationship with my brothers. I'm grateful you're here and whatever your stepmother might say, I think you're the most ladylike lady I've ever met."

She giggled. "Thank you. And you are the manliest man."

They burst into laughter again. When the laughter subsided, they lapsed once more into comfortable silence and watched the birds and squirrels play around the creek. Winona reached out and grasped Logan's hand. The world could have ended right then, and Winona would have died happy.

***

Once again, Winona's happiness was short-lived. She woke the next morning to find the house empty. The brothers had left early for their chores, it seemed. She woke and dressed, then headed to the well for water to wash in.

As soon as she stepped outside, she heard shouting coming from the direction of the stable. Her heart sank as she walked toward the sound. She hoped against hope it wasn't what she thought it was.

Of course, it was. Jay and Logan were fighting again. When she could make out their words, she realized they were fighting once more about whether the ranch should focus on cattle or horses.

"Blast it, Jay, we're a horse ranch! We breed horses! That's who we are!"

"That so? How's that working out for us? Huh? How many cattle have taken ill and died? Answer me that!"

Winona arrived then. Gregory turned to her and raised an eyebrow in greeting.

"What's going on?" she asked Gregory.

"Some of the horses have taken ill. No one knows what's wrong with them, but a dozen head died last night."

Logan shouted again before Winona could respond. "So, we isolate the sick ones, figure out what's wrong and solve it! We don't just turn tail and run like cowards!"

"It's not cowardly to admit when things need to change, Logan, it's smart. It's cowardly to avoid facing reality!"

Logan took a menacing step forward, but Winona had had enough. Before Logan could respond to Jay, she stepped in between them. "That's enough!" she shouted.

The two brothers recoiled in surprise.

Winona spoke firmly, surprised at her own courage, but refusing to stop now that she'd started. "I've had enough of the fighting between you two! You're not enemies, you're brothers. Jay, it's not Logan's fault the horses are dying. Logan, you need to listen to what Jay has to say. He has as much of a say in this family as you do! Enough bickering! Talk to each other like adults and solve this problem once and for all!"

The three of them stood silently for a moment. Finally, Logan said, "I guess it wouldn't do any harm to put some time into the cattle herd."

Jay nodded. "I'm sorry I blamed you for losing the horses."

They shuffled their feet awkwardly for a moment. Then Gregory interjected. "All right, now kiss and make up!"

The three of them turned to Gregory and stared at him. He grinned mischievously and all four of them burst into laughter. When Winona's laughter subsided, she shook her head. "I swear, you boys will be the death of me."

***

Logan sighed and drummed his fingers on the table. After a moment, Winona said, "You'll wear a hole in the table if you keep that up."

He chuckled and shook his head. "I don't know, Winona. A dance? It just seems like ..." His voice trailed off.

"Seems like what? Fun? A chance for us to spend some time together as a family? A chance to get your brothers off of the ranch for once? A chance to make this family a part of the community again?"

"That's just it," Logan said. "The community. It's one thing that we run errands together in town. No one's going to say anything to us during business hours but at a social function, parading our marriage around in front of all those snooty people? Aren't you worried about what people will say?"

"Not one bit," Winona said. "This is my family, and if people have a problem with that they can just learn to deal with it." Her voice softened and her face adopted a plaintive look. "Come on, Logan. It'll be fun. We haven't done anything fun outside of the ranch yet."

"What's wrong with the ranch?"

She rolled her eyes. "You know what I mean. Stop stalling and say yes."

Logan sighed and regarded his wife. He could no longer deny he was in love with her. The truth was the thought of dancing with her was perhaps the most exciting thing he could think of. He could only imagine how beautiful she would look dressed for a dance.

Most of his hesitation stemmed from guilt. When he invited Winona's parents over for lunch, he allowed Winona to think he was trying to mend fences, but the truth was he simply wanted to rub his marriage to Winona in their faces. He knew Winona admired him for being the bigger person, but he wasn't.

He was just as petty as Heath was. More so, in fact. Heath had overcome his discomfort with the marriage before Logan overcame his hatred for Heath. If Winona's parents were there, all he'd be able to do is focus on that guilt.

Then again, it wasn't like he still felt that way. He had reconciled his feelings about Heath Ross and Audrey's bark seemed worse than her bite so far. He couldn't deny it would be good for Gregory and Jay to get out a little bit. Besides, maybe Louise would be there, and he could finally convince Gregory to court her.

He sighed. "All right, I'll go to the dance."

Winona squealed and threw her arms around him. He closed his eyes and savored the feel of her soft, warm body pressed against his. Within moments, he'd forgotten all about his objections to the dance.

***

Logan fidgeted and tugged at the collar of his shirt. The dancehall was packed to the brim with members of Westridge's high society. He felt like he stood out like a sore thumb.

Jay wasted no time finding a pretty young girl and asking her to dance. For the first time in his life, Logan found himself admiring his brother's courage. He brought his wife, and he still couldn't work up the courage to dance.

He saw Heath and Audrey Ross standing on the opposite side of the dance floor. Their eyes seemed to bore into his and he felt heat rise up his neck.

A moment later, Winona's soft fingers slipped into his. "Hey," she whispered. "Forget about them. Forget about everyone. It's just us."

He looked down at her and wondered how on earth he could have noticed anything other than the beautiful woman who stood before him. She wore a light blue silk gown with lace on the collar and the sleeves. Her hair was tied exquisitely, and a gold pendant hung around her neck. She looked like a fairy tale princess and Logan was in love. He allowed her to lead him to the floor.

As they danced, Logan's anxiety fell away and by the second song, a lively two-step, he was laughing and dancing with abandon. He glanced to the side where Gregory waited, staring at Louise Parker. A glance at the young lady revealed her blushing and casting furtive glances Gregory's way.

Logan steered Winona close to Gregory and said, "Hey, go ask that girl to dance before I ask her for you."

Gregory reddened and shook his head.

"Come on, Gregory," Jay called as he and his partner whirled by. "Be a man!"

Gregory stared after his younger brother then heaved a sigh. He looked anxiously at Winona, who smiled encouragingly at him. Then he strode purposefully toward Louise Parker.

A moment later, the two of them were beaming and dancing, awkwardly but clearly happy to be in each other's company. Gregory smiled gratefully toward Winona and Logan felt a sudden rush of love for his wife. She turned to him to say something but before she could speak, Logan's lips were on hers.

Chapter Seventeen

Logan led Winona outside. Both of them were flushed from the dancing and the kiss, and the cool night air was a welcome caress on his cheeks. He said nothing for a while, fascinated by the feel of her hand in his and the sight of her next to him, her auburn hair flowing in waves over her shoulders while her dress flowed in similar waves around her legs.

She met his eyes and blushed. In the soft moonlight, the rose in her cheeks contrasted prettily with the blue of her dress and the burnished brown of her hair. She smiled up at him and squeezed his hand. He grinned and squeezed hers. She giggled softly and he laughed with her, then wrapped his arm around her shoulders and pulled her close. She leaned against him and sighed softly. A moment later, he felt her own arm snake around his waist.

They continued to walk in silence until the noise of the dance was a dim echo in the background. When they reached the edge of town, Logan turned so they walked along the outskirts.

"So, what is this?" Winona asked.

"What?" Logan replied.

"This. Us." She smiled at him, but her eyes were earnest and searching. "That kiss wasn't a kiss of convenience."

"No," Logan agreed. "It wasn't."

When he didn't continue, Winona asked again, "So what was it?"

He opened his mouth but couldn't say the words he knew she wanted to hear, the words he so desperately wanted to say. He swallowed and finally said, "I like you, Winona."

She smiled wryly at him, and his cheeks flamed. "I mean ..." he stammered. "I really like you. Like, a lot." Blast it, why couldn't he just say he—

He was pulled from his thoughts when Winona suddenly stood on her tiptoes and kissed him. This kiss was far softer and less urgent than the one they shared in the dance hall, but it carried just as much of the love he couldn't manage to put into words. She pulled away after a moment and lifted a hand to caress his cheek. "I really like you a lot too, Logan."

He chuckled and hung his head, then pulled her close to him. She melted into his embrace, laughing softly. "What are you laughing at?" he asked.

She shook her head. "I think it's painfully adorable how hard it is for you to say what you mean sometimes. You're going to have to learn not to be afraid of me."

"I'm not afraid of you," he said. "I just ..."

Just can't believe I found you.

Just can't believe I love you.

Just can't believe you're in my arms right now.

Just can't believe the world can be so perfect even though nothing's really changed.

It had changed, though. Since Winona, everything had changed. He and his brothers were happy again for the first time since their parents died. The ranch was in better shape than it had ever been and if Jay turned out to be right about the cattle after all, they would be far more comfortable than they had ever been. He gazed at the woman in his arms and wondered again how he could be so lucky.

She looked up at him. "Just what?"

He shook his head. "I'll never be able to explain it."

She caressed his cheek again. "I know. Try anyway."

Blast it, why couldn't he just tell her he loved her? What was he waiting for?

"Thank you," he finally replied. "You've made my life so much better since I met you."

She smiled again. There was tenderness still in her smile, but now there was a touch of sadness as well. "I'm glad, Logan," she said.

They began walking back to the dance. Logan looked at his feet for the first few minutes, ashamed he couldn't admit his feelings. After a minute, he felt Winona squeeze his hand and look up at him. She smiled, this time without sadness, and said, "It's okay. We have time."

Those five words meant as much to Logan in that moment as the other three would have. He smiled back at her and stood taller. His chest swelled with pride as he walked back with his wife—his wife!—to the dancehall.

His good feeling quickly faded when they entered the building. Gregory and Jay stood on the outskirts of the dance floor. Gregory kept a protective arm around Louise Sawyer, who clung to him like a raft at sea. They cast an anxious glance at Logan and Winona then turned back to the floor, where the majority of the attendees clustered around two newcomers.

One of the newcomers was an older man. He was tall, taller than Logan and despite his advanced age, held an erect bearing that accentuated his height, so he seemed to tower over everyone present. His hair was silver white and impeccably combed. His suit was also impeccable and was fashioned of a material that seemed softer and more vibrant than the wool suits common among high society. He smiled at the crowd in the genial, patronizing way Logan had seen politicians smile.

His smile stopped well below his eyes. A sharp, piercing blue, they scanned the crowd, stopping when they fell on Logan. Logan felt the hairs on the back of his neck prickle under the old man's gaze. His eyes seemed to bore through Logan, who felt his grip on Winona's hand tighten reflexively.

The older man turned and said something to the other newcomer. This man was younger, around Logan's age, and though not so tall as the other man, carried himself with the same royal bearing. His hair was combed in a similar style as well but was a jet black that was as dark as the older man's hair was light.

There was no mistaking the resemblance in those piercing blue eyes. After his father spoke to him, the younger man also scanned the crowd. His eyes stopped on Winona and a flash of pure hate ran through them before being replaced by an equally powerful lust.

Winona gasped and squeezed Logan's hand, and in an instant Logan knew who they were. The younger man approached them, his eyes never leaving Winona. Logan stepped protectively in front of her, but Jude Koch ignored him and lifted a hand in invitation to Winona. "Winona," he said, in a voice that dripped with honey and venom, "It's so good to see you."

Winona didn't respond. She looked at the floor and trembled slightly and Logan felt a surge of anger at Jude for daring to frighten his wife. He glared at Jude and said, "I don't think she wants to talk to you, Jude. Why don't you—"

"May I have this dance?" Jude asked, not even glancing in Logan's direction.

Logan felt the back of his neck grow cold. His hands slowly clenched into fists. How dare he? How dare he ask his wife to dance in front of him like that? How dare he frighten Winona?

Winona shook her head and shrank away slightly. Out of the corner of his eye, Logan saw Heath Ross take a step forward, but Audrey's arm shot out and stopped him.

"Winona, please," Jude repeated. "Let me have this one dance. I still love you. I—"

The ice in Logan's veins grew white-hot and before he could stop himself, he reached out and shoved Jude hard in the chest. Jude's eyes widened from the force of Logan's action and he fell hard, skidding backward to a stop a few yards away.

Gasps and cries echoed through the crowd. The music stopped as even the band looked on in shock at the two men. Logan blinked and looked around at the sea of disapproving scowls and looks of horror that showed on nearly every face. Gregory and Jay shifted uncomfortably on their feet. Louise clung even more tightly to Gregory, but a moment later was wrenched away by her parents, who led her quickly to the other side of the building. Gregory didn't confront them but the pain in his eyes crushed Logan.

He turned back to Jude who grinned smugly at him from the floor. He opened his mouth to tell the blasted cur to find his way out the door and he didn't care what anyone had to say about it. He stopped when a shadow fell over Jude. He looked up to see his father gazing at him, his expression inscrutable.

Sterling spoke in a voice as rich and poisonous as Jude's, tinged with a slight German accent. "Are you so uncouth as to assault a gentleman in public who has done you no wrong? Apologize to my son."

"That's all right, Father," Jude said. He grinned evilly at Logan. "A man can't help his upbringing."

Logan started forward but a strong hand gripped his arm, stopping him. He turned to see Gregory holding him. "Let it go, Logan."

Logan turned to Jude. Jude stared contemptuously at him. "That's right, Logan. Let it go."

Logan's hands clenched into fists, and he nearly wrenched his arm away from his brother so he could beat Jude senseless, but a softer hand gripped his other arm. He turned to see Winona's eyes pleading with him. "Please, Logan. Let's just go home."

Logan squeezed his fists together once more, then relaxed. Without a word, he allowed Gregory and Winona to lead them out of the dancehall. Jude stood up, grinning. He opened his mouth to speak, but Jay's fist crashed into his stomach. Unprepared for the blow, Jude doubled over gasping, the wind knocked out of him. Jay's lip curled in contempt before he turned and followed his family outside. Jude glared and made to go after him, but his father laid a hand on his shoulder to still him.

They rode back to the ranch in silence. Gregory stared into the night his face emotionless. Jay's expression alternated between anger and contempt. Winona's eyes remained downcast, grief and fear etched into her features. Logan, surprisingly, felt nothing anymore but a deep weariness.

When they arrived, Logan helped Winona from the wagon. She collapsed into his arms and began to sob deeply. Jay and

Gregory watched, helpless and shifted their feet. Finally, Gregory laid a comforting arm on her shoulder. A moment later, Jay followed and laid a hand on her other shoulder. The three brothers held her until her sobs had quieted and her shoulders no longer shook. Gregory and Jay took their leave then, nodding their goodbyes to Logan and heading to their rooms.

Logan held Winona for a long while, saying nothing but softly stroking her hair. His thoughts filled with anger once more as he recalled the contempt on the faces of the townspeople when he shoved Jude. So, everyone would side with a snake like Jude over him? Over Winona? Fine. It looked like wealth and status really were all that mattered in Westridge. Maybe Audrey wasn't so different from the other townspeople after all.

Well, if they wanted to shun his family that was fine with Logan. Neither he nor his brothers had any need for folks who would value a man's pocketbook more than they valued his character. They could keep their Jude Kochs and their Heath Rosses. Logan and his brothers would be just fine on their own.

When Winona stopped crying, she pulled away from Logan. She looked up at him and tried to smile but her lip still quivered, and her voice trembled when she spoke. "Thank you for a lovely evening."

His heart broke and he pulled her close again. "Don't worry about Jude, Winona. He's just a spoiled little brat. That's all he is. He can't hurt you. Not while I'm around."

She stood up and kissed his cheek, then pulled away and smiled, more steadily this time. "I believe you," she said softly. "I'm not afraid of him anymore. I'm just angry. I wanted tonight to be perfect."

"Tonight was perfect," Logan insisted. He took Winona's face in his hands and kissed her deeply. Her eyes were smoky and her cheeks were flushed when he pulled away. "You are perfect, and you are *my* wife and there ain't a blasted thing Jude Koch can do about that!"

She smiled and this time there was no grief. She brushed a lock of hair off his forehead and said, "Have I mentioned that I really like you, like a lot?"

He chuckled and looked down then met her eyes again. "I really like you a lot too."

They stood staring at each other a few more moments, then Winona whispered, "I think I should go to bed." She left, squeezing Logan's hand for a moment before finally parting. Logan watched her walk away. He felt a sudden urge to follow her, to take her in his arms and confirm once and for all that their marriage was more than just convenience.

He didn't though, and though Winona lingered in her doorway for a long moment before closing the door, he remained rooted in place, still unable to express the love he felt so strongly.

When her door closed, Logan sighed heavily and made his way to his own room. The events of the evening weighed on him. He'd made as though the townsfolks' reactions didn't bother him for Winona's sake, but the truth was they ate at him terribly.

Logan didn't feel a need for others to worship him the way Audrey desperately needed it, or the way Sterling and Jude Koch expected it. He didn't need them to love him or even like him. He had hoped only that the people of Westridge would respect him. At the very least, he hoped they would understand why he couldn't allow Jude's affront to Winona to go unanswered.

Instead, they had as one sided with Jude and Sterling Koch. Logan thought of the immaculate suit Sterling wore and his lip curled downward. So that's what people valued: wealth and status over character?

He shook his head, more determined than ever that his family should no longer have to suffer the contempt of the townsfolk. If they wanted to behave like sheep, led around by two wealthy, haughty, richly dressed wolves, that was their mistake. Logan wouldn't allow it to affect his wife or brothers anymore.

One thing his father had done right after Heath Ross's betrayal was withdraw from the community and pull away from the fake, money-worshipping leeches that populated Westridge. Logan had allowed his resolve to weaken momentarily, but now he was firm in his mind once more. As far as he was concerned, the Foley ranch bordered on Westridge but it and the family that resided on it were no longer a part of the town. He wouldn't cause trouble in Westridge, but neither would he allow any trouble from Westridge to come to his property. As of that moment, the Foley's were alone again.

As they should be.

Chapter Eighteen

Winona sat up and sighed. She was exhausted but her chores were nearly complete. A few more minutes of scrubbing and the stove would be clean, and she could complete her latest drawing. Now that the house was repaired and the years of caked-on dirt removed, it was rather easy to keep up with the cleaning and cooking. She resolved to ask Logan where else she could help around the ranch. Perhaps she could plow and replant the vegetable garden.

She heard a commotion coming from outside and stood to look out the kitchen window. Jay and Logan stood at the gate of the courtyard, arguing. Jay held a notebook in his hand and Winona realized he was trying to convince Logan to accept his plan for the cattle herd.

Logan had grudgingly acquiesced prior to the dance but since the spectacle with Jude, he'd balked once more. He gestured angrily at Jay and though Winona couldn't make out the words, she knew he was once more refusing to hear Jay out.

Jay lifted his hands in pleading and Winona was gratified to see he didn't return Logan's anger in kind. At least one Foley brother was learning to manage his emotions, she thought wryly. Logan listened for a minute, arms folded, then began shouting and gesturing again. After a minute, he strode angrily toward the house, leaving Jay standing at the gate, head hanging.

Winona quickly moved away from the window and sat at the table, fanning herself. She wanted to confront Logan about his conversation with Jay but didn't want him to know she'd been eavesdropping. When the door opened, she stood and smiled sweetly at her husband.

"Good afternoon, Logan!" she said brightly. "How are you?"

"Fine," he responded gruffly. Heavens above, were men always so dramatic?

She resisted the urge to roll her eyes and say something sarcastic and instead said, "How are things at the ranch? Everything okay with the horses?"

"Ten more dead," he replied tersely. "That brings the total to ninety-three head dead of illness this month."

Winona's irritation faded somewhat in the face of this news. She could understand now why Logan was in a bad mood. "I'm so sorry to hear that," she said. "Darrell still doesn't know what's wrong with them?"

Logan shook his head. "Best we can do is separate the ones that are ill but that doesn't seem to be helping."

Winona thought for a moment. Then her eyes brightened. "Cordelia mentioned there's a new doctor in town. He calls himself a veterinary. Maybe he can take a look at the horses."

"And how do you propose to pay for that, Winona?" Logan snapped. She stared at him, shocked into silence by his sudden outburst. He sighed and said, "I'm sorry. I didn't mean to snap. I just—we can't afford to hire a doctor right now. Darrell and the hands know this herd. We'll just have to hope that's enough."

He looked tired and drawn, and despite her frustration at his irritability she couldn't help but feel some sympathy. She hated seeing him stressed like this. Well, Jay had a way to make the ranch money again. Logan didn't listen to Jay but maybe he would listen to her.

"Logan," she began tentatively. "I was looking at the ledger with Jay and I think he might be on to something with the cattle."

He looked up sharply at her and she held a hand up and quickly continued. "I know you're set on breeding horses, but I think Jay's plan will allow the ranch to become profitable again. We can pay to finish fixing up the stable and care for both herds properly. We'll still breed horses, but we'll breed cattle too. At least long enough to—"

"Why was he showing you the ledger?" he barked suddenly.

Winona recoiled and protested. "He just wanted to show me his plan for the cattle. I used to help my father with his books and I thought I—"

"Jay had no right to do that!" Logan shouted.

Winona felt her anger rise and she raised her own voice in response. "Don't interrupt me like that! I asked him to show me the ledger, Logan. Like I was saying, I used to help my father balance the books at home and I thought—"

"This is your home now, Winona."

"Don't interrupt me!" Winona shouted. This time it was Logan's turn to recoil.

Winona glared at him and continued, her tone sharp and biting. She hated sounding like that, but he was so frustrating! "I thought I would try to see if I could help the ranch make money again, so you didn't have to worry all the time. It turns out, Jay actually has a pretty good head for numbers if you would just listen to him, Logan!"

"I don't want you to worry about that stuff, Winona," Logan retorted. "I'm more than able to take care of my wife. You won't have to worry you can't put bread on the table. You just focus on your chores. Leave me to take care of the rest."

Winona stared at him, once more shocked speechless. When she finally did find her voice, it trembled with rage. "Don't you dare treat me like property, Logan Foley. I am not some kept woman whose job is to keep her head down and focus on chores. I came here to be an equal part of this family.

Marriage of convenience or not, I will not sit idly by while my husband worries himself to death because he's too stubborn and proud to let anyone help him." Her face softened. "I'm not worried for myself, Logan. I'm worried for you. Ever since the dance, you've become morose and sullen again. I don't like seeing you like that."

"Well, I'm sorry I'm not always roses and sunshine, Winona." His voice was petulant, and Winona had to resist a sudden impulse to shake him senseless. "I'm trying to preserve my father's legacy and I'm the only one who seems to care."

"Is your father's legacy worth your family's future?"

Logan stood suddenly and glared down at her. "My father's legacy is everything!" he shouted.

Winona held his gaze as she stood to face him. She felt badly that he was upset and stressed but he needed to know that she would not succumb to bullying. She kept her voice even and replied, "No Logan. Your *family* is everything."

Logan glared at her for several moments before his gaze dropped. He sighed and rubbed his temples. "I know, I know. I'm sorry, Winona, it's just ..." he looked up as though searching for the answer in the air. When he didn't find it there, he sighed and said, "I just don't have time to think about the cattle right now. I need to focus on the horses."

He didn't meet her eyes as he said this, and Winona knew he was lying. She held him with her gaze until he shifted his feet uncomfortably. Then she said, "I won't force you to be honest with me, Logan and I won't force you to listen to your brother, but sooner or later, you're going to have to find room to let us in. I don't think you want to be alone as much as you think you do."

He opened his mouth but closed it without replying. Still avoiding her eyes, he mumbled, "I have to go check on the herd," and left the house.

Winona stood where she was until she could no longer hear Logan's boots walking away. Then she ran her hands through her hair and let loose a low frustrated growl from deep in her throat.

How could Logan be so pigheaded? What did he think he was gaining by insisting the ranch run as it had for the past twenty-five years? Was change so terrifying to him? Another thought occurred to her: maybe Logan still carried some resentment toward her father for betraying his father. Maybe the horses were important not because of his father's legacy but because of Logan's desire to beat Heath Ross.

Well, if that was the case, he was even more the fool. Spending his entire life fixated on Heath Ross would only mean her father's victory—if victory it even was—was complete. The only way to truly overcome that betrayal was to not allow it to consume him.

She would get nowhere trying to convince him of that, she knew. She would just have to be patient and continue trying to lead him down a better path.

She was so tired of being patient.

The door opened again, and she sighed, anticipating another argument but this time it was Gregory, not Logan, who entered the house. She brightened when she saw him. With Logan and Jay returned to their moody ways, Gregory was the only brother who seemed to have time for her anymore. She chuckled softly as she recalled that for the first few months she was here, Gregory barely seemed to register that she existed. Now he was the closest thing to an actual brother she'd ever had.

"What's so funny?" he asked.

"Your face," she replied. "It just has that effect on me."

He groaned and rolled his eyes. "I see Jay's been teaching you some jokes. Do yourself a favor and don't listen to him."

"Whatever, funny face," she retorted.

He shook his head but couldn't quite stifle a chuckle. "Well, Miss Full-of-Laughs, I was going to see if you wanted to join me on a ride but if you're going to poke fun the whole time, I might just go myself."

"Oh, stop," she laughed. "I swear, you Foley boys are worse than girls when someone teases you. Wait a moment, I'll change into my riding outfit."

Ten minutes later, she and Gregory rode leisurely across the west field. In a few days, they would move the horses here from the southeast pasture, and the smell of mint and thyme calmed and invigorated her at the same time. She and Gregory chatted amiably about little things. She asked his opinion on a pork rib recipe she wanted to try, and he spoke excitedly about a fishing trip he and Jay planned to take up the creek in a few days.

"You should come with us," he said. "I think it would be fun for you to get out of the house for a day."

"That sounds like fun," she said. "I think I might take you up on that offer." She grinned mischievously at him. "So, tell me what else is going on in your life?"

He reddened and looked away. "I don't know what you mean."

She laughed and brought her horse closer. "You know, you and Louise."

He grinned and shook his head. "I don't know what you're talking about."

"You know," she teased in a singsong voice. "Louise, your belle, your sweetheart, the love of your life, the pretty blonde girl you danced with—"

"Okay, okay," he laughed. "You've made your point." He grinned at her. "I can't believe I actually asked her to dance."

She laughed. "I know! It was almost like you were a man for a moment."

He ignored the jibe and smiled at Winona. "I owe it to you. You gave me the courage to start living again. After my parents died, I swore I'd never take another risk—well, you've heard all that before. The point is, I never would have had the gumption to ask her to dance if it weren't for you, so thank you."

She smiled warmly at him. "I just helped you see the courage that was already there."

He laughed. "What are you, a poet?"

She rolled her eyes. "Must you always be sarcastic?"

"Yes, it's a curse. Nothing we can do about it. I just have to live with it and now you do too."

"Oh, joy," she quipped. "So, when are you and Louise seeing each other again?"

His face fell. "I don't know. After that business with Jude and Logan, I'm worried she won't want to see me again. Her parents don't want her to see me, that's for sure."

Winona recalled how the Sawyers had pulled Louise away from Gregory during the altercation between Logan and Jude. Her lips thinned in anger, and she said, "Gregory, take it from someone who knows: if you want to be happy, you have to live your life without being concerned what others think of you. Louise's parents may not like it, but Louise is an adult, and she can see whomever she pleases. I think you should go talk to her. Tell her you intend to court her whatever anyone thinks. I think you'll find she'll admire a man with the courage to fight for her."

Gregory thought a moment, then straightened in his saddle. "Okay," he said. "I will. Thank you, Winona."

They completed the circle back to the corrals a few minutes later. Gregory bade Winona goodbye and headed off to complete his afternoon chores while Winona rode back to the house. She sent the horse away, knowing it would head to the stables by instinct, and walked inside.

Jay sat at the table, working on the ledger. His face was tired and sad, and though he'd proven himself a man and then some the past few weeks, he looked in that moment like a sad little boy, grieving at the hurt his older brother had caused him.

Winona sat across from him. He looked up at the noise and she smiled at him. "Hello, Jay."

He offered the ghost of a smile in return. "Hi, Winona."

"What are you working on?"

He sighed. "Logan's not going to go through with the plan for the cattle," he said, his voice hollow. "I'm trying to go through the numbers to budget accordingly."

Winona extended her hand. "May I?"

"Be my guest," he said, handing her the ledger.

In minutes, she had the ranch's finances properly sorted out. She felt a moment's satisfaction knowing she'd proven Logan wrong about her ability to help with the finances, but it faded quickly. The ledger painted a bleak story. Without the income projected from the cattle operations, the ranch would hover near the edge of bankruptcy, likely for years, before eventually collapsing. There was no way around it. Logan would have to come around.

"Jay," Winona said when she was done. "We need to convince Logan about the cattle."

He chuckled bitterly. "Well, how do you propose we do that?"

"Together," she replied. "Tonight. We talk to him together at dinner and make him understand. He wants to preserve your father's legacy and ensure the ranch stays in operation. Investing in the cattle herd is the only way to do that. You and I know that, and I think he knows it too He's just pigheaded. I think we can convince him if we both talk to him."

Jay didn't seem convinced, but he shrugged. "Well, it's worth a shot, I guess."

Winona smiled. "We'll convince him. You'll see."

She wasn't as confident as she sounded but after talking to Gregory, she was reminded how important this family was to her. She would succeed in saving the ranch or go to her grave trying.

Watch out, Logan Foley, she thought. *When it comes to pigheadedness, you've met your match in me.*

Chapter Nineteen

Winona checked the roast for perhaps the hundredth time. Just like the last ninety-nine times, the roast was still a long way from being done. She sighed and nearly ran her hands through her hair, preventing herself at the last second from ruining her hairdo, and by extension her outfit.

She'd chosen a white cotton-dress with a floral print that was both modest and flattering. She'd spent the morning starching it, polishing her boots and doing her hair until every part of her outfit was perfect. She had no idea if charming Logan with her appearance would make him more receptive to Jay's plan for the ranch, but it couldn't hurt.

She spent the afternoon preparing supper. She'd peeled and chopped potatoes and carrots to roast with the pork and baked a fresh loaf of bread with it. The bread finished hours ago and now rested on the counter. It had long since cooled and Winona made a note to put bread in the oven much closer to supper next time.

She paced the kitchen for a few minutes then checked the roast again. Shockingly, it still had a long way to go. She sat down heavily and sighed in exasperation. She hadn't felt this anxious in a while. She was nervous about her and Jay's conversation with Logan tonight. Logan was a caring man with a big heart and Winona knew he wanted only what was best for the family, but he could be so stubborn sometimes that he couldn't be made to listen to reason by anyone or anything. If he was in such a mood tonight, Winona could eat in front of him naked and it wouldn't make a difference.

She blushed crimson with embarrassment at the thought of being naked in front of Logan but only had to suffer for a moment because an instant later Jay walked into the kitchen.

He smiled at her and the anxiety in his face told her he shared her fear about tonight's conversation. "Hi, Winona," he said.

"Hi, Jay."

Jay sat across from her and breathed a sigh. Winona felt compassion override her worry and she placed a hand over his. "Don't worry. I'm sure he'll listen."

Jay chuckled bitterly. "Why? Why should tonight be any different?"

"Because," Winona said. "Tonight, you have me."

"Oh, so you're the key to his reason?"

"Don't be fooled by my demure behavior," Winona replied. "I can make myself irresistible if I want to." She batted her eyelashes coquettishly, eliciting a laugh from Jay.

"I sure hope you're right," Jay said. "Sometimes I feel like Logan wouldn't see daylight if he woke up on the sun."

This prompted Winona to laugh. "Don't worry. I can be very persuasive when I need to be."

Jay nodded. "Irresistible and persuasive. Good. We'll need both."

The door opened and a moment later, Gregory joined them in the kitchen. He sniffed the air and closed his eyes, smiling. "Mmm-mmm, whatever you're cooking, Winona, it smells delightful." He pinched his thumb and forefinger together and brought them to his lips as he said this.

Winona and Jay laughed, and Gregory grinned. "Seriously, though, what are you cooking? I'm starving."

"Well, you'll just have to be patient. I'm cooking a pork roast and it's not done yet."

Gregory rolled his eyes with pleasure and rubbed his stomach. "Oh, that sounds heavenly."

Jay laughed again. "You've been spending too much time with Louise. You're starting to sound like her."

"That's not true!" Gregory protested. "I haven't even seen her since the dance."

Jay stared at Gregory, nonplussed. "In that case, you haven't spent nearly enough time with her. Confound it man, why are you here and not courting her right now?"

"I know, I know," Gregory replied, lifting his hands defensively. "Winona already chewed me out about it. I'm going to call on her tomorrow."

"You better or I will," Jay said.

"Sounds good," Gregory replied cheerfully. "She's always wanted a pet. You're not nearly as adorable as a puppy but I'm sure you'll follow her around like one."

"Oh, like you don't?" Jay said. "Oh wait, that's right. You didn't have the guts to talk to her until Winona and I made you."

Gregory grinned and swung playfully at his brother. Jay dodged the slap and launched at Gregory. The two boys laughed and tussled while Winona tried frantically to keep them away from the stove.

"Boys! Boys!" she shouted through laughter. "If you're going to wrestle, do it outside and for heaven's sake, change before dinner!"

The two brothers separated, grinning. "No need to fear, milady," Gregory said. "We will both be in pristine condition for this evening's soiree."

Winona rolled her eyes. "I swear you boys will be the death of me."

"I feel like you say that a lot," Jay interjected.

"I feel like I mean it even more," Winona shot back. "Now get out of my kitchen, both of you, or I'll have Darrell tan both your hides."

Jay scoffed. "I'd mop the floor with that old man."

Winona smiled brightly and waved toward the doorway. "Oh, hi Darrell. I didn't see you there."

Jay quickly looked toward the door, eyes wide with fear. No one was there and when Gregory and Winona burst out laughing, Jay realized he'd been duped. He glared at Winona, who smiled sweetly at him. After a second, he too started laughing. "All right, Gregory. Let's give Winona some space before she tans our hides herself."

"You better believe I will," Winona assured him.

The two boys left, and Winona sat and shook her head. She was grateful for the distraction, even more so when she checked the roast and found it was noticeably closer to finished. She looked out the window toward the west field where Logan and Darrell were checking for any sign of wild animals that might pose a danger to the herd. Though not common, rattlesnakes, coyotes and cougars did occasionally wander into Westridge, and it was prudent to check frequently for unwanted visitors.

"Please be in a good mood tonight," she whispered.

***

An hour later, the four of them sat around the dinner table, chatting amiably as they feasted on the perfectly tender roast pork, steamed vegetables and the fresh bread Winona had warmed just prior to dinner. Everyone seemed to be in good spirits, including Logan, who happily informed them they had just gone through the herd and confirmed there were no more sick animals. It would take a few months for them to recover from their losses, but the mystery illness seemed to have moved on.

Winona looked at Jay. He met her eyes, worry etched all over his features. She smiled and nodded for him to go on. He took a deep breath, cleared his throat and called to his brother. "Logan?"

Logan looked at him and chuckled. "What's going on, Jay? You look like you've seen a ghost."

Jay swallowed and squared his shoulders. "Logan, I'd like to talk to you about my plan to grow the cattle herd and recoup some of the ranch's financial losses over the past few years."

Logan's smile faded. He stared wordlessly at his brother for several moments. Jay met his gaze and waited for his reply. Gregory glanced nervously between the two of them.

Winona reached out and laid a hand over Logan's arm. He glanced at her, and she smiled. "Just listen to him, Logan. He's just asking for a chance to be heard."

Logan didn't respond for several seconds. Finally, he sighed and nodded at Jay.

Jay's shoulders relaxed and he grinned excitedly at Winona before turning back to Logan. He pulled the ledger out from under the table and opened it to the page he and Winona had worked on when discussing the plan. Logan's eyes narrowed when he recognized Winona's handwriting, but he didn't say anything.

"So, this page here is the ranch's projected revenue and expenses if we focus entirely on the horse herd," Jay began. "Assuming we're able to sell the horses at market value and assuming we'll need to replenish our brood stock at the typical frequency then, factoring in the cost of feed for the winter months as well as supplies, tack, and typical odds and ends, the best we can hope for is to break even. Mind you, this is the best-case scenario and doesn't account for the likelihood that buyers would prefer Ross horses—"

"Likelihood?" Logan snapped.

"Possibility," Jay quickly corrected. "The possibility that buyers might purchase from Heath Ross instead of from us. In any case, it's more likely we lose money if we focus entirely on horses to the exclusion of the cattle. If things continue that way for another year, we'll be forced to sell the herd just to pay our debts. We'll have to let go of the hands and eventually sell the ranch itself. It's just too much risk."

Logan glared at Jay but said nothing, so Jay continued. "This page here," he said pointing to the opposite leaf, "shows our projected expenses and revenue if we invest in the cattle herd. If we increase our herd size to a thousand head and ensure consistent care, the herd should maintain a stable population without replenishment. Then we only have to replace what we sell or purchase more if we want to expand. Now, assuming current market prices for beef cattle, we stand to make a substantial profit, even if we only sell fifty percent of what I project."

Jay leaned forward, excited. "Here's the thing. We're the only cattle ranch within a hundred miles. In a few months, the railroad will pass through Westridge. We won't have to pay cattle drivers to move the herd to the railroad because it will be right here. We can charge lower prices than our non-regional competitors and monopolize the local beef market! Logan, forget about being comfortable, we could be rich!"

Jay stopped, grinning in anticipation of Logan's response. Logan didn't say anything for a long moment. Jay's grin faded and Winona glanced anxiously at Logan. Gregory cleared his throat nervously, the noise jarring in the tense silence.

Finally, Logan said, "Horse ranch."

"What?" Jay blinked, confused.

"We're a horse ranch. You said we're a cattle ranch. We're not a cattle ranch. We're a horse ranch."

Jay blinked again. "I know that, Logan. I mean if we become a cattle ranch."

"We're not going to become a cattle ranch," Logan said. "We've been through this, Jay. Over, and over again. Our father didn't found a cattle ranch, he founded a horse ranch. We're the finest horse ranch in West Texas and we're not going to allow a few years of hardship to force us out of the business that's earned us our reputation."

"Logan," Jay said, trying to remain calm, "The horse business here is failing. We've been through *that* before. There's just no way to remain profitable with the Rosses and the other large outfits encroaching on our business."

Logan slammed his fist on the table. "Blast it, Jay, enough with this talk of cattle! The Foley Ranch is a horse ranch, end of story."

Jay looked pleadingly at Winona. She turned to Logan, squeezing his arm. "Logan, please keep an open mind. I've looked at Jay's projections. He has some really good ideas. If you'd just listen—"

"Oh yes, I saw your handwriting on those pages. How long have you and Jay been planning to gang up on me?"

Winona stared at Logan, dumbfounded. "We're not ganging up on you, Logan! We're trying to save your father's ranch!"

"So now you're taking his side?" Logan thundered. "That's nice. My own wife and brother siding against me!"

"Logan, you're not listening!" Winona insisted, her voice rising. "Blast it, will you shut up for one second and let someone else have a say? We're trying to find a way to keep the ranch afloat so you don't have to watch the bank auction it off to the highest bidder."

Logan glared. He opened and closed his mouth several times without speaking. Finally, he angrily shook her hand off his arm and said, "I've had enough of this talk of cattle. We're a horse ranch. Period. Jay, I'm selling the rest of the cattle. That buyer from Arizona is back in town and I'm giving him the rest of the herd."

Jay's eyes widened. "No!" he shouted in protest. "You can't do that! Those aren't your cattle!"

"Yes, they are," Logan retorted.

"No," Jay insisted. "They're not! They belong to all of us! Pa left the ranch to all of us, not just you!"

"Well, since I'm the only one who cares about keeping the ranch focused on the business it was founded for, I'm the one who gets to make the decisions."

"That's not fair!" Jay shouted.

"Life's not fair," Logan replied.

"That's enough!" Winona interjected. "Logan Foley, I've had enough of your stubbornness. Jay and I are only trying to help but you're too stuck in your ways to see it. You're a bitter old man before your time, Logan, and your family is suffering for it."

Logan chuckled bitterly. He stood and tossed his fork onto the table. It clattered on his plate, then fell to the floor. Logan left it there and walked toward his room. "Great meal, Winona," he called over his shoulder. "Thanks."

The other three sat silently for several moments. Jay sighed and excused himself. "Thanks for trying," he said to Winona as he left for his own room.

Gregory offered Winona a wan smile. "Looks like Logan's back to his good old ways," he joked half-heartedly.

Winona sighed. "He'll come around," she said. "He just needs time."

Gregory didn't respond right away. Eventually, he smiled. "You know something? You're just as stubborn as he is. I think maybe he will come around yet."

Winona smiled and squeezed his hand briefly. "Thank you for saying that, Gregory. It's nice to know there's one Foley brother who isn't an utter fool."

"Always happy to help."

Chapter Twenty

Logan heard the crack of rifle fire and ducked behind their overturned wagon. Dust and splinters flew around him as the outlaws fired volley after volley at his family.

He turned to his father, who crouched next to him. "There's too many, Pa!"

Dale Foley peered through a crack in the wagon's floorboard. "No, not too many. Six, maybe seven. All firing at once, too. When they stop to reload, we'll take aim and fire at anyone who pokes his head out."

Logan nodded and looked around at his mother and brothers. Gregory's face was stoic, but tears ran down Jay's face. Logan's heart melted for the boy. A moment later, rage filled him. How dare these outlaws terrorize his family? His brother shouldn't have to cower in fear for his life because a few worthless bandits wanted his family's money.

Well, they would get what was coming to them. All Logan had to do was wait.

He waited but the fire didn't let up. How many rounds did their rifles carry?

He heard a cry and turned to see his mother collapse, blood spraying from her chest. He leapt up to run to her, but a hail of bullets shattered the boards around him, and he dove back for cover. He turned to his father only to find him dead as well.

This wasn't right.

Gregory let out a choking gasp and collapsed, clutching his stomach.

Logan tried once more to move, but the storm of rife fire forced him to remain where he was. Why hadn't they stopped to reload? This wasn't right. None of it was right. This wasn't what happened.

He looked at Jay. The boy's eyes were glassy with fear. "Logan," he whispered. Then his eyes flew wide. His mouth dropped open in a perfect O. He looked slowly down at his shirt, where a red stain appeared just below his right shoulder. He looked back up at Logan. "Logan," he whispered again. Then he fell.

"Jay!" Logan called. He ran to his brother's side. Miraculously, he managed to avoid the gunfire erupting all around him. He dropped to the ground next to Jay, his vision swimming with tears. He brushed Jay's hair out of his face. "It's okay, Jay," he lied. "I'm going to get us out of here. Don't you fret."

Jay, the focus slowly fading from his eyes, only looked at him and continued to whisper, "Logan ... Logan ..."

***

"Logan!"

Logan's eyes flew open. He sat up, gasping, and looked wildly around him. From a distance, he could still hear the outlaw's rifles. His brow furrowed. Why were they so far away? And where was he? He glanced around at the wooden furniture and the wool curtains that covered the bedroom's window. Gregory and Jay were there but they were different ... older.

"Logan, are you hearing me?"

Jay's voice snapped Logan fully awake. He was in his bedroom at the Foley Ranch. It was two years later, and his brothers Gregory and Jay were alive because they survived the outlaw attack that killed their parents.

"What's going on?" Logan demanded.

"The horses!" Jay shouted. "They're being rustled."

Logan's blood froze. He leapt out of bed and grabbed his gun belt, quickly tying it around his nightclothes. "Gregory, rouse Darrell and the others." He strode quickly to the doorway and began putting on his boots.

"They're already there," Jay replied. "Darrell sent me for you."

"How many?" Logan asked. He reached above the doorjamb for his rifle. When it wasn't there, he panicked for a moment, then remembered he moved it to the parlor when Winona was sleeping in his room. He swore and strode for the living room. "How many?" he called behind his back to Gregory and Jay.

He reached the parlor and grabbed his rifle from its hook above the mantel. He checked to ensure it was loaded then grabbed a handful of shells from the box on the mantel. He looked up where his brothers waited anxiously. "How many?" He repeated again.

Gregory opened his mouth to reply but stopped when the door to their parent's room opened and Winona walked out. "Logan? What's going on?" she asked. Worry etched her lovely features and in the midst of his fear, Logan felt a strange longing to wrap her in his arms and tell her everything was going to be okay.

He didn't have time to do that, so he only said. "The horses are being rustled. We're going to stop them. Blast it, how many?"

"I don't know," Gregory finally answered. "Twenty, maybe thirty."

Logan swore. He employed two dozen hands, not including Darrell. Including himself and his brothers, and assuming Gregory was correct, that meant he could meet the rustlers with equal force. He didn't like that, but it was better than being outnumbered. He shouldered his rifle and walked toward the door.

His brothers followed him, and Logan saw they'd brought him a horse. That was good thinking. He wouldn't have to stop by the stables for one. He lifted one foot into the stirrup and was about to swing into the saddle when Winona gripped his arm.

He looked at her. Her eyes were wide with fear. "Be careful, Logan," she said.

"I will," he promised. Then he swung into the saddle and rode off after his brothers.

His brothers led him to the west field. As they approached, Logan could see the bursts of gunfire in the distance. He spurred his horse and caught up to his brothers. "Which side of the battle are the rustlers?" he called.

Jay pointed to the right and Logan called. "Follow me! We're going to try to flank them!"

His brothers nodded consent. Logan veered to the right, riding parallel to the battle for a minute before swinging back west. He led them behind a small rise that would shield them from stray fire and hopefully allow them to get the drop on the rustlers.

When they reached the rise, Logan pulled to a stop. He dismounted and ran to the edge of the rise, dropping to his elbows just before cresting the top. His brothers dropped down on either side of him, each carrying their own rifles. Logan surveyed the battle ahead.

It wasn't going well. From their vantage point atop the rise, Logan couldn't see his own hands, but the rustlers were grinning triumphantly, and the herd was slowly but surely moving toward the edge of the ranch.

Logan brought his rifle to bear, aiming at the nearest outlaw, perhaps fifty yards. His brothers aimed their own rifles, sighting carefully at the rustlers. Logan waited until the outlaw slowed his horse, then fired. The man dropped and lay unmoving. An instant later, his brothers fired. One more outlaw fell from his horse. The second round felled an outlaw's horse. It fell, taking its rider with it. The rustler screamed in pain as his leg was crushed under the animal. The remaining rustlers looked around wildly, not knowing where the shots came from. One of them dropped, presumably felled by one of Logan's hands, and the others turned back to the battle.

Logan smoothly chambered another round and fired, catching another outlaw. Another fell, then another as his brothers' rounds found their home. The outlaws turned to the rise. One pointed in their direction and shouted before a spray of blood erupted from his chest. He clutched the wound and fell as the other rustlers raised their weapons toward the brothers.

Before they could fire, two of them fell, victims of the ranch hands' shooting. The others turned uncertainly between the two groups, allowing Logan and his brothers time to shoot three more.

Their numbers suddenly decimated, the remaining rustlers drove the herd forward. The spooked animals stampeded. Several of the animals trampled the outlaw stuck under his horse. The man released an earsplitting cry then fell silent.

Logan realized with a sinking feeling that any of his hands unable to avoid the stampeding herd had likely suffered the same gruesome fate.

He and his brothers ran back to their horses. They quickly mounted and galloped toward the fleeing rustlers. As they approached, Logan saw approximately half the herd break off from the others. A moment later, he saw Darrell and several of the hands firing into the fleeing rustlers. He noticed with grim satisfaction that several more of the outlaws fell.

The rest of the herd crashed into the fence that marked the border of the ranch. The stampede tore a long section of fence away and the surviving rustlers drove the herd onward into the wilderness.

They reached the hands a few seconds later. Darrell smiled grimly at Logan. "Much obliged to you, Logan" he said. "They'd have had us dead to rights if you boys hadn't shown up."

"How many did we lose?" Logan asked.

"Gomez and Henry went down at the beginning. Charlie and Parker are gone, so's Curly and Frazier. Luke's still alive but he's in a bad way. He won't make it through the night."

Logan felt as though the wind were knocked out of him. Seven men dead. He knew all of them. They were good men, loyal and capable. Gomez and Henry had worked at the ranch nearly as long as Darrell. Logan's stomach turned as he thought of Gomez's wife and children. They were likely waiting anxiously at home, praying, like Winona, for the safe return of their loved one.

Logan sighed heavily and swore. He took his hat off and threw it to the ground, swearing again. He looked around at the others. Gregory and Jay looked sick. They stared into space, their eyes glazed. Logan didn't blame them. Like him, they'd lost friends tonight.

Darrell lowered his head, his shoulders slumped. The other hands held similar postures. Logan's heart went out to them. They deserved better than this. Almost immediately, anger filled his chest. Those outlaws would pay. They would get what's coming to them.

"Get the rest of the horses into the corrals. We'll have to hold them there overnight. We'll rebuild the fence in the morning."

"What about the bodies?" Darrell asked.

"Take ours back to the ranch and lay them in the courtyard. Send someone to town for the sheriff."

"And the outlaws?"

"Leave them," Logan spat. "We'll burn them later."

"We can't wait," Gregory said.

"What?"

"If we leave them, they'll attract wolves and cougars. We have to burn them tonight. The horses too."

Logan swore. Gregory was right. "All right. Gregory, take five men and begin gathering the outlaws and dead horses for burning. Darrell, take eight more and get those horses into the corral. Jay, you and I and the other hands are going to bring our men back to the ranch and wait for the sheriff."

Everyone separated and got to work. Logan and Jay rode silently back to the ranch with the five remaining hands. Each man led a horse with a body draped over the top. Logan felt his anger rise the closer they got to the ranch.

Winona was waiting outside, pacing the courtyard anxiously. When she saw them, she ran to meet them, throwing her arms around Logan as soon as he dismounted. "Oh, Logan!" she cried. "Oh, I'm so glad you're safe!"

He held her tightly, closing his eyes and savoring her warmth against him. He allowed himself only a moment of comfort before pulling away. Winona looked at the others. Her eyes widened when she saw the bodies. "Oh Logan," she whispered.

Logan nodded. "Seven men dead. I'm going to send for the sheriff. Can you bring some linens out for the bodies?

"Of course," she said, welling with tears. "Oh, Logan."

He nodded, a lump forming in his throat. "It's okay now. The rustlers are gone."

Winona left for the linens. Logan sent Jackson into town for the sheriff and waited for Winona. When she returned, he, Jay, and the other hands gently lowered the bodies of their friends onto the linen sheets.

When they finished, Logan sent the other hands to help Gregory and turned to Jay. He meant to offer some words of encouragement but stopped when he saw his brother's expression. The younger man glared at Logan, his lips twisted in a snarl.

"This is your fault!" he shouted.

"Jay!" Winona cried, shocked.

"What in blazes are you talking about?" Logan asked incredulously. "My fault?"

"If you had listened to me, we would be a cattle ranch right now, not a horse ranch. We wouldn't be a threat to anyone, and no one would try to rustle us!"

"What are you talking about?" Logan repeated. "You think rustlers only rustle horses? We'd be in the same damned position whether we bred horses, cattle or elephants!"

"Logan!" Winona cried, shocked at his vulgarity.

"Yeah? And who's coming after our cattle business?" Jay pressed. "We're the smallest ranch in a sea of horse ranches a hundred miles square and you won't take advantage of the opportunity to be the only cattle ranch."

"Blast it, Jay, people died tonight. Now's not the time to argue about the cattle again."

"That so?" Jay said. "It never is the time, is it? Why would I ever get to have a say in things?"

"Grow up, Jay," Logan spat.

Jay's face flamed. He strode toward Logan, hands balled into fists.

Logan's eyes narrowed. "You raise your hands to me you best be prepared to use them," he warned.

Winona stepped in between them, placing her hands firmly on their chests. "Stop it! Both of you!" she snapped. "You're both acting like children!"

The two brothers stopped moving but continued to stare balefully at each other. Winona looked from one to the other, pleading in her eyes. "Boys, please. We can get through this. The sheriff will organize a posse. I'll talk to my father. He'll help. Rustlers are a threat to him too. We'll find the men who did this to us."

Her voice softened. "We've already come through so much together as a family. We can survive this, too."

"Oh please," Jay interrupted. "Family? We're not a family. My brothers and I aren't even family. You're just property."

Winona recoiled as though slapped. Before he could stop himself, Logan backhanded Jay hard. The younger man fell to the ground. Winona stood in front of Logan and hissed, "Logan, you stop it this instant!"

Jay sat up slowly, chuckling to himself. He smiled at Logan, hate filling his eyes. A trickle of blood ran down his chin. "Logan never told you how he ended up marrying you, did he?"

Winona stepped back, confused. "What ...?"

Logan's eyes widened. He flashed a warning glance at his brother, but Jay only grinned evilly and said, "He didn't tell you how he won you?"

"Won me?" Winona said. "What are you saying, Jay?"

"He won you in a game of jackstraws."

Winona glanced sharply at Logan. "Logan?" she whispered.

"That's right," Jay continued. "He didn't even want to marry you until Gregory and I showed an interest. Then he was all for the game. Just barely beat me, too. Guess he didn't mind the thought of a pretty little wife after all."

"Jay, watch your mouth," Logan said.

He reached for Winona, but she pulled away and walked backwards, shock and horror in her eyes. "Is this true?" she asked.

Logan didn't respond immediately. Finally, he said, "It was Jay's idea."

Winona doubled over, gasping with shock.

"Winona," Logan said. He strode toward her. "Please—"

"Don't you touch me!" she hissed. She spun on her heel and strode swiftly to the house.

Logan watched her leave. Jay laughed into the dirt next to him, but Logan felt no anger, only numbness.

Chapter Twenty-One

Logan paced slowly back and forth, hands on his hips. The horses were grazing contentedly, the events of the previous night forgotten. Logan envied them. It would be a long while before he forgot last night, if he ever did.

Darrell approached and said, "Six hundred ninety-three."

"That's how many they took or how many we have left?"

"That's what we have left."

Gregory counted twenty-four dead horses the night before. That meant the rustlers had escaped with an even seven hundred head.

Logan nodded. "Sheriff doesn't know anything?"

Darrell frowned. "I didn't talk to the sheriff, you did."

"Right," Logan said, rubbing his temples. "Well, he doesn't know anything, I guess."

Darrell looked closely at Logan. "You okay?" he asked.

"I reckon I'm just tired," Logan replied.

Darrell didn't seem convinced, but he didn't press the issue. "Why don't you go get some rest? I can supervise the fence repair and the horses, as you can see, are fine where they are. You need sleep."

Logan couldn't agree more. "All right. Much obliged."

Darrell tipped his hat and left for the fence.

Logan walked home, his shoulders slumped with defeat. Seven hundred head gone. This was going to ruin the ranch.

They were barely staying afloat as it was. The loss of half their herd was something from which they would never recover. They might manage to limp along a few more months, maybe even a year or two but eventually, they would fail.

They couldn't afford to replenish the herd. The best option available was to sell the remaining herd and use the money to support themselves until they could each find work. That wouldn't be a problem for three able-bodied young men used to hard work. It wouldn't be a problem with Winona either. She'd proven more than capable of hard work as well. Still, the ranch would be gone, and his family name would be nothing more than a memory. He would be a failure. Just like his father.

That thought knocked the wind out of him. He sat on the ground, and leaned forward, putting his head between his knees. His breath escaped in a rush, and he inhaled deeply before stilling, staring at the dirt.

An ant wandered slowly around, confused by the sudden shadow. It ventured a few tentative steps in each direction before choosing a course and proceeding confidently forward. Unfortunately, that route led it directly to the seat of Logan's canvas trousers and the creature once more was forced to try to navigate its way out.

He'd tried so hard. He'd worked his heart out to keep the ranch alive; to care for his family. He wanted so much for them to be safe and comfortable. He'd worked so hard, and he'd failed.

He took his hat off and tossed it on the ground in front of him. The warmth of the rising sun soothed his aching muscles slightly and a moment later he stood and continued toward the house.

If only he'd listened to Jay.

That thought hit like another whirlwind, and he stopped dead in his tracks. For the first time, he seriously considered the merits of Jay's interest in cattle and realized his younger brother was right the whole time. Jay was right and Logan was too—what's the word Winona used—*pigheaded* to see it. No, it was worse than that.

He did see it, but his pride wouldn't let him admit it. He wanted to beat Heath Ross at his own game, and he allowed his family's ranch to fail because of it. If he'd listened to Jay in the beginning and sold the horses to buy more cattle, they wouldn't be in this mess right now.

Then a thought hit him. They could still follow Jay's plan! They could sell the horses and buy another seven hundred head of cattle. That would make a thousand head total—more than enough to start—and since cattle were cheaper than horses, they would have money left over to finish repairing the stables and hire more hands to replace the ones that were lost.

They would have to expand to accommodate cattle, since cattle needed more room than horses, but they could pay for that when they began selling. They could still save the ranch.

He would have to tell Jay as soon as he could. Jay might not want to talk to him after Logan hit him the night before, but if Logan told him he was going to follow Jay's plan, that would get him to listen and give Logan a chance to apologize for his behavior. That was the least Jay deserved. From now on, Logan was going to treat his family as partners instead of employees. Heaven knew he needed their help.

There was someone he had to apologize to first, though. Winona was the best thing that had ever happened to Logan, and it was clear to him now more than ever that he didn't deserve her. She'd done more for his family over the past five months than he had over the past five years. She didn't deserve to be treated like an outsider or like property. He doubted she would be any more willing to listen at first than Jay would be, but if he began with a sincere apology, maybe she'd hear him out.

He walked faster toward the house, reaching it a few minutes later. Winona was in the kitchen, drawing in a small notebook she'd ordered from Cordelia a few weeks ago. She looked up when he entered.

"Hello, Winona," Logan said softly.

She looked down at her notebook and continued to draw without answering.

He walked around the table and sat across from her. She continued to ignore him. "Winona, I'm sorry. I'm so sorry for everything. I'm sorry for not trusting you. I'm sorry for breaking your trust. You deserve so much better than me, and I'll never forgive myself for the way I've treated you. I don't expect you to forgive me either, but I'd like to explain myself if you're willing to hear me out."

She smiled slightly but didn't look up. "What explanation could you possibly have?"

"Not a good one."

"I should think not. You won me playing a casino game."

"A what game?"

"Never mind," Winona snapped. "Look, if you have something to say, say it. Then leave me alone."

Logan nodded. The excitement he felt a moment ago had fled, replaced by apprehension. No turning back now, though. He took a deep breath and began.

"I didn't win the game."

Winona looked up from her notebook. "What?"

"The jackstraws game. I didn't win it. I mean, I did, but not fair and square. I cheated."

"You cheated at jackstraws to win my hand in marriage."

"Yes."

"How did you cheat at jackstraws?"

"When I dumped the sticks, I grabbed a few of the yellow sticks without letting my brothers see. As we played, I would add a stick every now and then. Because there are so many yellow sticks, my brothers never noticed I was adding more."

Winona stared at him for a moment. Then she laughed and looked up, shaking her head in disbelief. "Of all the crazy things ..." She looked back at him. "Okay, so what? You cheated at jackstraws to win my hand. Am I supposed to be flattered?"

"No, I'm not saying that."

"And I suppose I should be grateful you only wanted a marriage of convenience and didn't try to coerce me into romance."

"No!" Logan protested. "I'm not saying that, either."

"So, what are you saying?"

Logan hesitated for a moment. He had no idea how to say what he wanted to say. Finally, he just said, "It had to be me."

"What?"

"It had to be me. Marrying you. It had to be me. I couldn't let Gregory or Jay marry you. I just couldn't."

"Why not? At least they wanted to marry me."

"I wanted to marry you!" Logan blurted out.

"Then why didn't you say so?" Winona demanded. Tears welled in her eyes. "I asked to marry you. In front of my father and stepmother, I asked you and you said no. I asked you more than once and you said no. I pleaded with you, and you said no. Now I'm supposed to believe you wanted to all along? If that's the case, then where was your courage, Logan Foley?"

Logan shrugged. "I don't know. I guess it just didn't seem right to take advantage of a vulnerable young woman like that."

"Don't play the gentleman with me, Logan. Don't try to act like you're some chivalrous knight coming to the rescue of the damsel in distress. If you wanted to marry me, you should have said so."

"I should have," Logan agreed. "I should have said so a thousand times. I should have told you every day what an amazing, strong, courageous, beautiful woman you are. I should have told you every day how grateful I am to be by your side. I should have told you every day that you were the best thing to ever happen to me. I'm sorry I didn't. I was wrong."

"Yes," Winona spat. "You were. You were very wrong. You're still wrong. For someone as smart and strong as you seemed to be, Logan, you turned out to be quite the foolish coward."

Her words cut him like a knife. What cut worse was the knowledge he deserved them. "You're right," he said. "I allowed my insecurity and fear to rule me, and I pushed you away. I'm a fool and a coward." He looked up at her. "But I don't want to be anymore."

"Well, good for you," she said, sarcastically. "That's the first step to lasting change."

"Winona, I don't expect your forgiveness and I'm not asking for it. I just want you to know I'm not going to be the same man anymore. You're my partner. You deserve an equal say. So do Gregory and Jay. I've treated all of you like you're my subjects instead of my equals. Especially you and Jay. I should have listened to you guys from the beginning. It's my fault the ranch is suffering.

"I can't do this alone anymore. I can't take everything on all by myself and I can't keep secrets. If I want to earn your trust, I have to be totally honest with you." He paused. What he had to say next would be very hard. "I have to tell you something else."

"Oh boy," Winona said with mock excitement. "Another story."

"Part of the reason I wanted to marry you was to get back at your father."

Winona's face was unreadable. "What?" she breathed.

Logan nodded. "I hated your father. I hated him so much, Winona. I despised him for what he did to my Pa. I despised him and … I guess I despised my Pa a little bit, too. Your father ruined him, and Pa just rolled over and took it. He never tried to get what was due him or stop Heath from running roughshod all over their deal. He just rolled over, belly-up and let Heath destroy him. I don't think I've ever forgiven Pa for that. I thought if I could just get caught up with the ranch, I could eventually outgrow the Ross ranch with superior breeding. I wanted so much to succeed where

Pa had failed. I wanted to prove the Foleys were the better ranchers. Marrying you didn't exactly prove anything, but knowing that Heath Ross would have to see his daughter on my arm in public and one day acknowledge grandchildren that looked like me was thrilling to me."

"Grandchildren," Winona whispered, her face still blank.

"I wanted to hurt him. Not just him, but the entire town. I wanted people to see the son of the man they'd scandalized leading the daughter of the man they worshipped. I wanted them to know I had won."

Logan took Winona's hands in his. They remained limp in his grasp as she continued to stare ahead with that blank look. "Winona, I was wrong. I was so wrong. I should never have treated you like a prize or a token of some imagined victory. I should have married you.

The right way. Not a marriage of revenge or convenience, but of love. I should have courted you and cared for you and included you and supported you like a proper husband. I didn't do that, and I will always regret my behavior.

"Like I told you, I don't expect or deserve your forgiveness. What I did deserves no forgiveness. I only ask that you give me a chance to start over. Let me prove for the rest of my life that I can be the man you deserve and the man you need. I know I have a long way to go, but it's a journey I'm willing to take."

He stopped then and waited for Winona to respond. She stared silently at him, her face still expressionless. She didn't speak for several minutes. Logan's anxiety grew as he waited but he forced himself to remain still and silent.

Finally, Winona said, "Logan, I can't make sense of this. It's just so strange. I feel so ... out of sorts. I thought when I decided to stay here, I knew what I was doing. I thought I was so mature and grown-up; so ready to have my own life and make my own decisions, and now ... Logan, it doesn't make any sense! You wanted to marry me, but you refused to.

Then your brothers wanted to marry me, and you cheated to win my hand. You say you tried to tell me you love me while doing everything you can to avoid saying you love me. You tell me you want to spend the rest of your life with me, but you've insisted on a marriage of convenience. I thought when we kissed ... I don't know what I thought. It just doesn't make any sense."

She fell silent a moment. Logan stared ahead, avoiding her eyes. Her words cut deeply, especially the ones about telling her he loved her while doing everything he could not to say it. Why couldn't he just tell her he loved her?

Her face hardened. "You tried to use me to get revenge on my father. Logan, I ... I need to think." She pulled her hands away from his. He left his hands in front of him, staring stupidly, the lingering presence of her touching a weight on his palms and his heart.

Winona stood slowly. "I think you and I should take some time apart. We live with each other and neither of us can afford a room at the boarding house, so we should just avoid each other as much as possible for a while. I care about you, Logan but I don't know if you really care about me the way you say you do. I need to think. So do you."

She turned and left without another word. Logan sat where she left for a long while, his brain numbed once more. He sat until the sun peaked and continued to sit until it began to dip toward the horizon. Then he slowly, mechanically stood and walked to his room. That night, for the first time since his parents died, he cried himself to sleep.

Chapter Twenty-Two

The sun shone over Winona with a perfect amount of warmth that drove the chill of the morning from her bones without stifling her. The trees that lined the road on either side of the wagon displayed rich hues of red, gold and orange as they prepared to shed their leaves to conserve energy through the long, hard winter.

Winter was approaching quickly but today it didn't feel that way. Quails and groundhogs flitted around, foraging for seeds and grasses and—in the quails' case—insects to fill their bellies and their pantries during the months-long freeze. Winona heard songbirds calling to each other as they foraged the canopy. They sounded happy and free and alive.

Winona remembered how excited she would be as a child when the leaves began to change and the animals would grow bolder in their foraging, desperate to collect enough food for winter. She would ask her mother the names of the quails and groundhogs she saw, and her mother would give them names and tell stories about their lives in the wilderness while Winona listened with rapt attention.

Winona had loved rides with her parents. Her father would smile and laugh, and her mother would hold and kiss her tenderly. That was the last time she could remember feeling like a family. After her mother died, her father lost his smile and the animals no longer had names.

When her stepmother arrived, her father came alive again but not for Winona. She became the burden Audrey and Heath had to carry. At the same time, they drowned her in rules and expectations until the happy, imaginative girl Winona had been no longer existed.

She wanted so desperately to leave that house and find a family again—a family of her own that would establish itself on love and trust rather than status. She thought she'd found it with the Foleys. She'd been so excited to marry Logan! Now, she wasn't sure. They could hardly be said to have acted like a family the entire five months and more she'd been there, what with the constant fighting and the distrust that existed between all four of them. Now they were even further apart from each other.

After the horses were rustled and Jay revealed that Winona's marriage to Logan was the result of a parlor game, she was devastated but clung to the slight hope that it was all a mistake—that somehow Jay was wrong, and Logan really did feel something for her. Then Logan admitted to the game and the sliver of hope she held so tightly vanished.

She needed to clear her head, so early the next morning, she washed and drove into town. The cool morning air invigorated her, and the warming sun soothed her but neither helped her come to a satisfying answer in her head.

She reached the butcher shop just as Mr. Holt opened the door for business. He smiled broadly when he saw her. "Morning, Winona! It's so good to see you."

She returned a smile she didn't feel and said, "Good morning, Mr. Holt. How are you today?"

"Well, I'm fine, as fine china!" he replied in an animated voice. Winona wondered briefly if his cheerfulness was genuine or manufactured for her benefit as hers was for his. He walked behind the counter and tied on his apron. "Now what can I do for you today, Miss Winona?"

Winona purchased two dozen sausage links, twenty pounds of salt pork and four thick steaks. Mr. Holt packaged her order and threw in a rack of pork ribs. When the wagon was loaded, he beamed at Winona. "No charge today, Winona." His face became instantly somber. "I heard about what happened. You tell your husband I'm right sorry. Tell him a lot of people in this town are pulling for you and your family. If you folks ever need anything, don't hesitate to ask. I'm happy to help."

Winona wasn't sure how to respond, so she only said, "Thank you," and left. As she drove to the mercantile, she reflected on Mr. Holt's words. *A lot of people in this town are pulling for you and your family.* She realized suddenly that most of her time to this point had been spent in the company of high society.

Sure, she would take her walks through the poor quarters of town, and she would occasionally chat with the shopkeepers but most of her socializing had been with the wealthy elite, all of whom held the Foleys in disdain. The revelation that the other social classes didn't see it that way should have been gratifying.

It should have been, but she couldn't stop thinking about Logan's deception. To think her marriage was based on a silly game!

She'd understood when Logan offered only a marriage of convenience, free of romance. She couldn't deny even then that she was disappointed, but she understood. She was a stranger, and she was asking a lot of Logan, more than she had any right to. She could live without romance, at least long enough to allow it to grow naturally.

She'd admired Logan for his generosity in accepting her proposal. She wasn't under any illusion that he loved her, but she thought it noble that he had the decency to save her from scandal, and more importantly, a lifetime of misery with Jude. Learning yesterday that his acceptance was the result of a game rather than a genuine desire for her hand had crushed her.

What if Gregory or Jay had won? What if Logan's elaborate plan to cheat had failed and Winona were forced to marry one of his brothers? She shivered at the thought. Gregory was a good friend, at least until Winona learned of his culpability in the jackstraws game of the century, but Winona wasn't in love with him. Jay had a good heart, but he had a lot of growing up to do before he was ready to be anyone's husband, and in any case, she wasn't in love with him either.

She was in love with Logan.

A single tear coursed down her cheek at the thought, and she dabbed at it with her handkerchief. She was in love with him, and she could no longer pretend otherwise. Everything about him was a contradiction. He was so unlike any other man she'd ever met—strong, courageous and so tender and caring underneath that gruff exterior.

He was a rough-mannered, surly rancher but also a tender, caring companion. He could be petulant as a child one instant then stoic and resolute the next. He was the most frustrating person she'd ever known.

And she was in love with him. She was in love with him and, foolish girl that she was, she'd dared to hope he might eventually feel the same.

As usual, her hopes were disappointed. After everything, Winona finally knew she was nothing more than a pawn in Logan's personal vendetta against her father. So much for finding a handsome prince who would sweep her off her feet.

She reached the mercantile and quickly dabbed at her face with the handkerchief to remove any sign of tears. She took a deep breath and flashed a brilliant smile before dismounting and walking inside.

Mrs. Haversham looked up from her sewing machine. Her face lit up when she saw Winona. She stood and rushed over.

"Good morning, Mrs. Haversham," Winona said. "I was wondering—"

Mrs. Haversham threw her arms around Winona, stunning her and nearly knocking her off balance. The elderly woman fussed and cooed over her. "Oh, you poor dear. I heard about what happened with the horses. I'm so sorry."

"That—that's all right," Winona said, awkwardly returning her embrace.

Mrs. Haversham pulled away after a moment, holding Winona at arm's length. "Lucky you have a big, strong husband to protect you."

"Oh, yes," Winona replied. "Lucky."

Mrs. Haversham beamed and released Winona's arm. "Now then. What can I help you with?"

Winona purchased several yards of canvas fabric for new trousers and shirts, as well as several yards of cotton and linen for new dresses and nightclothes. She purchased a sewing kit as well. Starting tomorrow, she would mend their clothes and sew new outfits for each of the boys.

She left with a smile and a promise to return on Sunday for some of Mrs. Haversham's strawberry preserves. Her next stop was the general store. She wasn't particularly looking forward to seeing Cordelia. Of all the shopkeepers, Cordelia knew her best and would likely see through the façade of cheerfulness she carried. She didn't have a choice, though. They needed supplies, and whatever her future looked like at the ranch, she was there now.

She didn't mind living on the ranch. Even now, with her family fractured as it was, she didn't mind living there. She just couldn't get past how she ended up there. Aside from the stupid game where Logan "won" her hand in marriage, she had his motivations to consider. Using her as some sort of weapon against her father like that was simply unforgivable.

She sympathized more than anyone with Logan's humiliation at Heath's betrayal of her father, but to treat her like some sort of prize that he could shove in Heath's face was insulting and more hurtful even than the manner in which he won her hand.

What hurt the most was that prior to last night, she'd thought Logan at least respected her, even if he didn't really love her. She was so proud of the wife she'd been to him! Despite growing up in the lap of luxury and despite having no experience at all with chores or cooking, she'd cleaned and repaired the entire house almost by herself.

She'd assisted with the herd during the most recent storm. She'd begun tilling the vegetable garden again by herself, and she'd become at least a decent cook. Maybe she wouldn't win any prizes at the county fair, but she thought she'd done a decent job feeding the brothers. Certainly no one complained after the fiasco with Jay during the first dinner she cooked.

She laughed bitterly. Those boys seemed determined to sully every good thing she did. It's like they were afraid of happiness!

Her smile faded as she considered that all her hard work to this point had likely gone unnoticed. Logan hadn't seen her as a strong, capable, independent woman, whatever he had said during his ridiculous excuse for an apology. She wanted him to trust her so badly; to see her as a worthy companion and not just something fancy to wear on his arm. It seemed she was once again doomed to suffer disappointment.

She walked into the general store and smiled brightly at Cordelia. "Good morning, Cordelia!" she said with enthusiasm. "What a lovely day we're having!"

Cordelia returned the smile, but her eyes narrowed when she saw Winona's face and Winona knew she saw right through her mask of cheerful exterior. She didn't pry, however, but only said, "A lovely day indeed, Winona. It's so good to see you, as always. I'm so glad to hear you and your family are safe."

"Yes," Winona agreed. "We're very grateful." She produced her grocery list and handed it to Cordelia, hoping to finish her business quickly and avoid Cordelia's shrewd gaze. Cordelia took the list, smiling wryly but once again refused to pry and set about filling the order. Winona put on a show of perusing the shelves while Cordelia worked. She felt guilty for shunning the older woman, but she really didn't feel up to explaining herself to anyone at the moment.

After a few minutes, Cordelia finished preparing the order. "All right, Winona. We're all set."

"Thank you, Cordelia," Winona said, relieved. "How much do I owe you?"

Cordelia's smile widened. "A few minutes of your time is all I ask."

"Oh," Winona said. "Um ... I'm really in a hurry today, Cordelia but perhaps next time ..."

"It will only take a moment," Cordelia interrupted.

Her tone was gentle but left no room for refusal. Winona sighed and smiled. "Of course, Cordelia. I always have time for you."

"Wonderful," Cordelia beamed. "Winona, I can see you're in pain." She lifted her hand before Winona could protest. "I know you don't want to talk about it, and I won't press you. I'll only say this: one of the most beautiful and terrible things about being young is that the present moment is often the only moment you can see. It's beautiful because you get to experience each moment as richly as though it were an entire lifetime. It's terrible because when those experiences are sad or frightening, it's difficult to see a way out.

"Now, one of the beautiful and terrible things about being older is you begin to realize that each moment is only a moment. Life is not a moment, not even a series of moments. Life is a rich, full experience that is composed of moments but evolves to become something greater than those moments. Do you understand what I mean?"

"I think so," Winona said.

"Good. Now that's terrible in a sense because those moments no longer carry the same individual power they once did, so they no longer mean as much by themselves. In another sense, it's the most beautiful thing that will ever happen because when you experience a moment of suffering, you have the wisdom to recognize that it's only a moment that won't last forever.

Those moments aren't your life, only the soil from which your life grows, and the difficult moments are just as important to leading a full life as the easy ones."

She smiled at Winona and handed her the basket. "Now, I won't trouble you further. Just think about what I said and if it's of any help then I'm grateful to have shared this moment with you."

For the first time that day, Winona's smile was genuine when she said, "Thank you, Cordelia." She left the store, reflecting on what Cordelia said. She supposed it was true that this moment would pass, and she would not forever feel this pain. Still, since these moments were the soil from which her life would grow, could it possibly be the life she wanted?

She loved Logan dearly but no matter how she tried, she couldn't escape her nagging fear that she'd once more chosen to marry the wrong man.

Chapter Twenty-Three

Winona's last stop before home was an appointment with a merchant to arrange the sale of feed to the Foley Ranch on credit. She tried not to think about the implications of purchasing an entire winter's stores on credit. The horses needed feed to survive and with cold weather approaching any day now, that was a more pressing problem than finances.

She felt them before she saw them. The hairs on the back of her neck prickled and her heart began to beat faster in her chest. She lifted her hands to spur the horses faster but before she could snap the reins, a shadow fell over her face. Someone pulled a bag over her head, and she was pulled roughly from the wagon.

She drew in breath to scream, but a powerful hand closed over her mouth, silencing her. She kicked and struggled but a second pair of hands gripped her waist and lifted her off the ground. She was carried swiftly away but with her vision obscured; she didn't know where they were taking her. She beat at her attackers but if they felt her blows, they didn't react as they spirited her away.

A few seconds later, they threw her roughly into a wagon. She leapt up and tugged at the bag over her head, but a third pair of hands grabbed her from behind, pressing a cloth over her mouth. The cloth was scented with a cloyingly sweet perfume that nearly made her gag.

Her eyelids became heavy, and she felt her strength waning. She tried to struggle but her arms hung limply at her sides. The world spun around her. Then she fell into a deep, dreamless sleep.

***

The bag was lifted suddenly over her head. A brilliant white light blinded her, and a rush of fresh air invaded her nostrils. She gasped and opened her eyes, crying out when the searing force of the light assaulted her unprotected vision.

"Take your time," a voice said. "There's no need to hurry. You're safe here."

The voice promised safety but hearing it made Winona feel anything but safe. It was a rich, deep baritone that was at once gentle and resonant. It spoke in flawless English but with a slight German accent. Her heart pounded in her chest and a cold sweat broke out on her forehead.

Her vision slowly sharpened until she could clearly see Sterling Koch. He leaned against a rich, immaculately polished mahogany desk, dressed impeccably as always in a silk, Italian-made suit.

She glanced around her. She was in an office or a study of some sort. In addition to the desk and the chair behind it, there were four other chairs, all richly upholstered and all made of the same dark mahogany. A wine cabinet, also of mahogany, dominated half of the wall to Winona's right. To her left an occasional table as large as her dining table occupied the opposite wall.

Jude Koch stood in front of that table, staring at Winona with a look Winona imagined might be at home on the face of a cougar stalking a mule deer. Winona's skin crawled under his gaze but at the moment, her fear was reserved for Jude's father.

The older man stood with the air of medieval royalty, a noble observing a commoner. His expression wasn't arrogant, or hostile, or evil. It was merely a quiet self-assuredness, an intrinsic understanding that he was the superior and Winona the inferior.

He smiled pleasantly at Winona, and she shivered. "So, the prodigal daughter has returned. I missed you, *engelein.*"

The pet name sent a wave of nausea through Winona. She nearly retched but caught herself just in time. She avoided Sterling's eyes, trembling. She knew Jude was crazy and now she knew where he got it. Sterling may have greater self-control, but a man who would kidnap a woman from a public street in broad daylight was crazy to the bone.

She looked up at that calm, superior face and realized that wasn't the case at all. Sterling Koch wasn't crazy, and he didn't believe he was better than others. He knew it. He knew it as surely as Winona knew the sun would rise in the morning. He had the air of a man accustomed all his life to the abject, instant obedience of everyone around him. He kidnapped Winona because he could. It was that simple.

She shivered again.

"I do apologize for resorting to such base methods to talk to you, but I must confess, you and your husband have shown a great deal more resolve than I anticipated."

"Don't call him that!" Jude shouted.

Sterling lifted his hand and Jude quieted. "Temporary husband," he amended. He flashed his charming grin once more and continued. "You should know I initially intended a more civilized discussion with you and Mr. Foley, but after Mr. Foley's unfortunate assault on my son, I felt it was prudent to take more direct measures."

Winona's eyes widened in understanding. "You hired those rustlers," she whispered.

Sterling nodded. "I didn't intend for anyone to die. I am sorry for that. I did intend to force your hand. I thought if faced with a life of common servitude, as you most surely are if you remain with Mr. Foley, you would do the wise thing and reconsider my son's proposal. I'm sorry to see that isn't the case."

"Why?" Winona whispered. "Why me? Why my family?"

"Isn't it obvious?" Sterling gestured toward Jude. "Love."

Jude grinned at her, and she felt another wave of nausea pass through her.

"I must confess," Sterling continued. "It surprised me to learn of my son's attraction to you. You are an uncommonly beautiful woman, Winona, but there are many beautiful women in the world and Westridge is an unremarkable town filled with unremarkable people like your stepmother, who thinks a pearl necklace indicates wealth and a reserved pew at the church indicates power. I couldn't for the life of me understand why Jude would wish to settle with anyone in such a dreary place, even one so lovely as yourself.

"But then I considered the benefits of settling in such a boring locale. You see, a boring town like Westridge is very much like a blank sheet of paper. Jude tells me you draw."

Jude licked his lips lasciviously and a now-familiar bout of nausea coursed through Winona.

"If I settled in an exceptional city—New York, London, Paris—I should be but one of a great many exceptional people in that city. If, however, I settled in an unexceptional town like Westridge—" he smiled again—"I should be a prince. A beacon of light in a drab world."

Winona laughed in spite of her fear. "You small, small man. All your wealth and you can't find a better use for it then bullying a little frontier town. If you were to go to an exceptional city, you wouldn't be one of a great many exceptional people. You'd be a speck of dust. The exceptional city would hardly notice you were there and when you were trampled underfoot, it would hardly notice your passing."

Sterling smiled affably at her outburst. "Now, now, *engelein*. That's no way to speak to your father-in-law."

"I will never marry Jude!" Winona shouted.

"Yes, you will," Sterling insisted. His tone was one a patient teacher might use when addressing a willful child. "You will, and you will give me many grandsons to carry on my and my son's name."

"I'll die before I marry him!" Winona insisted.

Jude suddenly strode toward her. She shrank back but her bonds prevented her from moving and in a few seconds, Jude's hand was on her shoulder. He gazed intensely at her, his steel-blue eyes boring into her. "I love you, Winona Ross. I always have. From the moment I saw you, I loved you."

"I'm married to Logan Foley, Jude," Winona said. Her voice trembled but her gaze remained steady as she said, "That's final. I will never marry you."

Jude smiled and Winona was once more reminded of a cougar ready to pounce. "I know you loved me too, Winona. We were engaged to be married before ... before you made the rash decision to marry that rancher."

"I never loved you, Jude," Winona said quietly. "I liked you a little, I thought. Mostly I just wanted to escape my stepmother. I never loved you. Once I saw you beat that elderly man, I didn't even like you. You're a monster, and I would never do the world the disservice of bearing children for you."

Jude swallowed, his eyes blazing. He laughed nervously, "You're so passionate, Winona. I love that about you." He reached up to stroke her cheek and she pulled away, disgusted.

Jude's expression darkened. He lifted his hand high, and Winona steeled herself for the blow.

"Stop!" Sterling called. Jude froze, glaring at Winona.

"Save the discipline for after the wedding," Sterling instructed. "We can't have your bride come to her wedding day covered in bruises. Don't worry," he added, seeing Jude's face. "She'll learn her place soon enough."

"My place is by my husband's side," Winona said. "My husband will come for me. My family will come for me. You won't get away with this. When people hear you kidnapped and threatened me, they'll run you out of town."

"I admit, taking you the way we did does incur risk, but I learned early on that if one wishes to succeed, one must occasionally take calculated risks. I do anticipate that Mr. Foley will come looking for you but never fear," he flashed his charming smile again, "I've taken measures to protect myself and my son in the event of his interference."

"If you murder Logan, then Westridge will see you are brought to justice!"

Sterling approached slowly until he stood in front of her. He looked down and Winona shrank under the weight of his gaze. "You'd be surprised what people will accept when they see what happens to those who stand in my way."

"I don't care what you do to me," Winona said, "I will never marry Jude."

"Yes, you will," Sterling repeated.

"Pa has a friend," Jude said. "A circuit judge. He's on his way to town as we speak. He's going to annul your marriage to Logan so we can be together."

"I'll never sign an annulment."

"You will," Sterling repeated. "You will have no choice. Your marriage will be declared illegal by the state. You will agree to the annulment, or you will be charged with prostitution and imprisoned."

Winona stared in shock at the two of them.

Jude smiled and continued. "Once your fake marriage is done away with, you and I will be married in the church. Like a proper couple."

"Reverend Patrick will never agree to this!"

"He already has," Jude continued. "He never approved of your marriage to Logan. Surely you know that."

Winona didn't respond. Now that Jude mentioned it, she did recall the reverend was reluctant to marry her to Logan. Still, he couldn't force her to marry Jude!

You'd be surprised what people will accept when they see what happens to those who stand in my way.

"Once we're married, Westridge will be our town!" Jude declared. His eyes blazed madly. "People will have to do what we say. We'll rule them like kings and queens, Winona!"

"You're insane," she whispered.

"Am I?" Jude asked, grinning. "It doesn't matter. I win, Winona. I always win. If I say I'm not crazy, I'm not crazy. If I say you and I will be married, we'll be married. There's not a single thing anyone in this town or anywhere else can do to stop me."

"My father will stop you," Winona said. "He has money and influence too. He'll see to it this marriage never happens."

Sterling grinned, and in that moment the façade broke, and Winona could see the madness the father shared with the son. "You should know something, Winona. The annulment was not my idea."

Winona looked at Jude. He wore a grin that matched his father's and shook his head. Winona turned back to Sterling.

"Your stepmother," Sterling said.

Winona's heart dropped. Audrey had planned this?

"She approached me after the meal you shared with her some months ago. She mentioned the only witnesses to your marriage with Mr. Foley were Mr. Foley's brothers. It turns out that family members can be easily discredited as witnesses. Once you sign a statement revealing that you were coerced into the union, it will be quite simple to annul the marriage and allow you and Jude to wed."

Winona felt as though the wind were knocked out of her. She knew her stepmother was selfish, but she never expected her to go this far. How could she? Why? Why was it so important to her that Winona do what she say? She thought Audrey would be happy to be rid of her. There was nothing to pull Heath's attention away from her now and if people spoke ill of Winona, she could always remind them Winona was only her stepdaughter. Why would she go so far out of her way to ruin Winona's life? How could she be so cruel?

Tears welled in Winona's eyes. "There are others who will help us. Westridge isn't under your thumb, Sterling, and it isn't under Audrey's thumb either."

Sterling shook his head sadly. "Winona, *engelein,* how many times must I tell you? This is inevitable. You will marry Jude."

"I won't!" Winona shouted.

"You will," Sterling said. "Those rustlers were not the only associates I've hired. I've spent the past several weeks hiring gunfighters to protect my interests."

Winona's blood froze. "You can't do that," she whispered.

"I have," Sterling said.

"What will happen when word gets around you've built your own private army? Your judge friend won't be able to save you if the governor learns you're running Westridge like your own little kingdom."

"Actually, I'm quite close with the governor as well," Sterling said. "I brought that exact concern to him, and he assured me no one would fault me for taking steps to protect my perfectly legal business investments with force if absolutely necessary." His smile faded. "Will it be necessary, Winona?"

Winona didn't answer. She'd never felt so helpless. She wanted to refuse, to deny Sterling the satisfaction of her acquiescence, but if she did, what would happen to Logan?

She hung her head, defeated.

"Will it be necessary to use force, Winona?" Sterling repeated.

"No," she whispered.

"Good," Sterling said. "I'm pleased to hear you see things my way."

Winona stared at the floor, tears streaming down her cheeks. *Oh Logan, I'm so sorry.*

Chapter Twenty-Four

Logan scanned the street, searching for Winona. His heart beat rapidly in his chest and a cold sweat trickled down the back of his neck. On either side of him rode his brothers, both wearing the same anxious look. Gregory glanced toward the west, where the sun had already begun to sink below the horizon. He looked at Logan worriedly.

When Winona left early that morning to town, Logan didn't ask where she was going or why. He felt it was better to leave her alone as she'd asked, though it killed him to be so close to her but so far away. He expected she would arrive by dinner, early afternoon at the latest, but when the sun was halfway toward its rest and still no sign of Winona, he began to grow worried.

He hadn't yet told Jay of his intent to follow Jay's plan and his brother didn't want to talk to him at first. When he mentioned Winona hadn't returned from town yet, Jay's attitude changed, and he immediately offered to help look for her. Gregory was more easily convinced and within five minutes of alerting his brothers, the three of them were on their way to town.

They spoke with Mr. Holt at the butcher, who told them Winona was there at opening and left for the mercantile shortly after. They went to the mercantile, where Mrs. Haversham informed them that Winona left for the general store not twenty minutes after arriving at the mercantile.

They reached the general store just as Cordelia was boarding the door. "Well, good evening, Logan!" she cried when she saw them. "It's so nice to see you. It's been far too long. Is Winona with you?" The brothers' faces fell when she asked for Winona and she glanced between them, her smile fading. "Is something wrong?"

"Winona hasn't returned to the ranch," Logan said. "We're trying to retrace her steps and figure out where she's gone."

Cordelia's face widened with alarm. "Oh goodness! Oh, poor dear! Oh, I hope she's okay."

"Do you have any idea where she might have gone?" Logan asked.

"She mentioned she needed to meet with a grain farmer about purchasing feed for winter. Oh!" Her hand flew to her face. "You don't think he did something to her, do you?"

That was precisely the thought that worried Logan but there was no point in worrying Cordelia about it. "I'm sure it's nothing," he said. "She probably took a walk and lost track of time. You wouldn't happen to know where she was meeting this farmer, do you?"

Cordelia shook her head. "I assumed he was staying at the boarding house, and she was meeting him there. I didn't ask, though. Oh, I'm so sorry."

"That's okay, Miss Cordelia," Logan said. "I'm much obliged." He led his brothers away from the store and in the direction of the boarding house.

They reached the boarding house just as the sun finally dipped below the horizon. In the waning hours of twilight, they asked Mr. O'Leary, the proprietor, if there were any grain farmers staying at the hotel. O'Leary balked at first but when he learned Winona could be in danger, he quickly agreed to help.

A moment later, the brothers stood in front of a room while Logan knocked on the door. A tired-looking middle-aged man in a nightgown answered a moment later. "Yes," he asked irritably. He glanced between the brothers. "What is this?"

"You were supposed to meet a woman this afternoon," Logan said. "Winona Foley?"

"Yes," the farmer said. "I remember."

"Did you meet with her?" Logan asked. "When did she leave? Did she say where she was going?"

"As a matter of fact, I didn't see Mrs. Foley," the farmer replied. "I waited for over an hour, but she never arrived. I assume you are her husband?"

Logan nodded. "So, you have no idea where she is?"

"I'm afraid not," the farmer answered. "You can search my room if it'll make you feel more comfortable but I'm afraid I haven't seen hide nor hair of her."

Logan sighed and ran his hands through his hair. "That won't be necessary sir. Thank you for your time." He turned and left for the exit, Gregory and Jay close behind.

"Good luck!" the farmer called after them.

Outside, the brothers stopped and discussed what to do next.

"I say we call the sheriff," Jay said. "He'll round up a posse and we'll find her in no time."

Logan shook his head. "They won't round up a posse this time of night. Not to look for a woman who's only been missing half a day."

"What about the church? After you guys ... after yesterday, maybe she went there to pray or ..." His voice trailed off as he realized how ridiculous that thought was.

Logan sighed. "I hate to say it, but we have to go to her parents. I wouldn't think Winona would ever go to them for help but maybe you're right, Gregory. Maybe after yesterday, she thought she had nowhere else to turn."

That thought sent a wave of guilt coursing through Logan. He vowed silently that he would never allow Winona to feel so alone again. He would be the husband she deserved from here on out.

If he could find her.

He spurred his horse in the direction of the Ross ranch, his brothers close behind. They reached the ranch just as the first stars of night began to shine.

The gate was closed, so Logan shouted for Heath to let them in. When no one responded after several calls, he drew his pistol and fired into the air. A moment later, the door opened, and Heath strode outside, carrying a shotgun.

"What is the meaning of this?" he demanded. "Why are you here?"

"I'm looking for Winona," Logan said. "Is she here?"

"No," Heath said, "She's—you don't know where she is?"

"No," Logan said, his blood turning to ice. "I was hoping you did."

Heath lowered the shotgun and stared at Logan. "I haven't seen her since the dance last month."

Logan told Heath how they'd searched all evening and been unable to find her. Heath listened, worry growing in his countenance. When Logan finished, he said, "You'd better come inside. We need to make a plan." He pulled a key from the pocket of his nightshirt and opened the gate. The brothers dismounted and followed him inside.

Audrey met them in the parlor. "What is the meaning of this?" she demanded.

"Winona's missing," Heath said.

Audrey's face went white as a sheet. "Missing?"

"Since this morning," Logan confirmed. "We've asked all around town and no one's seen her."

Audrey slowly sat on the upholstered sofa in the center of the parlor. "Sterling has her," she whispered,

"What?" Logan said. "Sterling Koch? How do you know that?"

"I planned it," she whispered.

Logan was stunned. "You ... you *planned* to have Sterling Koch kidnap her?"

"Audrey what are you saying?" Heath said, eyes wide with shock.

"I planned to end Winona's marriage to Logan. I told Jude if he could get his father's judge friend to agree, we could claim that she was coerced into marriage by the brothers and the union wasn't valid. The plan was to convince Winona to annul the marriage and marry Jude."

"Convince?" Logan spat. "You mean coerce. Like how you were going to say we coerced her." Anger filled him and he raised his voice until he was nearly shouting. "You told everyone who would listen that I was going to be Winona's ruin but in the end, you were the one who ruined her, weren't you? Jude Koch is a madman, Audrey, and you delivered your stepdaughter right into his hands. Was it worth it? Are you proud?"

Audrey shook her head. "I wasn't going to go through with it. I thought I was doing what was best for Winona but after seeing you two at the dance, I couldn't do it. She was so happy! I'd never seen her so happy. More than that, she was confident, assertive, fulfilled. She was everything I'd ever hoped she would be, and I couldn't go through with it anymore. I told Sterling the deal was off."

Audrey maintained her poise and her voice remained even, but tears welled at the corners of her eyes. The tears convinced Logan of her sincerity but the anger still raged. Now, though, it was directed not toward her but to others. "There's no question in my mind. Jude is behind this. Agreed?"

Audrey nodded solemnly. Logan looked at the others. They nodded as well but there was no sadness nor regret. On the contrary, their faces showed the same anger that burned within Logan, and from their expressions, Logan could tell it was just as powerful as his own. Heath was angry as well, although Logan couldn't determine how much of that anger was reserved for the situation and how much was directed toward Audrey for her duplicity. His face also showed the same worry that filled Audrey's.

Logan couldn't bring himself to be angry with her. She'd behaved foolishly, thinking she acted in her daughter's best interests. Upon discovering Winona's best interests were served by her relationship with him, she'd changed her mind. If nothing else, it showed she acted with pure intent, though she'd done so in a reckless way. She avoided his gaze but finally turned her head and made eye contact.

Logan could see how difficult it was for her to accomplish that, and he almost felt sorry for her. "What ... what are we going to do?" she asked. He noted despair in her voice but also hope. There was something affirming about that hope being directed toward a decision Logan might make.

"We're going to get on our horses, go to Koch's ranch, and get my wife," Logan said.

"You got that right," Jay said.

"The Koch's are going to learn they don't run this town the way they think they do," Gregory said.

Logan nodded and said, "You don't worry. Your daughter will be safe." It felt strange to be sympathetic to them, but it somehow felt good as well. To Jay and Gregory, he said, "Mount up."

They turned but didn't make it three steps before Heath said, "Boys, wait."

Logan stopped and took a deep breath. He thought Heath was on their side. He turned around slowly, unhappy about a confrontation here delaying their trip. "What?" he asked, angrily.

"You probably haven't noticed it, but men have been arriving in town. Hard men, men with guns. The type of men who walk down the street and people step aside. I've seen them with Sterling and with Jude. One or two, and a man thinks it's normal. When you're a rancher, you hire a few men like that sometimes. Maybe there's a rustler threat. Maybe you want them on the roundup or when you deliver to market."

"But there's more than a few?" Logan asked?

Heath nodded. "Enough I've been uneasy about it over the last few weeks. I didn't know why Sterling would need that many but now ..." His eyes flashed and Logan saw the anger now. "If he and Jude were planning to kidnap Winona." He cursed suddenly, his face growing red with anger. Logan watched as he took a deep breath and then let it out slowly. "This needs to end."

"What does?"

"That man, his son, how they treat people. It needs to end, and I need to make up for things."

"What do you mean?" Logan asked.

Heath said, "I mean I need to come clean. I need to tell everyone the truth."

"About what?" Jay asked.

Heath pointed to Logan. "About that young man's father, one of the finest men this town's ever had. It's time I come clean and tell the truth about him, how he always treated me honestly and how ... well, how none of what people believe about him is true."

Logan stared in shock. "You ... you ..."

"Forgiveness," Heath said, "ain't nothing I deserve but I can't pretend anymore like it was okay, like I had to do it. My legacy now is a daughter in the hands of a wicked man. That's no legacy to protect at all. Maybe I can't get forgiveness and maybe I can't get redemption, but I can still make it right. I'm gonna go to the town and this community will know the truth about things, and they'll know the truth about Sterling Koch."

"You think they'll help?" Logan asked.

"I know they will," Heath said. "This community is filled with good people. They take sides with Sterling Koch because they think he's good people. They don't follow him because of his power or because of his name, at least not blindly. They think he's a good man. They won't take his side when they know the truth. Tomorrow, next day at latest, there will be a dozen men ready to go to the ranch to help."

"I don't want to wait," Audrey said. "I'll go there now."

All eyes turned to her. Logan didn't know what to say and the shock made him hesitate. Heath asked, "What do you mean? Why would you go there?"

"Heath Ross," she said firmly, though affectionately, "you aren't the only one of us needs to make things right. I need to make things right to. I'm going to the Kochs to find out what I can. I'm going over there to find out what's happening with my daughter and that's that."

"You can't do that, Audrey," Heath said.

"I agree," Logan said.

"It's too dangerous," Jay added. "I think Mr. Ross is right."

"Well, Mr. Ross can go right ahead with his plan," she replied, "and he should." She looked at her husband and while the adamant determination remained in her expression, Logan saw tenderness in her eyes, "And it's the right thing for him to do. He's wrong. He's not past redemption." She looked at all of them, "But I'm going to the ranch too. It's the best chance we have to get Winona back safe and sound."

Heath looked to Logan like he wanted to protest more but he finally sighed and simply said, "I don't like it."

"I know you don't," Audrey said, "but it's still happening like I say."

Heath nodded unhappily and Logan didn't protest. If her husband couldn't convince her, he certainly wouldn't. In addition, he thought perhaps Audrey was right. Whether or not it put the woman in danger, it might be the best way to get Winona back unharmed, and there was no question at all that both her parents had things to set right.

As did Logan.

Chapter Twenty-Five

Winona kept her eyes on the floor as tears continued to flow down her cheeks. She wanted to hold her head high, to meet Jude's eyes and show he hadn't broken her, but she couldn't bring herself to look at him or his snake of a father.

Oh Logan, I'm so sorry.

It occurred to her she didn't have anything to be sorry for. Not yet at least. She hadn't yet married Jude or signed anything that stated her marriage to Logan was invalid. There was still time.

Time to do what, exactly? Jude and Sterling had an army of gunfighters behind them, not to mention connections with judges and the governor's office. What could she possibly hope to do in the face of that kind of power? Her heart sank as the inevitability of her situation fully impressed itself on her. Sterling was right. She would marry Jude, even though she didn't love him. She would betray Logan, even though she did love him.

The townsfolk would do what Sterling asked of them, even if they didn't like it. All of these things would happen because there were people in this world, like the Kochs and her stepmother, who could impose their will on other people, either through influence or power, and there were people, like herself and the people of Westridge, who couldn't. Try as hard as she might, her life was only her own if others allowed her to have it.

"Don't be so upset, *engelein*," Sterling said. "This is happy news. Soon, you will wed my son and your future will be secure. You will live a life of privilege and comfort, free from poverty and worry. Free, too, from these lingering adolescent fantasies you feel for Mr. Foley. In time, you will see the wisdom of your decision."

Winona's lip curled slightly in contempt. She lifted her eyes and stared at Sterling. Sterling met her gaze with the same infuriatingly affable expression he always wore. To his right, Jude grinned evilly, licking his lips as he leered at her. She ignored him and responded to Sterling.

"My feelings for Logan are not adolescent, Mr. Koch, nor are they fantasy. They are born of a love more real than you, or your son could ever understand. I will marry your son, Mr. Koch, because I love Logan and wish to protect him from you, not because I love Jude. I will never love Jude."

Jude laughed, a sick, cackling sound, and took a step toward Winona. Sterling lifted a hand, but Jude stopped without approaching further. "Oh, Winona, you're so flighty. Of course you love me. You just need time to see that."

She turned her gaze toward Jude, and for a brief moment her fear and even her contempt faded. "You know, I feel sorry for you Jude. You'll never have anything or anyone who truly belongs to you."

Jude laughed again. "This whole town belongs to me, Winona."

"No," Winona replied. "It doesn't. You can terrorize people into doing your bidding. You can threaten, and hurt, and even kill people who refuse to submit to you. You can rule this town, but it will never belong to you, and neither will I. I'll never love you. I'll never give myself to you. You might have my obedience, but you'll never have my heart. People like you will never have real friends or loved ones. At best, you'll have sycophants like my stepmother who pretend to love you because they want your wealth or your influence. You'll never have true friends who will love you and care for you and fight for you for no reason other than that they care for you. You'll never know what it's like to truly belong.

Jude's face darkened and he looked as though he would try once more to hit Winona, but he stopped when the door to the study burst open and Audrey stepped in, closely followed by a flustered-looking butler in a suit nearly as immaculate as Sterling's.

Winona stared in shock at her stepmother. The shock quickly gave way to anger. Had Audrey come to gloat to Winona?

Jude's and Sterling's eyes widened in surprise as the butler apologized profusely. "Beg pardon, sir. I told Mrs. Ross you would attend to her in the parlor at your convenience, but she insisted on being seen right away." He glanced reproachfully at Audrey. "She was quite rude to me, sir."

"Sterling Koch," Audrey said, ignoring the butler. "I demand you release my daughter this instant!"

Release? Was Audrey here to rescue her?

"Audrey," Sterling replied calmly. "What a pleasant surprise. Please, have a seat."

"Release my daughter, Sterling," Audrey insisted.

"My father asked you to sit," Jude chimed in.

Without looking at him, Audrey said, "If you have nothing to add to the conversation, young man, please stay out of it."

Jude's face reddened but Sterling lifted a hand before he could retort. "Audrey, perhaps you and I should talk."

"I didn't come here to talk, Sterling. I came here for my daughter."

Her daughter. She'd called Winona her daughter three times now. Winona couldn't recall the last time Audrey referred to her as her daughter. She looked questioningly at her stepmother. Audrey flashed her a brief encouraging smile, then turned back to Sterling. "Sterling, for heaven's sake, what has gotten into you? Kidnapping Winona and holding her prisoner in your home? Have you gone completely mad?"

"As I recall, Audrey, this was your idea."

"It was my idea to have the marriage to Logan Foley annulled so she could marry Jude. I never agreed to having Winona ripped off the street like a common thief!"

Winona's heart sank. So that was the reason. Audrey wasn't here because she cared about Winona. She was just concerned that the Kochs would ruin her plans by not being careful.

"It was not my intent to proceed so directly," Sterling responded. "I initially desired to have a civil conversation with Mr. Foley but after his assault on Jude at the dance last month, I felt the chance for civility had passed. I cannot brook an assault on my son."

"And I should brook an assault on my daughter?"

There was that word again. How dare she call Winona her daughter? After everything, how could she still claim to be Winona's mother?

"Once more, Audrey, I must remind you this was your idea."

"Once more, Sterling, I must remind you it was my plan to annul the wedding, *not* to kidnap anyone!"

"Quibbling," Sterling said, waving his hand dismissively. "You desired for Winona's marriage to Logan Foley to end and for her marriage to Jude to proceed. I am taking decisive steps to ensure that happens."

"You're not the only one taking decisive steps," Audrey retorted.

Sterling raised an eyebrow.

"Oh yes," Audrey continued. "Logan knows you have his wife, Sterling."

"Don't call her his wife!" Jude shouted.

Audrey ignored him. "He knows you have her and if you think he'll sit idly by and allow you to coerce the woman he loves into a marriage with that—" she glanced disgustedly at Jude "—that animal, then you have another thing coming."

The woman he loves? Winona's heart began to beat faster. She sat straighter in her chair and looked hopefully at her stepmother. Logan loved her? After the revelation she was nothing more than a prize won in a game of jackstraws, she'd decided there was no way Logan saw her as anything more than a prize, or perhaps a weapon to torture her father with. Now her stepmother, of all people, was demanding her release because Logan loved her. She felt the briefest stirring of hope as Sterling and Audrey continued to argue.

"I'm sure Mr. Foley is quite distressed," Sterling said, his voice still maddeningly calm. "But he can hardly be after Winona as he doesn't know where Winona is."

"Yes, he does," Audrey replied. "I told him." She flashed Winona another encouraging smile then turned back to Sterling. "That's right. Logan and his brothers came to my house, and I told them you kidnapped Winona.

"Why?" Sterling asked. His voice remained even but his brow furrowed with concern. Winona's heart leapt. Logan knew where she was! He was coming for her! He did love her! Her excitement at the news temporarily overrode her fear for his safety.

"Why? Because he loves her, you jackass! Because I would rather my daughter belong to a man who will care for her the way she deserves and not an ape who wants her as nothing more than a trophy on his arm!"

Jude flashed Audrey a deadly smile but didn't respond to the insult. "What else does he know?"

"He knows everything, Sterling," Audrey replied, still ignoring Jude. "He knows you rustled his cattle and killed his ranch hands. He knows you've been scheming to end his marriage to Winona and force her to marry Jude."

"Does he know your part in this?" Jude interjected.

"He does. I told him."

"You told him?" Jude asked incredulously.

"I did. I told him I planned to assist you in ending his marriage but after I saw them dancing together I couldn't. Winona's become so strong and confident with Logan that I couldn't bear to separate them anymore." She turned back to Sterling. "I believe I also told both of you the deal was off."

"I apologize, Audrey," Sterling said stiffly, "if I gave you the impression you had a say in the matter. You do not. I appreciated your offer of aid, and had you kept your commitments things could have proceeded in a far more orderly fashion. That being said, this matter is my son's concern and with or without your help, Winona will marry Jude."

"Do you think Logan and his brothers will come alone?" Audrey protested. "They'll come with the entire town at their backs. You'll be putting Winona's life at risk, not to mention your own, by forcing a firefight."

"I assure you, Audrey, appropriate steps will be taken to protect Winona from harm."

"You'll forgive me if I'm somewhat less than relieved by your assurances."

Jude scoffed and stepped forward until he was inches from Audrey's face. Audrey met his eyes, but Winona could see her stepmother tremble with fear as Jude grinned evilly. "You're so weak," he said. "You never had the stomach for this, Audrey. You pretend to be powerful but you're just another little country-born farm girl who's in way over her head. Why don't you go hide at home and let my father and I take care of things?"

Audrey's voice remained steady despite her fear, "Logan Foley is coming for you, Jude. Will you smile when you see him?"

"Of course I will!" Jude threw his head back and laughed. "You don't think my father and I prepared for this? Logan coming for Winona is exactly what we're hoping for! In fact, why don't you take him a message? Tell him I will be marrying Winona at the church house in two days' time. Tell him he can show up if he wants. He can hear Winona tell the reverend that she takes me to be her lawfully wedded husband. He can hear her say *I do*. He can watch her kiss me."

"She will never marry you," Audrey protested.

"Yes, she will," Jude said in a sickening imitation of his father. "There's nothing either of you can do about it." His grin widened. "I can't wait to watch you two try."

"He won't be coming alone," Audrey retorted. "He'll have the whole town at his back."

Jude laughed again. "The town won't help him, Audrey. They're on our side."

"They won't be. Not after they learn what you two really are."

"Of course they will, Audrey. They will for the same reason you did. They want so desperately to believe they're important they'll do anything to gain the favor and attention of those who actually are important. My father and I could shoot Winona in the street and the town would still support us. Nothing talks like money and power, Audrey, and my father and I have more of that than the rest of the town combined.

"They won't stand for this!" Audrey insisted.

"Haven't you been listening? Of course they will!"

"No, they won't. At this very moment, my husband and the Foley brothers are preparing to tell the town everything about you. Once they hear the kind of lying snakes you two are, they'll gladly assist the Foleys in ruining you."

Sterling interjected. "It's been my experience that the Foley's are not regarded highly among the people of Westridge."

"Not regarded highly?" Jude added. "They're pariahs! The townsfolk won't support them. In fact, they'll be grateful to my father and me for finally ridding the town of its greatest embarrassment."

"You underestimate the people of Westridge," Audrey argued. "They'll never allow someone like you and your father to bully them and they definitely won't allow you to murder their own so you can kidnap his wife and force marriage upon her. They'll fight with Logan."

Jude waved his hand dismissively. "Even if Logan does manage to find a few supporters, my father and I are prepared. We've hired dozens of armed men to ride with us. Anyone who rides with Logan Foley will be crushed with him. That includes your husband."

"You're insane if you think you can get away with this. The law—"

"We are the law!" Jude shouted. He grinned again. "You know what? Let them come for us. The defeat they'll suffer at our hands will be the perfect message to Westridge that my father and I are the new law in this town and anyone who wishes to survive will do as we say. Take the message to Logan, Audrey. Winona will marry me at the church house in two days. If he, or anyone else, wants to try and stop us, they do so at their own risk. Now go. Run along before my father and I lose our patience and dispose of you here."

Audrey remained silent for a moment. Then she nodded. She turned to Winona. "Stay strong, Winona. Your husband is coming for you." She spun on her heel and left without another word.

Jude laughed when she left, and Sterling smiled. Winona's face remained expressionless but inside, she felt hope return to her for the first time since Sterling kidnapped her. Logan loved her. He loved her and he was coming for her.

"Don't worry, *engelein*," Sterling said when he and Jude stopped laughing. "Your uncouth barbarian of a husband stands no chance against us. You will marry Jude and live the life of power and luxury you were promised."

Winona met Sterling's eyes, her gaze without fear. Sterling's smile faded under Winona's gaze and Winona thought she detected a trace of fear in the older man's eyes. It was gone as soon as it appeared, but Winona now knew for sure that Audrey's news had rattled him.

Logan loved her. Logan was coming for her.

She smiled. "I'm not worried, Sterling. I'm not worried at all."

Chapter Twenty-Six

Logan glanced around at the others gathered in the room. Besides himself, his brothers, and Heath and Audrey, there was Sheriff Emmett Burke, Mayor Henry Josephson, Clarence Huxtable from the bank, Cordelia, Pat O'Leary from the hotel and Wyatt Custer, the proprietor of the livery.

Nearly everyone stared at Logan, despite the fact Heath Ross had called the meeting. Clarence and Cordelia offered encouraging smiles. The others seemed wary of him. Logan nodded curtly at the seated group. The sheriff and the mayor nodded in reply while the others remained stoic.

"Friends," Heath began. "I greatly appreciate everyone meeting on such short notice. By now, most of you are aware my daughter was kidnapped by Sterling and Jude Koch and is currently being held captive on his ranch. It is Sterling Koch's intent to force Winona into marriage with Jude."

"These are some serious accusations," Wyatt said. "Do you have any proof of these claims?"

"I saw her there," Audrey answered. "I went to Koch's ranch to beg for my daughter back. I saw her there with Jude and Sterling. She's being held against her will and will be forced to marry Jude—a man she does not love—in two days' time."

Wyatt opened his mouth to speak, then fell silent. Audrey stared at him as though daring him to question her honesty. He looked ready to do just that when Mayor Henry interjected. "I'm sure no one here would presume to question your integrity, Audrey, but it's not so simple as to whether or not they're guilty."

Audrey stared at Henry, shocked. Jay started forward angrily but Gregory stopped him. "Not so simple?" Audrey cried. "My daughter is being held prisoner as the trophy bride of a man she does not love. Honestly, Henry, she's being held prisoner. Did I even need to add the rest?"

"No," Sheriff Burke said. "You didn't. I've heard enough. Let's get these bastards."

"There's no need for foul language, Emmett," Cordelia chided. "But yes, I agree. Winona's kidnapping must not be tolerated. We must rescue her immediately."

Logan smiled gratefully at the two of them. Cordelia returned his smile with a warm one of her own while Emmett nodded gruffly.

"It's not so simple," Henry insisted. "Sterling Koch is a very powerful man. He attended the governor's daughter's wedding. He has connections with federal judges, congressmen …"

"You're worried about votes," Audrey spat. "That's it, isn't it? Next year's an election year and you're worried Sterling will influence the vote against you."

"I'm not running for reelection, Audrey," Henry answered tiredly. "But the point you made about him influencing the vote is valid. He has real influence, Audrey, influence beyond anything Westridge has ever seen before. If we take Winona by force, he could make a very successful case that he was trying to protect her from being forced to marry beneath her station and we assaulted him and kidnapped her."

Audrey shivered at the mayor's words. Ice ran through Logan's veins as well. Audrey had told him about Sterling's scheme to annul his marriage to Winona and it was unnervingly close to Henry's speculation.

"That's outrageous!" Cordelia said. "No judge will believe that!"

"Probably not," Henry admitted. "But they'll rule in his favor, nonetheless."

"They won't," Jay chimed in. All eyes in the room riveted instantly on the youngest individual present. Jay held his head high and his voice remained firm as he spoke. "Winona will tell them our side of the story is correct. The judge won't be able to rule against her then."

Logan felt a swelling of pride for his brother. Though his fear for Winona was in the front of his mind, he felt a small pang of guilt. His brother had become a man and Logan had been too busy focusing on himself to see it.

"Yes, he will," Henry said. "He absolutely will."

"How?" Gregory said. "What, a federal judge is just going to blatantly allow Sterling to force Winona into marriage with Jude?

"You don't understand," Henry repeated. "People like the Kochs don't live by the same rules we do."

"They don't live by the rule of law?" Audrey asked incredulously.

"They don't," Henry replied. "They live by an entirely different set of rules. People like Sterling can manipulate the law to mean whatever they want it to mean. All it takes is a little bit of money and knowing the right people and they can exist outside of the law in everything other than appearances."

"So what?" Logan asked, incensed. "We just give up? Just throw our hands in the air and say, 'Oh well, it'd be nice to save you, Winona, but Sterling's just too rich and powerful?'"

"No, I'm not saying that," Henry said. "I'm saying we take our time with this and be smart. We gather evidence. We build a case. Clarence, you have some connections of your own. You find a good councilor at law and a judge who will be sympathetic to our case. When Winona is forced to marry Jude—"

"Not going to happen," Logan snapped. "Let's make that clear. Winona is not going to marry Jude Koch. We're not here to decide if we're going to stop Sterling, we're here to talk about how."

"You don't understand," Henry repeated softly.

His voice carried a strange mixture of exhaustion and desperation and though Logan was furious with him for arguing against rescuing Winona, he somehow managed also to feel sympathy for the old man. A lifetime in politics had broken him. Logan could understand why Henry would choose to retire rather than run for mayor again.

"There's not just the legal side to consider," Pat O'Leary added. "Sterling's railroad station is nearly finished. By next season, the Grand Central Railroad will pass directly through our town. Sterling Koch is a conniving old snake but he's going to put Westridge on the map."

"So we're going to sacrifice my daughter to Sterling's violent oaf of a son as payment for his railroad?"

"That railroad is the town's future, ma'am," Pat retorted. "And I'll be honest. I can think of far worse fates for Winona then being wed to the wealthiest, most powerful young man within two hundred miles."

Logan started forward, and this time Gregory stopped him. Logan realized wryly that Gregory had positioned himself between Jay and Logan for a reason.

"You're right, Pat," Heath said.

Logan, his brothers and Audrey turned to stare incredulously at Heath. Cordelia looked shocked.

Heath held up a hand for silence and continued. "You're right, Pat. That railroad is the town's future. It's the thing that's going to take us from being a tiny little frontier town to being an important city like Austin or San Antonio. It's the biggest, most important change this town will ever experience, and Sterling and Jude Koch have the power to bring that change. Is that what we really want, though?"

"Yes, Heath," Wyatt insisted. "It is."

"Are you sure? Look what it's doing to us. I remember a day when what mattered to the people of this town wasn't the size of a man's wallet but the integrity of his spirit."

"Fine words, Heath, but fine words don't put food on the table."

Clarence spoke for the first time, his rich, sonorous bass echoing across the room. "I'm the most recent arrival to Westridge represented in this room," he said. "So, I can't pretend to know this town as well as others present. I have, however, had the privilege of managing the finances of the majority of this town's residents and while I can't discuss individual financial circumstances, I can say that if we behave with some generosity to those less fortunate, the people here have more than enough to survive a fortnight of poor seasons and harsh winters. Sterling Koch can enrich this town, but this town will survive quite comfortably without his wealth."

"Look at what we've become," Heath repeated. "Pat, Sterling Koch has kidnapped my daughter. Look me in the eye and tell me you're willing to accept that."

There was not a trace of anger in Heath's voice, but Pat averted his eyes anyway. When he didn't respond for several seconds, Heath continued. "I fear very strongly that Sterling has corrupted this town nearly beyond repair. He's taken fine, neighborly, generous people and turned them into self-centered, money-worshipping fools. That includes me. We're all so blinded by the presence of such wealth that we refuse to see how easily Sterling manipulates us to his own ends with no regard for our own. He kidnapped my daughter. He kidnapped Logan's wife and we're all willing to accept that for the hope of a share of the profit."

"With all due respect," Wyatt said, in a tone that made it clear he thought very little, if any, respect was due, "but I find it strange you would side with the Foleys in this case. I understand wanting to rescue your daughter, but wanting to also return her to the bed of a criminal whose father nearly bankrupted you?"

Gregory leapt to his feet and this time it was Logan and Jay who stopped him from attacking Wyatt.

Heath sighed. "Friends, it's time I told the truth about my falling out with Dale Foley."

Logan's heart began to beat faster. Heath Ross was really going to admit to stealing from Logan's father. He couldn't believe it. He felt a newfound respect for Heath. It had taken longer than it should have for Heath to do the right thing but when the time finally came, he didn't shy away from it.

Audrey laid a supportive hand on Heath's shoulder. Heath smiled at her and began. "Friends, Dale Foley was not at fault in the disagreement we had five years ago. I was the one who stole from Dale. You all know I started my fortune with the proceeds from a major deal with the U.S. Army. What you don't know is that the deal was initially with both Dale and me together. Dale and I were scheduled to meet with the lieutenant colonel in charge of the purchase to finalize the deal. Unbeknownst to Dale, I moved the meeting up. When I arrived, I told them Dale had withdrawn and the Ross ranch would be handling the entire contract. He changed the paperwork accordingly and Dale Foley was written completely out of the deal. When Dale protested, I paid men to act as witnesses and claim Dale had tried to write me out of the deal and I only acted out of self-preservation."

There were a few murmurs and gasps of surprise at this admission. Cordelia's hand flew to her mouth and a soft "Oh!" escaped her lips.

Wyatt still appeared dubious. "Dale had five years to seek satisfaction but as I recall, once the initial case was dismissed, he let it go. If what you're saying is true, why didn't he fight for his half of the sale? You're no Sterling Koch, Heath. I doubt you have any judges in your pocket."

"No," Heath said. He hung his head and took a deep breath. "Dale let the case drop because I asked him to."

Logan's breath escaped in a rush. He leaned back heavily and stared wide-eyed at Heath. He'd never known this part of the story.

"It's true," Heath said. "I asked Dale to let go of the case because I didn't want Winona to spend the last years of her childhood visiting her father in jail. He agreed not to put Winona through that pain."

Logan kept staring at Heath, stunned. He understood now why Dale had never tried to get his money back. All these years he'd thought his father was a coward and a pushover and the truth was he cared more about a young woman's happiness than his own wealth.

"Dale was a better man than I'll ever be," Heath continued. "And his sons are as fine as he was. It's an honor for Winona to be married to Logan and it will be an honor to be allowed to remedy the wrong I've done Logan's family by cheating his father. It will also be an honor to remedy the wrong I did Winona when I first agreed to give her hand to Jude Koch in marriage. I ask all of you now to stand with me and fight the men who've terrorized our town. Sterling Koch may be powerful but if we all unite against him, even he can't stand. What do you say?"

For a moment, everyone was silent. Then Cordelia spoke. "I'm with you, Heath, and you Foley boys as well."

"As am I," Clarence affirmed.

"I'm in," Emmett said. "Like I said earlier, let's get these bastards."

"I'm with you," Henry said. He chuckled. "Hell, it's not like I have anything to lose now that I'm retiring."

Pat nodded slowly. "You're right, Heath. Seeing the kind of wealth Koch has ... Well, it makes a man positively green. But a man who would act out of envy is no man at all. I'm with you.

They turned to Wyatt. Wyatt's face showed signs of the internal struggle raging within. Eventually, though, Wyatt took a deep breath and nodded. "I'm in."

Logan and his brothers clapped and cheered, and Audrey and Heath smiled gratefully.

"All right," Emmett said after a moment. "We're going to get Winona back. The question is how?"

"We wait for her to come to us," Audrey said.

The others turned to look at her. She outlined everything Sterling and Jude had told her at the ranch, how Sterling had bought a judge to annul Winona's marriage to Logan, how they planned to force the reverend to marry the two of them, how they had hired a small army of gunmen to force Westridge to comply with their leadership of the town and how they had threatened to kill Logan if Winona didn't go along with them. She told them how they planned to marry Winona and Jude at the church the next day.

"That's when we stop them," Audrey said. "They have a lot of armed men but if we take them by surprise, we can stop them before they have a chance to fight."

"It'll be no trouble putting together a posse," Emmett said. "Especially after I tell everyone the truth about the Kochs. I've been keeping tabs on the boys he's hiring. They're hard men and there are a lot of them, but there are more of us. We'll win if it comes to a fight."

"It's settled then," Audrey said. "We're going to rescue Winona tomorrow before she is forced to marry that animal, Jude Koch."

"You can bet your life on it, ma'am," Emmett assured her. "Sterling Koch will never know what hit him."

Hearing the leaders of Westridge agree to help him brought a surge of hope to Logan. He smiled. *Don't worry, Winona. I'm coming for you.*

Chapter Twenty-Seven

A memory stirred in Logan's mind. He remembered his father taking him to town when he was a boy. A store under construction had a false front created, a tall front with gables that didn't represent the architecture of the squat, single-story rectangle of the actual building behind it. The false front even had windows with drapes and a wooden box behind the window. His father said the box was to keep it from being obvious the front was false.

At the time, Logan thought the false front was a silly thing, something he couldn't understand at all. Why would someone want to pretend to be something other than they were? Why would someone want to pretend a store was something other than it was? His father explained the façades were something that would make the store seem established, more than it was, so people would feel more confident about shopping there.

Since people came from larger towns and cities back East, they were used to seeing larger buildings and nicer decorations. It made people comfortable and in most of the towns in the west, when stores became successful, they would move to larger buildings that didn't need a façade to be grandiose. Even with that understanding, Logan hadn't been able to get past the idea of a customer stepping into the store and realizing the outside was all a lie.

The memory came to him because he stood on the roof of Smythe's Haberdashery, a one-story building. The false front came up eight feet above the roof itself. The building was joined to another, sharing a wall. The second store, a seamstress shop that had changed hands four times since Logan first noticed it as a child, had a false front as well, and the space between the false fronts provided perfect cover from which Logan could observe the church.

His father had been wrong. Smythe's Haberdashery was very successful, successful enough the general store stopped selling hats, belts, suspenders and ties, and left those products to Smythe's. The building still wore a false front, though. Logan imagined false fronts eventually grew so identifiable with a store that changing them seemed an unthinkable thing to do. The part that he still didn't understand, though, was how a man could step right in and buy a bolo tie or how a woman could step right in and buy a feathered hat just like those worn in Paris. How could they do that and not immediately be put off by the false front?

He supposed he understood the recalcitrance of the folks in town to act immediately against Koch. When his false front was revealed, there were still consequences to consider—consequences that had the potential to take food from tables or livelihoods from families. They'd come around, though, once they'd become fully convinced of just how false the Koch front was.

On the other hand, the process required also tearing down an altogether different false front, the one Heath constructed for Logan's family name and then tore down in front of the town.

He thought about how free he felt now, how the shame of his family history was gone, or if not gone yet definitely on its way to being gone. He thought about how powerfully that dark cloud had followed him around, had followed his entire family. Now, there was brightness upon them, and it was love for Winona that made it happen. Not only Logan's love for her but her father's love, stronger than his pride and shame, such that he was willing to confess and set things right.

To think all of it—what happened with his family as well as what happened at this very moment—came from greed. It made what the preachers said about love and money and the root of evil make a great deal more sense. Positioned on the roof because of the excellent but concealed view of the church it offered, Logan looked down and saw preparations for the wedding.

Ten guards. Logan knew there were ten guards outside of the church because he'd counted them almost a dozen times by now.

It occurred to him the Koch family was brazen in its behavior. They were so confident in their façade, their false front, that they could put armed guards in front of a church without bothering to think about how it would look. Of course, over the years they'd developed the front in such a way that people in town would likely make excuses, essentially thinking if the Koch family put guards in front of the church there had to be an important reason.

Logan imagined there were plenty who would just assume future weddings ought to have guards as well. Now, all of that façade was falling apart, and the Koch truth was revealed to everyone, or if not to everyone, to enough that everyone would soon see it.

The sight of an approaching stagecoach immediately drew him from his musings and Logan watched as it pulled in front of the church. Two people emerged but the angle and the distance made it impossible to be certain of them.

But he felt certain nonetheless that one of the two was Winona, the woman he loved.

Loved.

Absolutely. There was no way for Logan to deny that now. It became clear the moment she was taken from him. The clarity settled on him then and solidified now. He loved Winona more than he loved himself, and she was in the clutches of a madman. He felt energetic as rage filled him—anger mingled with a protective urge that was almost panic-inducing in its desperation.

He'd spent days in agony fighting to keep himself from charging the Koch ranch alone. Now, the sight of what had to be Winona forced to participate in this farce fueled even greater anger, greater panic and greater agony. He stood without thinking and then crouched again behind cover. The best shot he had was to follow the plan, he reminded himself.

Logan heard the long, low whistle from Gregory. The men were gathered. He scrambled from the roof down the back and to the ground where the groups now emerged. He nodded to Gregory and Heath and then rushed around the side of the building. Things would have to move very quickly now. He moved toward the front of the building and then into the high brush in the vacant lot next to it.

He ducked back on Willow Lane and ran about fifty yards away from the church before crossing the street, passing between the druggist's shop and a vacant home and into the trees beyond. From there, he ran toward Main Street, emerging about a hundred yards from the church. Nobody appeared to be looking his direction, so he rushed across the street and into the brush on the other side.

He hurried as fast as he dared until he was behind the church, confident he was undetected. A lone guard seemed bored, leaning against the back porch rail, rifle slack at his side. Logan rushed up as silently as he could and a blow from his pistol knocked the man to the ground, unconscious. Thankfully his rifle slid through the railings and landed with a dull, quiet thud on the ground instead of the sharp clatter that might have happened had it landed on the porch.

He took a moment to breathe. Four minutes, maybe five had passed, he thought, from the time he left the others. Everything moved quickly, according to plan. Things were proceeding exactly as they should, and he felt a surge of triumph as he climbed onto the porch and threw the door open. In a moment, Winona would see he was there.

But Winona was not there. Nor was Jude.

A trap.

Logan's heart sank as he saw the men, smiling wickedly and triumphantly at him, guns drawn. There were two of them. He could almost feel the barrel of a pistol one of them held against the preacher's temple. The other said, "If you ever want to see you pretty little wife alive again, you're coming with me."

"Coming where?" Logan asked. It seemed to him his voice came from somewhere other than his mouth.

"We're going to Mr. Koch's ranch, just you and me, and you're not going to give me no trouble at all because you love that little wife of yours and you don't want nothing to happen to her." There were a great many things about the situation worthy of hate, but Logan believed he hated most of all that the man was right.

Certainly, there was a great deal of frustration about the situation, but the smugness in the man's expression really grated on him. It grated enough that Logan had to remind himself of the stakes involved as he holstered his gun.

The gun remained in his holster as he exited the rear of the church along with the man with the smug smile. He found that surprising. He found it even more surprising that the man didn't take it from him when they mounted horses hitched at the edge of the church and set off toward the Koch ranch.

As they rode, Logan found his hand moving time and time again toward his holster only to stop and return to the reins when he thought about the man's words. The effect was terribly distracting and more than just a little bit frustrating. It added to the anger, specifically to the anger at the smugness of the bastard who'd tricked him or, at least, been the voice of the trick.

The journey to the Koch ranch seemed particularly strange. On one level, it seemed to take forever. It seemed as though time slowed and for some reason, despite the danger of his current state, Logan felt like he had to get to Winona immediately. On another level, though, it seemed as though no time passed at all before they passed guards posted at the courtyard of the Koch farmhouse. They called the two to a stop and one said, "Why the hell didn't you disarm him?" as he reached up and removed Logan's revolver from his holster.

"He's been a good boy," the other man said. "He knows what happens if he's not."

"All the same, you should've disarmed him."

"Why don't you stand your post and shut up," the man said. To Logan he said, "Come with me and keep being a good little boy." Logan wanted to punch the man. He wanted it more than he could recall ever wanting anything, but the emptiness in his holster had an effect. The precariousness of the situation grew stronger. The man led him right to the front porch of the ranch house and a moment later led him into the house.

The moment he stepped inside; he saw Winona. She sat on a high-backed chair, the kind very much in fashion among the wealthy at present. Beside her stood Sterling Koch, who had his hand on her shoulder. From the look on her face and the way her shoulder was slightly depressed, Logan could tell he held her down. "Let her go, Koch," Logan growled.

Winona breathed out, "Logan!" and the hope in her voice might have been the most encouraging thing Logan had ever heard.

"Glad you could join us, Logan," Jude said. Logan turned and saw him with two other men. Jude said, "You know, every man has a price, Logan. This here's Judge Petticock. I know, it's a funny name but he's a judge and he's going to help us out with your annulment." He gestured to the other man, "and this here is the Right Reverend Arthur Pent. He's here to marry me and Winona."

Logan looked at Winona, looking her up and down quickly. She nodded slightly and Logan realized she knew he wanted to know if she was okay, and she'd responded. Neither of them had to use words to make that clear.

He loved her.

He loved her and he'd do anything for her. It was that simple.

"You should be ashamed of yourself," he said.

"Save it, young man," Sterling Koch said. "You're beaten. Just accept it and get it over with."

"No, Pa," Jude said. "I'd love to hear this trash tell me how ashamed I ought to be."

"I'm not talking to you, Jude," Logan said. He looked at the judge and shook his head. "You took an oath before God to be honorable and just." He looked at the priest. "And you took an oath to God. I seem to recall something in the Good Book about it being better not to make a vow to God than to make it and fail to live up to it." He saw the expression on both faces change. There was shame. Logan doubted there was enough to make a difference, though.

"You know, you're right," Jude said. "And I don't want to be responsible for them breaking their vows. You did me a real favor here. Winona won't need an annulment at all. Why bother with an annulment if she's a widow?" he laughed as he leveled his pistol at Logan, and Logan realized dying for Winona was something he was willing to do.

Gunfire sounded suddenly from outside, though. Jude was very clearly startled, and Logan ducked behind a settee as the man fired. He heard the shot impact the wall. Outside someone screamed in a panicked voice, "Mr. Koch! There's too many! Mr. Koch!"

"The whole town's against you now, Sterling," Logan said. "It's all over. You're beaten, old man. Just accept it and get it over with."

He peeked from the side of the settee and cursed as he saw Jude pulling Winona away. He held his still smoking gun against her head. "We're going out the back," he said. "I'd hate to have to ruin your wedding night, so you behave."

Logan stood as they ducked around a corner. Sterling Koch stared at him with his pistol trained on his chest. Logan rushed forward, startling him, shouting, "I said you're beat!" He crashed into him, and they fell against the high-backed chair. Koch beat at his sides, but Logan forced himself back and stood. Sterling stood as well but Logan lunged toward him, his swing a wide arc and aided by the momentum of his lunge. His fist impacted the man's face and caught Koch as he tried to stand. Koch's gun fell to the floor and his face seemed for just a moment uncomprehending, as though he'd never felt a punch in his life. Logan imagined that was possible. Then, Koch crumpled to the ground and was still. Logan reached down and took the old man's pistol. He glanced at the priest and the judge. They stood wide-eyed and lifted their hands. "Shame on you," Logan spat.

Then he ran from the room to find his wife.

Chapter Twenty-Eight

Jude's arm wrapped around Winona like a vise, holding her immobile against him as he dragged her away from the house. She screamed for Logan and an instant later Jude shifted his grip and clamped her hand around his mouth, silencing her and restricting her breathing so she gasped for air.

"Hold on, Winona," Jude said. "We're almost out of here." His voice shook, whether from fear or his rapidly eroding façade of sanity Winona couldn't tell. He dragged her toward the stable a few hundred yards distant. A wagon and team of horses waited in front of the stable, tied to a post.

"We'll make for Ohai," Jude said as he pulled her along. "My father has business associates there who will protect us until my father sorts things out in Westridge." He looked down at her, his face contorted in a sick mockery of affection. "Don't worry, my love."

In looking at her, he stopped paying attention to where he was going. A moment later, he stumbled over a rock. He slipped and cried out and though he didn't fall, his grip around Winona loosened.

This was her chance.

She bit down hard on the hand covering her mouth. Jude cried out again and released her. The sudden loss of support caused Winona to lose her balance. She fell backward, landing heavily on her backside in front of Jude. Jude snarled, enraged, and reached for her. She kicked forward, hard. The blow landed cleanly on Jude's chest and sent him sprawling, a surprised expression on his face.

Winona got up quickly and ran back toward the ranch, where sporadic gunfire and shouting could still be heard. She made it only a few yards before a shot rang out and a bullet whizzed past her head. She kept running but the shot disoriented her, and she stumbled and fell heavily to the ground.

"Don't you move!" Jude shouted. "Or I'll put the next round through your knee."

Tears streaming, Winona rolled onto her back.

Jude approached her, a crazed smile on his face. "Winona, love, that's enough nonsense. Now get up and come with me so we can get out of here."

Winona looked at Jude, but her thoughts were fixed on Logan: his awkwardness around her, his strength, his rough manners, his courage, that surprisingly sweet smile he wore on those rare occasions when time spent with her was enough to drive away his demons for a few moments.

She looked at Jude and there was no longer any fear in her heart. "Jude Koch. Go to hell."

Jude's eyes widened in shock. Then they narrowed in anger. His grin turned malicious. "I'll meet you there, my love."

He raised his pistol and Winona closed her eyes, ready to accept her fate. A shot rang out, but Winona felt no pain. She wondered why that was until she heard Jude's piercing scream.

She opened her eyes to see him clutching his hand to his chest. Blood seeped between his fingers and his gun lay on the ground a few yards away.

"Winona!" Logan's voice called.

She turned to see him rushing toward her, smoke rising from the barrel of his drawn pistol. "Logan!" she cried.

"Get behind me, Winona," he said.

She rose to her feet and ran behind him. She wanted nothing more than to wrap her arms around him and cover him in kisses. "Oh, Logan, you came for me!"

"Of course, I did," Logan said. "You're my wife."

She was bruised, bloody and exhausted from her fight with Jude and her days of imprisonment. Behind her the battle between Sterling's men and the posse continued to rage. In front of her, Jude glared hatefully, teeth bared as he cradled his wounded arm. Despite all this, Winona was happier than she could ever recall being.

"I'll kill you!" Jude shrieked at Logan. "I'll kill you!"

"You can try," Logan said sardonically. He holstered his pistol. "If I were you, I would come quietly and throw yourself at the judge's mercy rather than mine, but a man's got to do what he thinks is right. Not that you're much of a man."

Jude's face turned a deep shade of red. "I'm more of a man in my sleep than you'll ever be, Logan Foley." He turned to Winona. "This is what you want? Fine. You can die with him." He snarled and dove for his pistol.

In an instant, Logan drew and fired, his movements a blur. The round struck Jude in the chest, knocking him backward. He sat up slowly as a red stain appeared on his shirt below his shoulder, slowly spreading across his chest. He looked at the stain, a confused expression on his face. Then he looked up at Winona. He opened his mouth, but no words came out. He swayed for a second or two. Then he fell and lay unmoving.

Logan holstered his pistol and turned to Winona. "I'm so sorry, Win—"

Before he could finish, she threw her arms around him and kissed him deeply. He wrapped his arms around her and pulled her tightly to him. They kissed for several long moments, both overcome with the joy of reuniting. When they finally pulled away, Winona laid her head on Logan's shoulder. "I knew you'd come for me."

"I love you, Winona," he said in response.

"I know," she said. "I love you too."

They remained in each other's arms for a long while. The gunfire at the house slowed, then stopped. A minute later, several of Sterling's gunmen left the house, arms raised. They were followed by several members of the posse, led by Jay. Jay waved when he saw them. He said something to the man next to him.

Winona couldn't be sure from this distance, but it looked like Pat O'Leary from the hotel. Pat nodded to Jay and led the posse toward the gate of the ranch, where the posse's horses waited along with two wagons meant for transporting prisoners. Winona noticed grimly that very few of Sterling's men appeared to have survived to be taken prisoner.

Jay arrived a moment later. Logan released Winona and shared a brief but heartfelt embrace with his brother. After that, Jay hugged Winona. "It's so good to see you," she said.

"You too," Jay said.

"How did you get here so quickly?" Logan asked.

"When Audrey told us about Jude's plan at the ranch, I felt a little suspicious," Jay replied. "Not of Audrey, but of Jude and Sterling. The Kochs are arrogant but they're also cowards. It didn't make sense to me that they would so brazenly advertise their plans and give you even the slightest chance to beat them. I figured they were trying to bait us into a fight on their terms and I figured those terms would most likely not include putting themselves in harm's way.

"So, Gregory and I decided we would split the posse in half. Gregory and Sheriff Burke would lead one half to the church in case Jude was telling Audrey the truth after all. Pat and I would lead the other half to the Koch ranch in case my suspicions were correct, and the Koch's were lying after all." He looked contemptuously at Jude's body. "I guess it was a good thing we did."

"I'll say," Logan replied. He looked at Jay, his expression a mixture of pride, love and gratitude. "You saved my life, Jay. Winona's too. I owe you a debt I can never repay."

Jay shrugged. "It was what any man would have done for his family."

"You're a good man, Jay," Logan added. "I'm sorry I've been too blind to see it. From now on, I'm going to treat you the way you deserve to be treated: as an equal partner in the ranch. We're going to follow your plan with the cattle. It's a good idea and it deserves to be acted on."

"Well, we'll worry about that later," Jay said. "Right now, you need to get Winona back to the ranch for some much-needed rest, and Pat and I need to get these outlaws to jail. We'll talk about the cattle later."

Despite his words, Jay couldn't stop the grin that spread across his face. Winona's heart warmed as she witnessed the two brothers make up to each other. How lucky she was to be part of such a wonderful family.

She heard the sound of footsteps and turned to see Pat approaching. He tipped his hat to Winona. "Miss Winona, I'm happy to see you're safe."

She smiled at him. "Thank you for helping my husband, Pat. I'll never forget what you did for us today."

Pat returned a smile of his own. "It's the least I could do." He turned to Jay. "The prisoners are secured in the wagons. We kept Sterling separate from them, bound to one of the horses. Better not to risk him inspiring some sort of revolt with that forked tongue of his."

"I agree," Jay said. "We'll take them to jail and hold him there until he can stand trial, him and that no-account judge and priest he hired. We'll let Sheriff Burke figure out what to do with the gunfighters." He turned to Logan and Winona. "Why don't you two take that wagon Jude was going to use and ride back to the ranch? We can take it from here."

Logan nodded, pride and love for Jay still etched on his features. He laid a hand on Jay's shoulder and thanked him again, then led Winona to the wagon.

They spent the ride to the ranch in comfortable silence. Winona lay against Logan's shoulder. After a few minutes, he shifted in the seat and wrapped his arm around her so she could lay on his chest. She closed her eyes and drank in the feel of him, his strength and gentleness comforting her. The fear, and pain, and worry of the past two days seemed only a distant memory. She was safe now. She was with the man she loved—the man she was truly meant to be with, and all was right with the world.

She smiled at the thought and drifted slowly into a deep sleep.

She woke to the sound of Logan's voice. It was close by but muffled. She stirred and opened her eyes. She was in Logan's room at the ranch, the room she'd occupied when she first arrived what seemed like a lifetime ago. Logan's voice came from the parlor. She recognized several other voices: Gregory, Jay, her parents and the sheriff.

She relaxed a moment longer, her body luxuriating in the softness of the mattress after days spent strapped to a chair. Then she got out of bed and walked into the parlor.

Logan stood in the middle of the room, talking with Sheriff Burke. Gregory and Jay stood a few feet from them. Her parents sat on the couch. Heath had his arm around Audrey, who leaned against him, her eyes red from crying. Winona couldn't recall ever seeing her stepmother look so vulnerable. She felt a wave of compassion for Audrey. She was far from a good mother to Winona growing up but after her intervention at the Koch ranch yesterday, Winona could see now that in her own way, Audrey did love her after all.

When Audrey saw Winona, she stood and ran to her, throwing her arms around Winona and sobbing. "Oh, Winona!" she cried. "I'm so glad you're safe!"

Winona held her stepmother as the older woman cried in her arms. "It's okay, Audrey," she said. "I'm okay."

Audrey wiped her eyes tremulously. "There's more, I'm afraid, and I want to get it all off my chest." She looked at Logan briefly but couldn't hold his gaze and dropped hers to the floor. "When the Kochs and I were conspiring against the Foley Ranch, we planted a ranch hand among your help when you hired two or three new men. His name was Tom. He didn't stay long—just long enough to introduce some tainted feed. That's why you lost some of your herd to sickness. Tom lost his nerve, however; that's why he disappeared so suddenly."

Heath's head snapped up and he shot a startled look at his wife. He said nothing, but a deep frown creased his face.

"I'm so sorry—sorrier than I can say," Audrey continued, pale from her husband's sudden reaction to her unexpected revelation. She also met Logan's shocked expression with remorse and honesty.

"Well, that explains it," he said. "I couldn't figure how it happened so sudden, and why isolating the sick horses didn't help." He was silent for a moment, and then he looked up at Audrey. "The important thing is that we got Winona back and the Kochs are out of our hair."

Heath looked at Audrey, and then Logan. "Son, just let me know how many head you lost, and I'll make it right," he said with a nod. Logan nodded back.

Then Heath took a deep breath, stood, and walked over to his family, smiling. His expression was tired almost to the point of haggardness, but he stood tall, as though a weight he'd carried for years was finally lifted from his shoulders.

"Hi, Pa," Winona whispered.

Heath's smile wavered and as tears came to his eyes, he wrapped both Winona and Audrey in a bear hug, holding them for a long time. Winona squealed and the others laughed as the Rosses relished their long-awaited reunion.

When her parents finally released her, Winona turned to Gregory. "It's so good to see you."

The middle Foley brother smiled and walked to her, sharing his own embrace. "Same to you," he said. "You had us worried senseless for a while there."

"Really? From the way you and Jay handled everything you seem to have kept your senses about you rather well."

Gregory chuckled. "Well, what can I say? I guess we just had the right motivation."

Winona turned to Logan who smiled lovingly at her. "Good morning, Winona."

"Morning?" she asked. "How long was I asleep?"

"Since yesterday afternoon," Logan replied. "I brought you to bed when we arrived at the ranch. I figured it was best to let you sleep as long as you needed."

Considering how refreshed she felt, Winona couldn't argue with that. "Thank you, Logan," she said. "Thank you all."

Sheriff Burke nodded. He wore his typical stoic expression, a slight smile the only indication of his own happiness. "We're all right pleased to see you home safe," he said.

"What happened yesterday?" Winona asked. "At the church, I mean?"

"Well," Gregory said. "We were waiting on a signal from Logan to attack the men guarding the church. When we never got that signal, we knew something had gone wrong. We came out of hiding and told the men guarding the church they could come quietly and live through the day, or they could try to fight and we'd bury every one of them. We outnumbered them about five to one, so they decided to live."

"Where are they now?" Winona asked.

"Sterling, Petticock, and Pent are in jail awaiting trial. We've sent word to the Texas Supreme Court. We allowed all but a few of the gunfighters to leave town after taking their weapons and making them promise never to come back. Some were wanted for previous crimes. We've held those men for trial."

"You let them leave?" Winona cried, aghast.

"They won't be back," Burke assured her. "Men like that are opportunists. They won't pick a fight when there's no money involved. You won't have to worry about them coming back."

Winona nodded. She paused a moment then looked at Burke. "Sheriff, I want to be there when Sterling stands trial. I want to see him put away for the crimes he's committed against this town and against my family."

"We'll all be there," Audrey added. "We all deserve to see that rat put away for good."

Burke nodded at Winona and Audrey in turn. "You can count on it."

Gregory rubbed his stomach and interrupted. "All this talk of trials and gunfighters is making me hungry. What do you guys say we break for dinner?"

Logan smiled. "That just might be the best idea you've ever had."

Gregory chuckled. "Well, I might not be a future cattle baron like Jay over here, but I've been known to have a good idea or two."

They all laughed, and Winona smiled gratefully at her family. At long last, she had the life she'd always wanted, the one she'd dreamed of since she was a little girl.

She was home.

Chapter Twenty-Nine

As he sat at the courthouse, Logan realized he didn't actually believe there was such as a thing as liberty and justice for all, at least not for normal people, small people. The realization came upon him suddenly, and with it came a dramatic sense of certainty that Sterling Koch would walk away from this trial with no consequences for his behavior. He hadn't expected this feeling.

He certainly didn't expect it after feeling such a sense of victory and triumph after the town came together to help him rescue Winona from the clutches of Koch and his son. He hadn't experienced that certainty at all during the trial. In fact, he'd felt the opposite certainty, that somehow despite all of the walls built in front of him over the course of his life, he'd prevailed and Koch wasn't just foiled in his attempts to hurt Logan and others in town but would actually be held accountable for his actions.

Logan still believed Koch was foiled. The man had no sway or power over Logan or his family now. He had no wicked son who could terrorize anyone and his hired guns were all either driven from town or in cells where they belonged. Some were already hanged for past crimes come to light after their arrests.

Koch couldn't hurt anyone anymore. Logan understood that and felt a measure of pride that he'd been involved in the events that brought those circumstances to pass. He felt a powerful sense of pride, in fact.

But none of that meant Koch would face justice. As the sheriff said, "Settle down, now! Settle down! The judge is coming in! Settle down," and the crowd quieted, Logan realized he believed the man would face no real consequences. He'd get a slap on the wrist, a fine or house arrest, something like that. He hadn't felt that way about the verdict. He knew all of the people that sat on the jury.

They were good people, although just a few months ago they were also people who would turn their heads and look away if he came into town. As much as they'd turned their heads away from him and looked to Koch for leadership before, though, they'd rallied behind him when the truth about his family and Koch's behavior came to light.

He knew the jury would find Koch guilty, but he also knew that guilty or not, Koch's fate lay in the hands of the judge, Hancock Taylor.

Logan knew nothing about Taylor except that he traveled from the state capitol in order to handle the trial. Paul knew enough about the capitol to know the government there believed the railroad was the key to progress. Koch, guilty or not, would not be easily replaced to lay the tracks, so to speak, for the railroad's path through town. He knew the jury would find Koch guilty, but he felt certain suddenly the judge would reverse all that meant for Koch. A sick feeling settled in his stomach, and when he rose along with everyone else in the courthouse at the sheriff's urging, he felt unsteady on his feet. The judge, a small man with a too-full beard and a too-important expression said, "This court will come to order. You may be seated."

As much as the sight of the judge struck Paul as a man filled with himself and puffed up with purpose and regality, the judge got to business quickly. He looked at Koch, who sat next to his expensive lawyer all the way from Boston and said, "Sterling Koch, you were found guilty of conspiracy to commit murder, extortion, kidnapping and … Well, you know all the charges. If you'd stolen a horse instead of a person, a gallows would already be under construction and, like your devil of a son, you'd be dead and justice would be served. I can't sentence you to death for these crimes, though, as much as I wish the laws allowed it. Maybe it will change. Since that Philadelphia boy was kidnapped in July, there's some noise in the legislature about changing the law. For now, I can only sentence you according to the rules I have. Sterling Koch, you are remanded to the custody of the Texas marshals, who will escort you to the Texas State Penitentiary in Huntsville, where you will serve a sentence of not less than twenty-five years." He brought his gavel down and the sound of it hitting the bench seemed sharper than a gunshot.

The courtroom erupted in cheers at the news. Judge Taylor adopted an almost comical expression of affront and brought his gavel down. "Order!" he called. "Order!"

There was no order to be had for several moments as the townspeople cheered the sentencing of their tormentor. Sterling sat and stared straight ahead, his face expressionless.

Logan wore a similar look as he tried to process what he'd just heard. Twenty-five years? That was incredible! For a man of Sterling's age, that was essentially a life sentence. Logan had never seen the inside of a state penitentiary, but he'd heard from others who had that conditions in those facilities were adequate at best and usually far less than. It was conceivable that Sterling could live another twenty-five years under normal circumstances but in state prison the chances were slim to none. It was then that Logan knew he and his family were safe.

The realization brought a grin to Logan's face. He turned to Winona who smiled gleefully at him as she cheered. Then he too pumped his fist in the air and whooped and hollered with the rest of the crowd.

"Can we please have order!" Judge Taylor cried, his tone similar to one a parent might take with a particularly troublesome toddler. "This is a court of law!"

The noise died down and within a minute, Judge Taylor was finally allowed to continue. "As I was saying," he said, voice stiff with dignity, "Mr. Koch, you are sentenced to not less than twenty-five years in the State Penitentiary at Huntsville. You will be remanded to the custody of the local U.S. Marshals office pending transportation to the facility. This court is now adjourned."

He banged his gavel once more and the court erupted with renewed cheers. Sterling and his lawyer left swiftly, escorted by two U.S. Marshals. Several in the crowd taunted and jeered at Sterling as he left.

Logan watched him leave and wondered how he could have been so afraid of him. Minutes ago, he had seemed so formidable, larger-than-life, a force to be reckoned with cautiously, if indeed at all. Now, he seemed only like a small old man.

All that wealth, Logan thought. All that power. For what? Now he would spend the rest of his life languishing in a bleak prison cell, his influence and richness useless to him. What a sad life to be spent the way it had and end the way it would.

He turned to Winona. She smiled at him, her expression radiating pure love. He extended his arm, and she took it, her smile widening.

"Shall we head home, my love?" he suggested.

"Yes," Winona replied softly. "Let's go home."

***

Logan laughed as Gregory recounted the first time Jay had attempted to ride a horse. "He couldn't lift himself up on to the saddle. He tried and tried but he couldn't do it."

"None of you offered to help?" Winona asked through her own laughter.

"He wouldn' let us!" Logan protested. "He kept saying he wanted to do it himself."

"He couldn't do it, though," Gregory repeated. "He just kept sliding off."

"Hey, I was five years old!" Jay protested, pink with embarrassment.

"That's right," Logan said. "Five years old and already a stubborn sonofa—"

"Logan!" Winona warned. "Language!"

"Alright, alright," Logan relented. "The point is you were as stubborn a kid as you are as a man."

"Hey, I figured it out eventually."

"No you didn't!" Gregory said. "Pa finally got frustrated and put you on the saddle himself. You threw such a huge tantrum about not being allowed to do it yourself that the horse got spooked and took off, throwing you from the saddle. If Pa hadn't caught you quick as he did, you would've broken an arm."

"Ma was so upset with Pa when she found out!" Logan said. "Oh, those were good days."

"If you say so," Winona said dubiously.

"A toast!" Gregory cried suddenly, lifting his glass.

"You want to toast with water?" Logan asked.

"Why not? It's not about the drink, it's about the meaning of the toast."

"Let him make his toast!" Winona chided. "For heaven's sake, Logan you sound like a crabby old man sometimes."

"I'm your crabby old man," he said smiling.

"Mine, all mine," she joked, smiling at him.

"Ahem," Gregory said, "If you two don't mind …"

"Of course, Gregory, dear," Winona said. "My apologies. Do continue."

He smiled and bowed slightly. "Thank you. As I was saying, I would like to raise a toast. To good days."

"To good days," Winona responded.

"To good days," Logan and Jay echoed.

The four of them raised their glasses and solemnly sipped their water. Gregory whistled and made a face. "Whew," he said. "The drinks are always stronger in Texas."

The other three groaned and rolled their eyes and Gregory bowed his head with a flourish.

"Not your best effort, Gregory," Winona quipped.

"An artist is never appreciated in his own time," Gregory retorted.

They spent the rest of dinner laughing and talking good-naturedly. Logan couldn't recall a time he'd ever felt this happy. He'd thought after his parents died that he'd never feel happy again. Now it felt like the best part of his life was only just beginning.

After dinner, Logan and Winona remained at the table while Gregory and Jay excused themselves and headed for bed.

Winona smiled bashfully at Logan across the table. When he smiled back, she blushed and lowered her eyes.

Logan regarded his wife with an admiration that bordered on worship. What had he done to deserve so perfect a woman?

Nothing. That was the answer. He'd done nothing to deserve her and quite a few things that deserved losing her, but she loved him anyway. That, he thought, was perhaps the most remarkable thing about her.

"If you're going to stare at me, you might as well say something," Winona said. "Instead of just ogling me boorishly."

"Thank you," Logan said.

Winona's eyebrows raised. "Not what I had in mind, but certainly not unwelcome. And for what are you thanking me?"

"For saving me," Logan responded. "For saving my family. For a long time, I thought my brothers and I were done for. We didn't get along. We bickered constantly, we barely spent any time together that wasn't spent working or fighting, we disagreed all the time. I really didn't feel like we were a family anymore.

"Until you came. You brought us the courage and the desire to unite as brothers again. You gave us a reason not to quit on ourselves. You'll never know how much that means to me.

"I love you, Winona. I love you more than I ever thought I could possibly love anyone. You're the most beautiful woman I've ever seen but more than that, you're strong, and wise, and caring. Without you, I would have been alone. Now, thanks to you, I not only have the most wonderful wife a man could ask for, but I have my brothers back too. I owe everything to you and from now on, you have everything of me."

Winona didn't respond for a moment. When she finally did, tears welled at the corners of her eyes. "You know, when you rescued me from that storm six months ago, I woke up for a moment before you brought me into the house."

"Really?" Logan said. She'd never mentioned this to him before.

"I did," she affirmed. "Just long enough to open my eyes and look at the man who had rescued me. You seemed so perfect then," she said. "Like something out of a fairy tale, a knight in shining armor come to the aid of the beautiful princess in distress. I think I fell in love with you then."

"Really?" Logan said again. "That fast? You didn't even know me."

"I didn't," she agreed. "And believe me, once I did get to know you, there were times I felt fairly certain it would be impossible for me to love you, but I did. No matter what happened, I loved you. Even when it hurt. Even when I didn't want to. Even when I was so angry with you the sight of you made me want to run away, I still loved you. You know, you've saved me three times."

"Three times?" Logan asked.

"Yes," Winona asserted. "Once with the storm, once when you rescued me from Jude Koch."

"And the third?"

"The third is every day," Winona replied. "Every day you save me from a future alone with no purpose and no meaning and nowhere to belong. Every day I look at your adorable infuriating face—" Logan chuckled softly at that "—and thank

God that I found you and pray for Him to give me a hundred thousand more days like it.

"I think we really were meant to be together, Logan. Like people talk about: two souls fated to spend their lives together from birth who have finally found each other. I used to think that was just fantasy, but I don't think that anymore. You're my true calling, Logan. All my life I've searched desperately for the life I thought I wanted, and it was given to me before I even knew what was happening.

"I love you, Logan Foley. I love you more than life itself. You are my life." She reached forward and took his hand in hers. "And I'm so glad I found you."

Logan didn't respond right away. The love and joy and gratitude he felt was so powerful it nearly overwhelmed him. He lifted his hand and gently caressed his wife's face. There was so much he wanted to say but no words seemed adequate to express the love he felt for this woman.

So, he said the only words that really mattered. "I love you, Winona Foley."

At the use of her married name, Winona burst into a smile. Logan returned it for a second, then leaned forward and kissed her.

Chapter Thirty

Winona almost felt like a fairy tale princess from a storybook, rescued from a dragon, or a troll, or an evil king by a knight with a silvery sword, a bright chest plate, and a tall, white stallion with wild eyes and hooves like thunder. It was foolish, of course. In books like that, the adventure was all that mattered.

A lovely princess was spirited away, and a strong and handsome prince came along to rescue her. It was all the stuff of legends, and it was all very beautiful and sweet. In stories like those, there was only a line or two about how frightened the princess was, hoping against hope for a happy ending. The story was always about the quest to rescue her, the gallantry of the hero and the reward of the maiden's love.

None of those stories ever talked about how terrifying it was to be in the hands of a monster. None of those stories ever talked about what it meant for the princess to be completely helpless.

None of those stories ever talked about how the fear of the moment could be so strong that the desire for all of it to end, even with death, was something that the princess actually entertained.

Her "fairy tale" troll was dead. Winona would never have to fear Jude Koch again. She no longer faced the prospect of marrying the monster. Her knight vanquished him not with a silver sword but with an 1860 Remington New Army Model forty-four caliber revolver. Winona knew that because it was the "evil king's" gun, and Sterling Koch bragged about it while they held her captive. The evil king was deposed now, and he'd probably spend the rest of his life in prison. She couldn't imagine him living another twenty-five years, at least not when he had to live those years there, away from his creature comforts and his power.

In the storybooks, the adventure always ended when the evil villain was vanquished. Then, there was usually a kiss and that was that. Another sentence or two summarized the happy ending ... *and they lived happily ever after.* Her tormentors were dead or vanquished, but happily ever after wasn't as simple as it was in the storybooks. Winona couldn't remember a fairy tale where the princess's parents sided with the troll and the evil king. Maybe those stories existed, but she didn't know about them at all. Her parents had, though. Winona's parents had done that, and it hurt deeply. They'd changed course thanks to her hero, but a simple sentence about living happily ever after wasn't going to salve the wounds of their betrayal.

But what would?

Winona wanted those wounds to heal. Logan had lived his life filled with shame about his father. In many ways, his family and their legacy had been restored to him during this whole princess-rescuing adventure. On the other hand, Winona's family legacy was revealed to be a legacy of shame and her parents weren't restored to her but torn away.

She wanted desperately for a different outcome, something sweeter on the way to her very own happily ever after, but what could make that happen? The thoughts filled her as she sat on her porch and watched as her parents' wagon slowly grew larger and more distinct as it approached her home.

Logan and his brothers were away from the house for the day inspecting the stables and corrals to ensure they were prepared for the winter storms that were only a few weeks away.

Winona felt this would be an excellent opportunity for her to have a private conversation with her parents where they could be free to speak their minds without worrying about what Logan might hear.

As their wagon approached, she wished she had reconsidered and asked her parents to come when Logan could be there to support her. She felt in her heart that her parents had changed and were no longer the wealth-obsessed fools they seemed to be before, but that didn't necessarily mean they were ready to atone for their past mistakes or that Winona was ready to hear it. Well, they were nearly here now. There was no point in running anymore.

When the wagon arrived, Winona stood. She smiled and waved to her father and stepmother as they alighted from the wagon. She took a deep breath and willed herself to remain cheerful and not show her anxiety at the discussion she knew was coming.

Heath tethered their wagon to the post in the courtyard. Then he and Audrey approached the house. Audrey smiled and embraced Winona. "It's so good to see you, Winona," she said.

Winona returned the embrace awkwardly, still unused to this kind of affection from her stepmother. "It's good to see you too," she said. "Won't you come inside? There's a kettle on the fire if you'd like tea."

"I'd love some tea," Heath replied. "Thank you."

A few minutes later, they sat in front of the fire in the parlor, each savoring a cup of tea with a bit of honey and lemon. Winona recalled that the lemon was a tip Audrey showed her years ago, something she'd learned from her travels in Europe, she'd said. At the time, Winona had merely thought her pretentious. Now she wondered if maybe Audrey had, in her own way, tried to connect with Winona and Winona was simply too hurt by the loss of her mother and put off by Audrey's airs to notice the attempt.

Well, after today, she would no longer have to wonder. She set her tea down and said, "Dad, Mom," it sounded so strange to call Audrey by that name, "I know you came here to talk to me in private and I'm fairly certain I know what about. I don't know how to begin this conversation without being awkward, so I think we should just get on with it and hope for the best. It might be hard, but at least it will be done."

Heath smiled at her, and there was pride in his voice when he said, "You've grown up to be such a wise and strong woman, Winona. I'm very proud of you."

In spite of her anxiety, Winona smiled at her father's praise. "Thank you."

Audrey took a deep breath. "I might as well go first. I believe I have the most to apologize for. In fact, I'll start there."

She took another breath and met Winona's eyes. "Winona, I am so sorry for the way I've acted toward you all of these years. I've made you feel that you're inadequate and worthless, that the only thing that mattered about you or anyone else was how much money you had and how highly thought of you were among high society. I ridiculed every dream you ever had because none of those dreams involved accumulating wealth or influence. I never should have done that and I'm so sorry."

She hesitated a moment and continued. "The worst thing I ever did was try to force you to marry Jude Koch. The man was a monster, and his father was even worse. I knew they were bad people and I still tried to force you to marry Jude. Oh, I never thought that they were so vicious and monstrous as to kidnap and threaten you the way you did, but I knew they cared only for themselves and their own wealth and power." She laughed bitterly. "I even admired that." She looked back at Winona. "But I never should have forced that on you. I'm so very sorry."

She waited for Winona to respond. Winona couldn't for several moments. Her head was reeling. She was hearing exactly what she wanted to hear but it wasn't enough. It only left her with more questions.

"Why?" she finally asked. "Why was wealth and power so important to you? Why did it matter if I didn't want to be wealthy above all else?"

Audrey smiled softly. "I've never told you about my life growing up, have I?"

"No," Winona said. She realized she actually knew almost nothing about Audrey prior to her stepmother's marriage to her father.

"Well, you know when I met your father, I had some money left me by my first husband."

"No," Winona said. "I didn't know you were married before you met my father."

"Oh," Audrey said. "I guess I never told you that, either. Well, I was, briefly, to a much older gentleman with a modest fortune. His fortune dwindled throughout the course of our marriage, as he was past retirement and lived off his estate without enriching it. I tried, of course, to manage things as best I could but the world is not ready, it seems, for a woman to command wealth and influence the way a man does. That's part of the reason I was so keen for you to marry into wealth. Anyway, he died and left me the remainder of his fortune. It was modest, but enough to keep me in comfort until I met your father. Before my first marriage, I was very poor."

Winona's eyes widened in surprise. "You were?"

"I was," Audrey confirmed. "And when I say poor, I mean poor. We lived in a tar paper shack just outside of a little town called Belcher. There were nine of us living in a space about the size of your parlor. There was no fireplace and no stove. No floor or foundation either, just packed dirt. In the winter, we'd have to sleep huddled together in the middle of the room, relying on each other for warmth. For clothing, my mother would cut holes in flour sacks. When we got bigger, she'd have to stitch two sacks together."

Winona listened to her stepmother in shock. She couldn't imagine her fancy stepmother living in such squalor. The image would almost have been comical if it weren't so heartbreaking.

"My parents both worked from sunup to sundown every day but Sunday to provide for us. Even then, we barely had enough for food and sometimes not enough even for that. When we couldn't afford food, my mother would take us kids to the soup kitchen so we could get a ration of beans. Half the time, that was all we had to eat.

"The worst part was Sunday, because on Sunday my parents would insist on taking us to church so we could give thanks to God for his many blessings." There was the faintest trace of bitterness in Audrey's voice as she relayed this news. "Every Sunday I would beg to stay home and every Sunday my parents would drag us to service in our canvas sacks, barefoot, and sit us right up front so all of the wealthy children in their pressed suits, cotton dresses, and polished leather shoes could stare at us.

"I hated going to church. I hated looking around and seeing all those other people live easy, comfortable lives, knowing that the rest of my life would almost certainly be spent in destitution, like my parents.

"As I got older, I resolved to never allow any child of mine to live like this. I made it my mission to find a way out of that house. When I was old enough to work, I took a position at a boarding house. My parents were only too grateful to have one less mouth to feed. I saved a portion of my wages until I had enough to buy a halfway decent dress.

"Once I could afford to look more presentable, I took a position with the local bank as a teller. After that, my fortunes slowly improved. I never approached anything resembling wealth, but I could at least provide a roof over my head, decent food, and a change of clothes.

"It was never enough, though. I would constantly see the wealthy patrons and patronesses of the bank and feel the same shame and envy I felt as a child wearing my canvas sacks surrounded by a sea of cotton dresses and wool suits. I had more now than I had ever had, but it wasn't enough. I wanted to be free of that feeling of shame and guilt.

"So, when my chance finally came, I took it. Jonathan was nearly forty years older than I, but he was kind and demanded little of me. Most importantly, he was wealthy. Modestly wealthy but wealthy enough I would never need to work again unless I chose to. He died four years after we married. Two years after that I met your father."

She looked at Winona, tears brimming in her eyes. "I never meant to hurt you. All I wanted was to ensure you would never have to live a life of squalor like I did. When Jude Koch showed an interest in you, I thought this was the best chance you would ever have to ensure you would live in comfort. I see now how wrong I was. I'm so sorry."

After she finished, Heath spoke. "I have to apologize as well. When your mother died, I felt like I died with her. I withdrew from everyone, you included. I left you alone to deal with your mother's loss. When you needed me the most, I wasn't there. I can never make that up to you. I'm so sorry. It's not fair of us to ask this but I'm asking anyway. Is there any chance you can forgive us and allow us a second chance to be the parents you deserve?"

Winona didn't answer for a long time. Her head reeled from everything she'd just been told. She felt sympathy for her parents. Both had endured immense hardship. It was understandable that both of them had reacted as poorly as they did.

It was understandable, but was it forgivable? Winona had to endure the brunt of her parents' suffering. Maybe they had their reasons for being so hard on her, but did that really make up for everything?

No, it didn't. They deserved sympathy for their suffering, but that didn't justify the suffering they caused her. Feeling sorry for their behavior didn't make up for the years of pain Winona had endured.

Despite knowing this and despite knowing that she had every right to deny her parents the forgiveness they craved so terribly, she could feel nothing but compassion for them. They had tried the best they could. Maybe they hadn't always done well, but Winona could see now how much they cared for her. They didn't deserve forgiveness, but she would forgive them anyway.

She took one of Audrey's hands and one of Heath's hands and said, "I forgive you."

Instantly, their arms were around her. A moment later, all three were crying and holding each other tightly. No more words were said. No more words needed to be said.

I have my new family back, Winona thought. *And now I have my old family back too.*

Through the parlor window, the setting sun cast a warm glow over the three of them as they held each other and wounds that had festered for years finally healed.

Chapter Thirty-One

Life was funny sometimes. That was all there was to it. Oh, it wasn't the kind of funny a man felt sitting around to a campfire listening to old-timers sharing knee-slapping tales about when they were young, or funny the way some men just brought a smile to everyone's face when they talked. It was more like the kind of funny that made a man shake his head in wonder at how things arrived at wherever they arrived.

Gregory chuckled and shook his head as he reflected on that. Overnight, his family had gone from being outcasts to being heroes. They'd gone from carrying around shame that didn't belong to them and wearing it like a big smudge of mud on a clean white shirt to attracting glances of admiration from people in town.

And it all happened because a girl ran away from home.

That was the funny part. Winona ran away and met and married Logan and suddenly everything in life was just fine. Oh, that wasn't fair, really. Winona ran away and held onto Logan the way a man holds onto the reins when a horse is running out of control. She didn't sink hooks into him, at least not on purpose.

For that matter, it would be just as true to say Logan got his hooks into her. Those two were a couple of lovebirds, and Gregory didn't think anyone could ever pry the two of them apart. They were two peas now, nestled together in the pod, and that was how they would be forever.

And it all started just because a girl ran away. That was funny.

But there was more to it that was funny. This girl ran away, and it wasn't just her ma and pa who made her want to run. Instead, she had put Logan into a real sticky situation. She put him right in the middle of a test of wills with the most powerful family in the area so suddenly that Gregory and his brothers all had to stand up to a man even the bravest men in Texas would be afraid to face.

That should have been something that hurt them instead of helping them. But it didn't hurt them. It made Winona's father finally come clean about what really happened with their Pa, and that changed everything about how people saw them. The whole town came together, and Sterling Koch and his family weren't powerful enough to stand against them.

Gregory was pretty sure the town coming together like that did a great deal more for everyone than any of Koch's plan for the railroad would have done. It could have just been that he looked at the world with eyes that were a little brighter now than they used to be, but it seemed to him the whole town seemed a lot happier and a lot stronger.

He certainly felt stronger.

He'd been head over heels for Louise Sawyer ever since he first saw her in Mrs. Crenshaw's class seven years ago, but he'd been too scared to approach her. His parents never even knew he liked her. His brothers didn't even know he liked her until a year ago when he'd finally found the strength to approach her in public and ask if he could call on her. He had nearly died of shock when she said yes!

It was another month before he finally worked up the courage to call on her and he'd only seen her five times before the fiasco with the Kochs at the social had spoiled everything.

Except it hadn't spoiled everything. Gregory had. Louise had made it clear she liked him even before Gregory had gained enough gumption to court her. She'd given no indication her feelings had changed after the dance, but Gregory had avoided her nonetheless, certain that her parents would disapprove, and their relationship would eventually succumb to their pressure.

Gregory realized now that his pride as much as his fear was to blame for his mistakes. He might not show it the way Jay and Logan did, but he had tremendous pride in his family name, and it hurt him terribly to see the people of Westridge abuse it for so long. So rather than risk learning that Louise felt the same, he shunned her so he'd never have to feel the pain that would come with hearing his family besmirched by someone he loved so much.

He did love her. Today, he would tell her.

In the month since Winona's rescue from Jude Koch, Gregory had seen Louise no fewer than seventeen times. Watching Logan and Winona overcome tremendous adversity and remain close with one another inspired him. The fear and the pride were still there, but they no longer held the same power over him they once did.

So, the day after Winona's rescue, Gregory had woken early, washed, brushed his best suit and polished his boots until they gleamed. Then he'd saddled the most beautiful horse they owned—a blood bay with a shimmering coat and a spirited attitude—and ridden straight for the Sawyer's house. When he arrived, he declared his intention to court Louise and asked if she would be so kind as to accompany him on a ride.

Of course, she'd accepted, and things had been wonderful between them ever since. The more time they spent together the more deeply he fell in love. She was the most fascinating person he'd ever met: sweet and gentle one moment, fiery and spirited the next, but always fair and possessed of a maturity that far exceeded her years. She was everything Gregory had ever wanted and more than he'd ever hoped to find. Today, he would tell her so.

He reached into his pocket, where the small felt box Logan and Winona had given him the night before remained securely shut. He recalled his surprise when they'd given it to him.

"I can't take this!" he'd exclaimed to Winona said, wide-eyed. "This was Ma's engagement ring! She'd want you to have it."

"Well, I want you to have it," Winona said in that self-assured way she had when she knew she was right and whoever she happened to be talking to at the moment would just have to deal with it. "Logan and I are already married, and I think this ring would mean more to you than it does to me."

He'd wanted so much to accept the gift, but he didn't until he looked at Logan and his older brother said, "Take it. Show Louise how much she means to you. Show her every day."

Winona had rolled her eyes at that and laid a hand on Logan's chest. "Okay, Tennyson, I think Gregory can handle it from here."

"Tenny-who?"

"Never mind," Winona said, kissing him softly on the cheek. Logan's face had lit up in a wide, boyish grin at her touch, as it usually did. Gregory wondered idly if Logan was aware of that reaction or if it was as subconscious as the grin that would come unawares to Gregory himself whenever he saw Louise.

He wore that grin now as he pulled the wagon to a stop in front of the Sawyers' porch, despite the fact his heart pounded with anxiety. Louise waved when she saw him, smiling brightly and practically bounding down the steps. She opened her arms as though to embrace him but caught herself at the least second and let them drop to her sides awkwardly.

"Good afternoon, Gregory," she said, her voice as awkward as her posture.

Gregory stared at the beautifully awkward girl in front of him and momentarily forgot his nervousness for the joy of seeing her once more. He grinned and replied, in an exaggeratedly formal tone, "And a very pleasant afternoon to you, Miss Louise. I've come to see if you would care to enjoy a scenic ramble through the local countryside. The day is terribly lovely, and it would be such a pity to waste it confined to one's house."

Louise rolled her eyes. "You're insufferable, Gregory."

"And yet you suffer me," he replied.

"Miracles abound," Louise quipped. "Since you ask, I am available for a ride, but it will have to be brief. My parents are expecting company for supper."

"Oh? Someone I know?"

She laughed. "There are only a few hundred people in town, Gregory. Odds are you know them."

"Who is it?"

"Jeb Cain."

Gregory's eyes widened in shock. "Jeb Cain? I knew it! He's sweet on you, isn't he? Your parents invited him over so he could court you! Admit it!"

Jeb Cain was nearly seventy years old and happily married to their former schoolteacher, the erstwhile Mrs. Crenshaw. Louise rolled her eyes again but couldn't stifle a chuckle. "I swear, Greg Foley, you'll be the death of me one day."

"Greg? Since when am I Greg?"

"Since I said so," Louise replied pertly. "Now are you going to take me for a ride or are we going to stand here all day jawing at each other?"

Gregory grinned and offered her his arm. She took it and he led her to the wagon. He helped her into the seat then hopped in from the other side.

They drove slowly through the town, stopping every so often to chat with their friends and neighbors. They ran into Cordelia and Clarence Huxtable in front of the general store.

"Cordelia!" Louise cried, waving at them. "You've returned from your honeymoon!"

"Why Louise!" Cordelia said, beaming. "I swear you grow prettier every time I see you. Isn't she pretty, Clarence?"

"Pretty as a cactus rose during the first bloom of spring," Clarence confirmed in his delightfully sonorous voice.

Louise blushed prettily and Gregory thought that a cactus rose was a pretty fair comparison after all. "Not nearly as pretty as you, Cordelia."

"Well now," Clarence chuckled. "That's hardly a fair comparison. The world has never known beauty like Cordelia's."

"Oh, go on with you," Cordelia said, blushing like a ripe tomato.

Clarence smiled down at his wife and said, "I'm a slave to the truth dear and can't help but share it."

"My heavens," Cordelia said, shaking her head. "I don't know what I'm going to do with you." She looked up at Louise and Gregory. "So, what are you two lovely young people up to today?"

"Gregory's taking me for a ride through the countryside," Louise said.

"Well, how lovely!" Cordelia said. Everything was lovely to Cordelia since she and Clarence married three weeks ago.

"It's a beautiful day for it," Clarence agreed.

"Well," Cordelia said, beaming once more. "Don't let two old folks like us interrupt your ride. Have a lovely day and we'll see you both at church on Sunday."

Gregory and Louise said their goodbyes to Clarence and Cordelia, then proceeded out of town. The first winter storm had not yet arrived, and the road was in excellent condition, offering them a smooth ride as they proceeded through the rolling hills and fields of prairie grass, broken here and there by stands of pine or maple and patches of sunflowers or thimbleweed.

When they reached a particularly beautiful meadow with sundrops, columbine, and prickly poppy generously complementing the ubiquitous thimbleweed, Gregory stopped.

"Why are we stopping?" Louise asked.

"Well, I figure this would be as good a place as any," Gregory responded.

"For what?" Louise asked.

Gregory smiled and dismounted from the wagon. He walked to the other side and held out a hand to help Louise descend. She smiled quizzically at him but allowed him to lead her several paces into the meadow.

The anxiety that left Gregory when he picked Louise up earlier returned in full force and his knees fairly knocked when he finally stopped and turned to Louise. He opened his mouth to speak but no words came out at first.

Louise smiled softly. Without warning, she leaned forward and kissed him. Her lips were soft and cool on his and it felt as though all his senses tingled under her touch. When she pulled away, he opened his mouth again and this time there was no hesitation in his voice.

"Louise, you're the most beautiful girl I've ever met. I thought that the moment I first saw you in Mrs. Crenshaw's classroom. I wish I'd had the courage then to tell you how I feel about you. I wish I had the courage a thousand times over the past seven years.

"Now that I know you, I know you're not only beautiful. You're smart, and strong ,and kind. You're too good for me."

"Oh, Gregory," Louise said. She reached up and softly stroked his hair.

"It's true," he insisted. "You're too good for me but you like me anyway. You'll never know how much I appreciate you for that." He reached into his pocket and fished out the little felt box.

When Louise saw it, she gasped, her hands flying to her mouth.

Gregory got down on one knee and lifted the box. "Louise Sawyer, I love you. I've been in love with you for seven years and I'll be in love with you for seventy more. You're the most perfect woman on earth and if you'll do me the honor of becoming my wife, I promise you I will spend every day for the rest of my life doing everything I can to be a husband worthy of you. Will you marry me?"

Louise's eyes were suddenly dewy with tears. She didn't respond immediately and for a terrible moment, Gregory thought she would refuse. Then she threw her arms around him and kissed him everywhere—his cheeks, his neck, his face, his forehead, saying over, and over again, "Yes, yes, yes, I will!"

Finally, she simply held him, laughing and crying. Gregory smiled through his own tears of joy. When Louise whispered, "I love you," he squeezed her tightly, his heart full.

They held each other for a long time, saying nothing, each savoring the feel of the other in their arms. After several minutes, Gregory started laughing.

Louise pulled away. "What's so funny?" she asked.

"I never put the ring on your finger," he said. "It's still in the box. I got so nervous, I forgot to put the ring on your finger."

Louise smiled radiantly and offered her left hand, fingers pointed downward.

Gregory grinned and got back on one knee. He opened the box with a flourish, eliciting a giggle from Louise. Then he gently retrieved the ring and placed it carefully on her finger. Louise lifted the ring and gasped. "Oh, Gregory! It's beautiful!"

"You're beautiful," Gregory said.

She smiled down at him. "I love you, Gregory Foley."

"I love you too, Louise Foley."

Chapter Thirty-Two

As they walked along the fence and looked over the ranch, Logan realized his entire perspective on the place had changed. It was beautiful now. Oh, it had always been beautiful. He knew that. It had always been lovely, but now it seemed he could see it clearly. What had happened in the Bible?

A man had been blind, and Jesus touched his eyes (or something like that), and the scales fell away. That was it, Logan thought. Scales fell away and he could see. It seemed to Logan he was a lot like that man, only the scales were the shame of their circumstances and the way he had to live his life in such isolation. The ranch was just as much a prison back then as the prison Sterling Koch now called home.

For a moment, Logan thought about how Koch's face must have looked when he arrived there. Would that be the moment realization had finally set in for the old man? Did he now understand he was finished? Had he internalized it completely, so he wore that knowledge now the same way Logan and his family had worn false shame for so many years?

Logan realized as the thoughts occurred to him that he didn't feel any satisfaction about that. There was relief that the man had been brought to justice, that he'd rescued Winona and even that he'd killed Jude. There was gratitude that Koch's money couldn't buy him a life free of punishment for what he'd done. There wasn't satisfaction, however, in the man's misery. Logan wondered why.

"Beautiful day," Jay said from beside him.

"Feels kind of like every day is a beautiful day now," Logan said.

"Guess every day can be now," Jay replied.

Logan took a breath. "I was wrong, Jay."

Jay stopped walking. "You don't think it's a beautiful day?"

Logan turned and looked at his brother. "Not about that. I'm right about that. There aren't a whole lot of things I've been right about, but it *is* a beautiful day."

"You're right about Winona, Logan. You were right about needing to take a stand against Jude and his father. You're right about a lot."

"Damn it, Jay, stop being nice to me. I've got to tell you something."

Jay lifted up his hands. "Okay. I'll be mean to you. You missed some spots when you were shaving this morning. You look scruffy. You're an important rancher now and you ought to take more care with how you look. Better?"

Logan shook his head with a smile. "Okay. Maybe don't stop being nice to me, but can I get through this? I need to tell you something."

"All right, then," Jay said. "Talk to me. I'll listen quiet-like. I'll be a mouse."

Logan said, "I don't know where to start."

"For a man demanding I shut up so he can talk, you seem pretty set on staying quiet."

"I never trusted you. I never trusted anyone. I let what Heath Ross did to us keep me from believing anyone could be trusted at all. I didn't listen when you tried to talk to me. I didn't listen to anything at all, and for years you've been trying to help this ranch succeed and I've just treated you like

..." he shrugged. "I don't know what it was like, but I didn't treat you like I should have."

"We all had a hard time of it, Logan," Jay said, "every one of us. You were just trying to do the best you could for the family."

Logan said, "You're right about that, but it doesn't make it right. Heath Ross was trying to do the best he could for his family. Winona's mother was trying to do the best for her. That doesn't mean what they did wasn't wrong, and it doesn't mean what I did wasn't wrong."

He looked up at the sky for a moment. He only wanted to break eye contact with Jay for a little break but as he looked up into the clouds, he surprised himself by saying a quick prayer that he might be given the right words to say. He wasn't entirely sure if the petition was for God's ears or for his father's. "Jay," he said when he looked back down, "the last thing our pa said to me was to take care of you and Greg. He said he wanted me to take care of my brothers and to take care of his horse ranch."

Jay stared at him for a long moment and finally said, "I understand."

"Maybe you do. Maybe but the part of what he said that stuck with me so much was that he said it was a horse ranch. Horse. That's why I've held so fast to that. He said his horse ranch was important to him and he wanted me to take care of his horse ranch. Whenever you would come to me and you'd want to talk about anything else, it didn't matter at all what you said. It had to be horses. I was stubborn like half a horse about that, like a mule. I didn't want to hear about anything else."

Jay chuckled. "No. I guess you didn't."

"I didn't want to hear about it, and I was so angry with Ross that I couldn't think clearly anyway. I couldn't trust anyone, and that meant I couldn't even trust you. I swear Jay, it felt like trying to change things around here was just the same as trying to destroy the place." He held up a hand, "It wasn't, of course. I'm not saying anyone was trying to destroy the ranch, least of all you and Greg. I'm just saying I haven't been in my right mind. I've been so busy thinking about what the ranch shouldn't be and what people shouldn't be, I haven't paid attention to what really mattered."

He looked around at the beautiful landscape and noted to the north a few deer at the tree line. To the south, he could see some of their stock. "Well, I've just kept talking and just talked myself into a circle, so I lost my place," he said. "Jay, I didn't trust you. I didn't trust anyone. That was wrong. I should have trusted you, and I should have trusted Gregory. Maybe if I had, I wouldn't have failed so badly at taking care of the ranch."

"You didn't fail, Logan," Jay said.

"Yes, I did," Logan said. "Sure, I kept the ranch running where others might not have, but I still failed. If I'd trusted you and Gregory to have an equal say, we wouldn't have had to endure the hardship and fear of the past few years. Winona wouldn't have had to suffer through my pigheadedness for six months before I finally saw reason."

Jay smiled wryly. "I'd say Winona seems fine with the way things turned out."

"I know that," Logan said, "And I'm happy with the way things turned out too. All except one thing."

"What's that?"

"I need to do what I should have done in the first place and let you and Gregory become equal partners in the business.

So that's what I'm going to do. You were right about the cattle, Jay. You were right the whole time. Gregory saw it. Winona saw it. Any fool could see it. I saw it, but I just didn't want to admit it because I was so hung up on the need to save Pa's horse ranch."

Logan chuckled. "You know, it only now occurred to me that Pa just meant to take care of the ranch and only called it a horse ranch because that happened to be the only animal we had at the time. The point is you were right. We should invest in cattle. I've already talked to Winona and Gregory, and they agree. We're going to arrange for a buyer for the horses and we're going to purchase another seven hundred head of cattle. Heath and Wyatt are going to send some hands to help Darrell convert the stables to cattle pens and Winona and Gregory are making plans to replant the pastures with clover and alfalfa. We're going to be a cattle ranch and by God we're going to be the best cattle ranch this side of the Mississippi."

Jay's eyes widened and a grin spread across his face as Logan spoke. By the end, he was beaming from ear to ear. "You mean it?"

"I mean it," Logan said. "I'm so sorry it took me so long to see the light, but I see it now."

Jay threw his arms around his brother and hugged him hard. Logan returned the embrace, the first he and Jay had shared in years. It felt good. It felt like they were family again. Logan would trade in everything he owned for that feeling.

When they released each other, Jay smiled and said, "Thank you, Logan. It means a lot to me to hear you say that."

Logan smiled. "It's the least I can do." He looked up at the slowly descending sun. "We should head back. I promised

Winona we'd be home in time for supper. She's making pork roast again."

Jay's eyes lit up. "My favorite!"

Logan suppressed a smile. Pork roast was the meal Winona had made for their first dinner as a family, the meal Jay had eschewed for a meal in town. "Make sure you tell Winona," he said.

Jay smiled. "I will."

They walked in comfortable silence for a while. After a few minutes, Logan cleared his throat and said, "So do you want to head to town on Thursday? To buy the cattle, I mean? There's a breeder there offering to sell on consignment. The cattle wouldn't arrive until the railway station opens, but that shouldn't be more than another few months. I'd go myself but I don't know what I'm looking for as well as you do."

"I would love to," Jay said.

"Much obliged," Logan replied.

They fell into silence again. A few minutes later, Jay said, "You know, it doesn't have to be either/or."

"What?"

"It doesn't have to be either/or. The ranch, I mean."

"What does that mean? Either/or?"

"Either cattle or horses. It doesn't have to be one or the other."

"You want to raise both? We don't have the room."

"Actually, we do," Jay said. "There's at least twenty thousand acres of prime pastureland to the northwest that's just lying fallow. If we talk to Clarence, I'm sure we could secure a loan for the purchase. It's a hefty sum, but if all goes well with the cattle, we can pay the loan off in a few years and still have enough to pay for new fencing, buildings and to hire a few dozen more hands. We could recoup every dollar we invest in five years and then some."

Logan looked at his brother, pride and love swelling his chest. "You know something, Jay? Pa would be proud."

"Oh, I always knew that," Jay replied. "You're the only one too pigheaded to see that."

Logan chuckled and rolled his eyes. "Nice to know you're still going to be a pain in my backside."

"Hey, a tiger can't change its stripes."

"What?"

"Something Winona says sometimes."

"She's never said that to me."

"Really? You should pay more attention to your wife."

Logan shoved Jay playfully. The younger man stumbled, laughing as Logan called after him. "You may be all grown up, but I can still whup you."

"You'll have to catch me first," Jay said. He took off toward the house.

Logan sprinted after him, barely managing to keep up. "Not fair!" he called after Jay. "I'm forty pounds heavier than you. I can't move like that."

"Excuses!" Jay called over his shoulder.

They reached the house a few seconds later. Jay burst in the front door, nearly colliding with Winona, who shrieked and nearly dropped the large pot she held. "Jay Foley!" she chided. "This is a house, not a play yard!"

Though he'd seen it happen, his momentum carried Logan forward as though he were intent on proving his wife wrong. Play yard or house, Winona had another close call, this time as Logan burst through the door following his brother. She shook her head and shrieked again, narrowly avoiding Logan as he bounded into the parlor. It seemed almost miraculous to him she didn't drop the pot, and comical enough he needed the miracle to keep himself from laughing and to show the appropriate contrition.

"Sorry, honey," Logan said.

"Don't sorry me!" Winona scolded. Despite her tone, Logan could see a smile her in her eyes. She allowed Logan to kiss her cheek before setting the pot down. "When you boys have finished roughhousing, will you go tell Gregory dinner is ready in ten minutes?"

"Yes, ma'am," Jay said meekly, on his best behavior in a way that made Logan smile.

"What are you smiling about?" Winona said. "Now you go find a basin and wash up. I won't have men sitting at my dinner table looking like they ought to be eating in the barn!" She couldn't keep the smile from her face again.

He smiled and said in his best boy voice, "Aw ... do I have to?"

Her eyes flashed but then she shook her head with a laugh. "Go on with you before all you get for supper is a crust of bread."

Logan smiled, leaned forward to give her another kiss on the cheek. She turned her head as he did, so the kiss ended up on her lips and Logan felt like a boy because of the thrill that gave him. "Now get!" she said. "Right now!"

Ten minutes later, they sat around the table enjoying steaming hot pork roast with mashed potatoes, roasted carrots and thick, creamy gravy Winona ladled generously over the plates. After one bite, Jay said, "Logan, I think we'll need to raise hogs now. If Winona's going to cook like this, we definitely need to raise hogs."

"All right," Winona said, "you three are forgiven for roughhousing."

"I wasn't roughhousing!" Gregory protested.

"Not today," Winona said, "But you probably need forgiveness for something."

Logan chuckled, "She's right about that." He supposed they all needed forgiveness and imagined they'd need it for some time to come. They'd get it, too.

That fact made him pause and put down his fork.

He hadn't even known Winona watched him closely but the moment his fork was down she asked, "Is everything okay? What's wrong?"

"Nothing's wrong," he said. "Nothing at all. For the first time in as long as I can remember, nothing's wrong at all. Everything's ... everything's just fine." He smiled at her and said, "In fact, everything is just about perfect."

Jay said, "This supper is perfect. That's for sure."

Gregory quipped, "Not all of us think with our stomachs, Jay."

Logan smiled and picked up his fork. "I do. You can believe that." He lifted a piece of pork to his mouth and kept his eyes on Winona. "I certainly do."

He saw a faint blush in Winona's cheeks as she said, "Now stop being foolish, you three, and eat your supper." She couldn't manage even the slightest sternness in her tone.

Chapter Thirty-Three

Gregory cleaned up nice.

Winona thought it probably made her a silly girl to think about such a thing at the moment, but she couldn't help herself. Gregory looked a fine gentleman in his new suit. It was very snappy, from the black and grey striped trousers extending up from his new polished black boots, to his waist. There, a matching vest with beautiful brass buttons added to the picture.

The buttons shone in stark contrast to the material, and added a dapper brightness to the look, polishing the outfit just as the buttons were polished. He looked like a proper, successful rancher as well, because he had his father's pocket watch with the brass chain visible from a loop on the vest until it disappeared into his pocket. His jacket was solid black and quite fine as well.

His shirt was stiff and white and the black bow tie with its thick cloth made it look even whiter. On top of his head, he wore a lovely black derby, which suited him more than the regular Stetson he ordinarily wore.

Of course, the most attractive thing Gregory wore was on his face. It was the bright smile that seemed to carry with it all the happiness any man could hope to have in this life. She smiled at the sight. Gregory got that happiness on his wedding day like most people did instead of through the roundabout way she and her husband had found it.

Her brother-in-law looked very nice, and she realized he was a fine man. Louise had captured the heart of a very fine man indeed. It felt a little strange to have known him for as long as she had only to just now really notice it. She blushed, chastising herself for not having noticed it sooner.

She thought there were a great many things she probably ought to have noticed sooner than she did. The conversation with her mother and father ought not to have been so revelatory, really. Parents behaved in the best interests of their children. At least, they tried to behave in their children's best interests, although oftentimes their actions had the opposite effect.

Even Sterling Koch acted in favor of Jude's best interests. The problem, she imagined, wasn't really the intent of parents. Their intentions were always good, Winona guessed. At some point, the actions took over and became the goal in and of themselves. At some point, how the child reflected on them meant more than what the child needed or wanted.

Good intentions.

There was something someone used to say. Winona thought perhaps it was an old schoolteacher. Hell was full of good intent, but heaven was full of good works. Something like that. A book of proverbs in the Koch house said the road to hell is paved with good intentions and said it was first suggested by some ancient Roman king. Winona didn't know who said it, but she imagined it was true. She imagined everyone wanted to be judged by their intentions.

But everyone wanted to judge others by their actions, didn't they? Didn't she?

She pressed her lips together and forced her mind back to the moment, to notice again that Louise had captured the heart of a very fine man. Of course, it was easy to notice things now that the Kochs weren't a part of her life and now that she didn't have to live like some kind of outcast, someone clothed in shame and driven away rather than someone welcomed.

And that was remarkable.

She didn't know if she were welcome before all of this and her time fully removed from the town and the people had simply made the welcome more obvious to her now that she was back. Winona suspected, though, that the town as a whole was closer now. They didn't have a leader to cling to, a man to check with before making a decision one way or another. Instead, they had to rely on neighbors, friends and loved ones. She thought it made the town blossom, and she felt like a part of Westridge in ways she never had before.

And Greg, the fine man in front of her, looking at his bride as though she were Aphrodite risen from the sea, was a part of Westridge now, too. The church was full of people who'd probably looked down on him and his entire family or, if not actively looking down on him, nevertheless didn't want to draw attention to themselves by welcoming him.

A fine man, that one. And, of course, Winona was also very aware of Gregory's involvement in her rescue, how he'd stood right by Logan's side, and she owed more than one brother for her freedom. She was glad Gregory smiled, so glad he was happy. She hoped he was able to remain happy for the rest of his life, to have a perfect happily ever after like in the storybooks. The thought was pleasant—a happily ever after for everyone. She smiled as she looked at him and then let her eyes move to the two men who stood beside him.

Jay also cleaned up very nicely indeed.

Jay's outfit was as light as Gregory's was dark. Both appeared youthful and vibrant, but Jay appeared more of a man about town, a man who was involved, a man who likely spoke to everyone he saw and left them smiling afterward. Above his boots, he wore brown, brushed cotton trousers with a high waist.

A gold-colored Spencer vest just barely extended below the waistband. He wore a pocket watch with a chain as well, although with his lighter clothing it didn't stand out as much. His coat was long, a light tan frock coat that almost looked white compared to his brother's jacket. He wore the same starch-stiff white shirt, although once again it didn't stand out quite the same as it did next to the black of Gregory's vest and jacket.

He had a puffy silk tie, almost like an ascot. That tie was black, blacker than anything Gregory wore, and made for such a lovely sharp contrast with the rest of his outfit that it automatically drew the eye there. Without that black tie, Jay might have appeared a bit of a dandy. With it, the outfit gave him an almost distinguished air. On his head, he wore a cream-colored straw derby, and the overall effect was to make him seem a proper gentleman.

What a change!

What a change to see the two of them there at the front of the altar, dressed in fine clothes, clothes she knew her father bought for them. She imagined her father would spend some time trying to make up for what he'd done to their father, although none of them held him accountable for it now.

In fact, she'd insisted they accept the clothes, insisted that they take the gift, because her father had used her as the excuse for his behavior and because he had prevailed upon their father to keep the truth hidden. She'd insisted they help her redeem the role she unwittingly played, and she was glad she did. Of course, she also knew enough of herself that she not only wanted them to have the clothes but also wanted her father to be out the money it took to buy them.

And then there was Logan.

As she looked at him next to his brother, her heart swelled. His brothers looked like gentleman ranchers, heavy on the gentleman and light on the rancher. Logan, too, looked like a gentleman rancher but his outfit, while just as formal, tipped to the other side so the rancher part of the look was far more evident. He wore a long black frock coat over a grey and black striped vest.

He wore the same puffed silk tie as Jay, but with the coat, vest, and black trousers, it blended with the outfit and didn't serve as a focal point. He wore a black Stetson high enough that it might have seemed a top hat if not for the wideness of the brim. The lambskin black gloves he wore added an air of importance to the look. His brothers seemed like part of a wealthy ranching family. Logan looked like the patriarch of that family.

She realized she wore an obvious smile on her face, and she wasn't able to control it. Just looking at her husband made her mind race crazily, traveling over all their interactions. Even the painful interactions that seemed rewritten by her mind, a lovely trick that made her feel a bit like a silly romantic. She didn't mind that at all, though. In fact, she liked the thought of being silly over Logan.

They were building a home together now, and she would be a strong woman. She would cook and keep the house. She would help with the ranch, and she would use whatever talents she had to manage the household and, where appropriate, the business of the ranch. She would stand by Logan's side in the bad years, and she would help him celebrate the good years. He was the patriarch, and by God, Winona would be the matriarch. She would do all of those things.

But for now, it felt wonderful to instead behave like one of the heroines in a traveling melodrama and just be filled with silly, overly emotional wonder that the hero in the ten-gallon hat belonged to her. She turned her attention back to Gregory but couldn't keep her attention there and looked at her husband again.

The focal point of Gregory's outfit unquestionably had to be the line of brass buttons on his vest. The focal point of Jay's outfit was, of course, his tie. As for Logan, there was no focal point at all. The whole outfit was the focal point or perhaps, the whole outfit made the man himself the focal point. He stood proudly by his brothers, and Winona thought the pride he showed was well-earned.

She smiled as she looked at him and smiled when she thought he probably drew far more eyes than the groom. In fact, he likely drew more eyes than the bride! Winona thought Louise looked lovely as well, though, and it seemed such a strange and wonderful change to be able to appreciate loveliness in anything again.

It didn't seem strange at all to see Logan as the man he was now, although she might have believed it strange had she imagined seeing him this way just a few months before.

She was finally free.

She wasn't only free from Jude but free from everything he represented, everything she'd run away from and everything her running had caused. The wedding was lovely because life was lovely. Life was finally unequivocally lovely, and the man who stood in the front of the church like the patriarch of a noble ranching family was *her* man.

Hers.

Dear God, that felt wonderful. Logan was hers and, perhaps more importantly, she was his. That felt better than just about anything she could imagine. She was resolved, as well. She had every intention of being his for the rest of her life.

She'd run away and ended up with him. She'd remained to keep herself from a fate that was worse. He wasn't an alternative to something worse anymore. He was everything she wanted, everything she could possibly hope to have.

Louise Sawyer, who was about to become Louise Foley, looked absolutely stunning, Winona thought. Her eyes traveled to Logan's mother's ring on Louise's finger, and she felt a burst of pride she'd prevailed upon Gregory to take it. It made the moment more than their wedding. It made the moment also about the addition of someone to her family.

Her family!

That thought gave her pause. It described her marriage to Logan, too, didn't it? At least, it described her now, after all the Koch business was behind them. She looked at the men again, Gregory in his dark clothes and Jay in his brighter clothes. She loved them both, already thinking of them as brothers. Did they love her as well? Again, she smiled at the thought. She'd become an addition to their family finally and now that family was hers.

Of course, there remained no doubt at all that she loved the oldest brother at the altar.

She returned her gaze to Louise, admiring the beautiful, cream-colored taffeta gown. There was a great deal of fabric, and Winona wondered at that. Winona never wore a bustle. Nonetheless, she knew such accoutrements grew more popular, and even expected in the larger towns in the West, and she imagined there would come a time when they were expected in Westridge. In the wedding gown, it was certainly pretty but she was happy to keep from having to walk around with such a thing behind her. She tried to focus her thoughts and to keep her mind on the ceremony. It wasn't an easy thing to do. Even with only a month or so passing since Koch's trial ended with him sent to prison, her mind still swirled with the newness of all her joy, and it made it difficult now to focus on the joy of Gregory and Louise. It was like the Bible, though, she thought. All things were made new.

She heard soft weeping and turned to see her stepmother beside her, dabbing at her eyes with her father's handkerchief. She reached over and gently touched her stepmother's hand. Her stepmother looked at her and smiled in embarrassment at her tears and then turned her attention back to the couple. Surprisingly, when Winona moved her hand back, her father replaced it with his and her stepmother turned hers toward her father's.

In a moment their fingers interlaced, and Winona felt certain the moment represented the first time she'd ever seen her parents hold hands. She smiled at the sight. She noticed also that her stepmother leaned in slightly toward her father, and though he kept his eyes forward when she did, his features softened a bit in satisfaction. She'd certainly never seen that before.

All things were made new, indeed.

Epilogue

Logan thought he probably should have understood the power of the community coming together because of the way they joined up to help him take on Sterling Koch and his devil of a son. So, he felt just a touch of embarrassment to feel amazed as he watched the steam in the distance as the first train approached the new Westridge Station.

Of course, that embarrassment didn't measure up anywhere close to the amount of joy he felt or the pride he felt at the sight of the finished railroad. The community had risen up and driven away Sterling Koch. They'd done that fully expecting their expectation that the railroad would stop in down would be dashed. They'd weighed the sacrifice and found doing what was right to be more important than doing what was profitable.

And yet, they'd gotten the profit anyway.

It seemed to Logan taking on Sterling and Jude breathed life into the community unlike anything they had before. It empowered everyone to accomplish things they didn't know could be accomplished. They came up with the money to finish laying the tracks and came up with the money for the station. He wouldn't have been surprised if he learned every single family in town owned at least one share of the Westridge Rail Station Company.

He owned a hundred shares himself. He knew Heath Ross owned a thousand. His brothers each owned fifty. The town raised all the money at two dollars a share. It seemed such an easy undertaking when all was said and done that he imagined a number of people felt foolish, as he did thinking they needed a man like Sterling Koch to do it in the first place.

Logan didn't understand all of the financial implications but Cody Pickwell, an associate of Clarence Huxtable's who relocated to Westridge to help Clarence provide financial services to the people and businesses that would grow as a result of the station, said the station would be added to the bond issuances at the capitol. The State of Texas would end up buying all of the shares from the shareholders.

They stood to make a profit from that in a year or so, and already the railroad company had arranged to operate the station so the station would cost Westridge nothing. The process was so much easier than anyone could have anticipated, and it made the way everyone had bowed before the Koch family seem even more ludicrous. People had been held in sway by nothing more than the force of an evil man's personality, when all was said and done.

Pickwell said other changes would come. Goods could travel by rail now, and that meant there would be fewer middlemen between ranchers, farmers, and others. The general store would soon have some of the conveniences people in the East took for granted. There would likely be a stockyard somewhere along the line soon so ranchers wouldn't have long cattle drives to bring their beef to market. People would arrive soon. The new catalog company, Montgomery Ward, would begin delivering so people could order things the general store didn't necessarily want to stock.

Koch had been right about the impact of the railroad station. He just wasn't necessary for it.

That fact, that the town could prosper without Koch was accepted now, although Logan knew it was the hardest thing for the community to accept. Some had accepted it, especially after the meeting. Most of those who came together, though, to help rescue Winona believed that in doing so, they were condemning the town to obscurity.

Logan appreciated everyone who helped, but he appreciated even more those who helped believing the entire time they did so against their own interests. They were men and women who acted out of a strong sense of what was right and what was wrong, and that moral core was more important to them than their own ease.

How easy it was for him now to appreciate people! How easy he found it to look at people in the best possible light, to give them all the benefit of the doubt. The town had changed into something brighter and more beautiful; there was no doubt about that at all. Logan felt he'd changed into something brighter as well, with an outlook far more beautiful than he possessed before. There was simply no doubt about that at all.

"It'll be here any minute now," Winona said from beside him.

He turned to her, eyes wide and sudden panic filling him. "What are you doing on your feet?" He asked. He put his arm around her shoulder and said, "You shouldn't be on your feet!"

She smiled tolerantly and said, "Logan Foley, I'm pregnant. I'm not on my deathbed."

Logan said, "Just the same, I'll feel better if you're sitting down." He ushered her to a bench in front of Talbot's saloon and said, "Let me get you a drink."

"I don't want a drink right now," she said.

"I don't mean whiskey or gin. I mean maybe some milk or, if Charles has some of Rebecca's lemonade, maybe a glass of that."

"All right," Winona said, "Lemonade, but stop acting like I'm going to faint dead away, Logan."

"No promises," he said with a smile and walked through the batwing doors.

Charles stood behind the bar, mopping the wood with a rag. He was portly and balding slightly. With his starched shirt and striped red suspenders, he looked the part of a saloonkeeper. He fit the role perfectly. It seemed impossible to look at him without feeling good. "Morning, Logan," Charles said with a smile.

"It's just past noon, my friend," Logan said.

"Then a good afternoon to you," the man replied. "Big day today."

"You know, having your place right here is going to be good for your business. When people get off the train, your saloon will be the first thing they see."

"Let's hope they have a taste for gin and beef, then," Charles said with a grin. "Whiskey, too."

"Well, right now, I've a taste for gin. Winona has a taste for your wife's lemonade, too. Do you have any here?"

Charles smiled and put a glass on the table. As he poured the gin he said, "She just made a new batch." Logan brought the shot to his lips and downed it as Charles got a tall glass for the lemonade. "And I just got my ice delivered this morning, too," he said. He turned around and stabbed at a thick block with an ice pick.

"Just fine, then," Logan said. He smiled as the gin warmed him and when Charles turned around again, he put the shot glass on the bar. Charles put shards of ice in the tall glass and then poured another shot of gin. Logan drank it as Charles lifted a large clear jug from behind the counter and poured from it to fill the lemonade glass.

"Much obliged, Charles," Logan said. He reached in his pocket for some coins, but Charles shook his head.

"No charge, Logan," he said.

"You won't stay in business very long if you give everyone free drinks," Logan said.

"Not everyone, Logan. Just you."

"You should let me pay," Logan protested.

Charles looked at him and shook his head adamantly. "Do you know what this town is? This town is not the Westridge filled with people under Koch's thumb, not anymore. This town isn't filled with ruffians keeping everyone in line with their guns who wouldn't fall in line with promises.

This town came together for everyone to succeed and not for the vanity of one man and his damnable family. That's all because of you, Logan. You and your family will drink for free at Talbot's for as long as it stands. I won't hear any more about it." He lifted a finger. "Not one more word."

Logan just stared at him for a moment but then nodded. "Much obliged, Charlie," he said. The gin felt warm in his stomach as he lifted the glass of lemonade. The glass was cold, and he marveled at that. Charles didn't often have ice. He imagined he would have ice far more often now with the railroad.

He imagined a lot of business would have a lot of things now with the railroad station so close. He nodded to the barkeep one more time and then walked to the swinging doors and back out. He sat next to Winona and handed her the lemonade.

She took it and said, "Oh! It's cold."

"Charlie has ice in today."

She took a sip and said, "I'll have to find a way to convince Rebecca to share her recipe with me."

"I think taking on the Kochs was probably an easier battle," Logan said.

"I'll just join the library committee and convince her it ought to preserved for our grandchildren and their children, too."

Grandchildren. Logan looked at her with a smile. The thought wasn't farfetched anymore. In fact, the idea of children, grandchildren and even great grandchildren almost felt like an inevitable fact now. He asked, "Does the baby feel like a boy or like a girl?"

Winona laughed softly and said, "Logan Foley, just how many times do you plan on asking me that question?"

He smiled and put his hand on her swollen belly and said, "Probably until the baby arrives." He left his hand there for a moment and leaned forward to kiss her cheek tenderly. It still seemed impossible to him, having a child. He found it interesting how he desperately wanted a boy. He fantasized about teaching him to ride, to hunt. He fantasized about teaching him how to shoe a horse, how to mend a fence.

He fantasized about teaching his son to shoot and to fish. He could spend an hour just contemplating telling him stories about his grandfather. Then, almost abruptly, his mind would change, and he suddenly wanted a daughter. He thought of buying her dresses and taking her into town. He thought of teaching her to ride and telling her it didn't matter what people wanted to say or think.

She'd be able to ride a normal saddle or she could ride like a boy rode, and not turned the side. He even thought about teaching her to hunt and all the disapproving glances she'd be sure to get from Winona. Of course, he'd get a lot of disapproving glances one way or the other, because he knew without a doubt he was going to spoil the child whether it turned out to be a son or a daughter.

Dear God, a daughter!

He laughed and Winona turned to him with a raised eyebrow. "I was just thinking about how if we have a Winona Junior—"

She chuckled, "Girls aren't named after their mothers, dear," she said.

"Okay. If we have an Edith, or a Hattie, or an Anna, or a Cora, then."

Winona smiled and said, "I think we'll want to settle on one name, Logan. Maybe two."

He laughed and watched her take a sip of the lemonade. Condensation on the glass surprised him. Ice! The town would be full of it when the trains ran regularly. "I was thinking when she's old enough and boys want to court her, they'll really be in for it. Between me, Gregory and Jay ... well, I imagine they'll have to be really committed to face all that."

"It's here," she said, lifting her hand and pointing.

"Well would you look at that," Logan said, but by then the hissing sound of the arriving train drowned out his voice. The sight was still quite impressive, a giant engine clothed in steam and smoke, and a crowd of onlookers staring in awe as it came to rest. When the noise died down, Logan said, "A week or two ago, Merle Cuttard told me a train crossed the whole country in just eighty-four hours. Can you imagine that? Eighty-four hours! It's something called an express train, so they don't stop at every station."

"Do you think they would stop here?"

"I'm not sure it's on the same track."

"What a remarkable time we live in, Logan," Winona said.

"And what a remarkable woman to live in it with," he replied and kissed her cheek again.

"Oh, go on with you." He could see her cheeks color a bit. He liked that very much. "Do you want to go see the train?"

Logan said, "Why don't you finish your lemonade. I just wanted to see it arrive. I imagine we'll see the train plenty. Maybe we'll even take a trip."

"Logan!" He looked up and saw Gregory across the street. He waved and Logan waved back. Louise was pregnant as well, not as far along as Winona.

The two made their way over and Winona said, "Will you come to supper tonight?"

Louise said, "I was going to invite you and Logan over."

Logan laughed and said, "That's fine but why don't you two come over first. Jay wants to show you the cattle."

"I see them all the time," Gregory said.

"Well, I haven't," Louise said, "and he's right to be proud of it."

"He is indeed," Logan said with a smile. "A year. That's all it's taken him. A year getting to do what he thinks ought to be done and the herd's thriving better than anyone can imagine."

"You're doing a fine job, too, Logan," Gregory said.

"Oh, no," Logan said. "That herd is all his."

"The cattle herd, sure, but the horses ... that's the two of you, and mostly you."

"We've made a little progress there," Logan said.

"Pa would be proud," Gregory said.

Louise pointed to the sky and said, "He is. You can count on it."

"Ride to the ranch with us?" Winona asked. "Logan put cushions in the wagon. You can spend the night at the ranch or take the wagon home. Logan's riding into town tomorrow anyway, so he could bring it back."

Logan said, "Fine by me," mostly so he felt like he actually had a say in the plan. Later, as the four of them reached the edge of the ranch, he thought about how true those words were. He'd given Jay complete authority to handle the cattle as he saw fit. Now, his land was filled with steers. When they sold, they might fetch as much as twenty-five dollars a head, maybe more. He glanced at Louise, whose eyes were wide as she looked at the herd. Jay had been right all along, and he'd done a job worthy of his pride in it. He smiled at Winona, and she smiled back. It seemed to him sometimes she could read his thoughts.

Fine by me.

Things were fine by Logan.

Logan was certain things had never been as fine as they were right then. He clucked his tongue and snapped the reins softly as he approached the ranch house, his home.

THE END

Also by Ava Winters

Thank you for reading **"An Uninvited Bride on his Doorstep"**!

I hope you enjoyed it! If you did, here are some of my other books!

Some of my Best-Selling Books

#1 Brave Western Brides [Boxset]

#2 The Courageous Bride's Unexpected Family

#3 Healing the Rancher's Cold Heart

#4 A Redeeming Love in the West

#5 The Rancher's Unexpected Love

#6 A Bounty on Their Scarred Hearts

Also, if you liked this book, you can also check out **my full Amazon Book Catalogue at:**
https://go.avawinters.com/bc-authorpage

Thank you for allowing me to keep doing what I love! ❤

Printed in Great Britain
by Amazon